KINE

At the core of the frost that night was silence. A round moon shone on the covert, its rays mirrored by the snow so that branch and twig, the last berry of winter, were conspicuous. Lanes were quiet. In thickest hawthorn, finches roosted: dark balls of puffed feather, rimed claw. In burrow and tree bole, rodents shivered. It was quiet cold, silent as a lurcher, cruel, insidious. Such a cold stilled the sap, seized the weakened beast and froze the perched bird.

The weasel stepped briskly, with goblin energy. His place in the valley was traditional; his name, Kine, an English weasel name for centuries. Through history his family had hunted there . . .

Kine

A. R. Lloyd

Hamlyn Paperbacks

KINE

ISBN 0 600 20467 7

First published in Great Britain 1982
by Hamlyn Paperbacks
Third printing 1982
Copyright © 1982 by A. R. Lloyd

Hamlyn Paperbacks are published by
The Hamlyn Publishing Group Ltd,
Astronaut House, Feltham,
Middlesex, England

Reproduced, printed and bound in Great Britain by
Hazell Watson & Viney Ltd, Aylesbury, Bucks

*To Tessa,
Sophie and Laura –
with love*

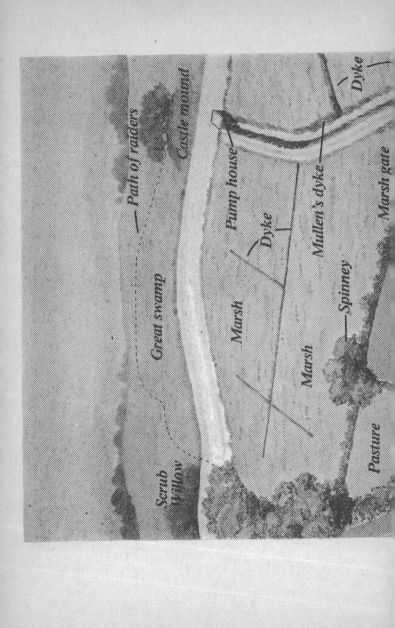

Pasture

The Lea

Moor pond

Gibbet

Stunted Ash

Path to marsh

Hayfield

Cornfield

1st Mink killed

Ploughman's Cottage

Woodpiles

Owl barn

Farm lane

Poacher's orchard

Poacher's cottage

Dar'st thou die?
The sense of death is most in apprehension,
And the poor beetle, that we tread upon,
In corporal sufferance finds a pang as great
As when a giant dies.

Shakespeare *Measure for Measure*

Part One

KINE'S COUNTRY

CHAPTER ONE

THE revenge-takers stopped on the crest and surveyed the valley. It had, by moonlight, a frosty
ghostliness. There, where a grey wood straddled
the far ridge, the wild forest of Anderidan had once
ranged above the river, the *Lemanus* of Caesar's
ordinance. And there, where dykes and sedge-banks
raked the levels, ancient peoples, Cantii, Bibroci, had
guarded frontiers.

To that marshy bottom and wooded eminence had
come Romans, Saxons, Danes and Normans, as alien as
the vengeful marauders who now gazed at it. Men had
passed there in arms and in search of trade. They had
passed on the pennoned barges of medieval times, and
on foot in rebellion when Wat Tyler marched. But they
had long gone. Of mankind there were few signs: a
ploughman's cottage, chimney smoking; a poacher's den.

It was still a place of wildlife, the oldest life; a place
where the heron fished as he had fished in the days of
woad, and crows flew as they had flown for half a million
years. By moonlight it seemed to the aliens a promised
land, a glistening image of their far-off and lost home.
From the crest they intended to invade and possess that
land.

They were implacable. Trapped and caged, their forebears had been shipped from North America to squalid
fur-farms across the world, their offspring slaughtered
and flayed for the coats they bore. People knew them by
different names – nertz, sumpf-otters, mink – and for
their savagery. Unremitting in resistance to captivity,
they had met brutality with bitter hatred, snarling and
hissing in their prisons, cursing the bleak dome of
foreign skies. Some, large as cats, had gnawed the mesh
of their cages until their mouths bled.

The first to escape had made for water. Powerful

amphibians, they were safe from pursuit in streams and channels, adept at seizing fish in their shark-like jaws. By night they raided poultry runs, slaughtering voraciously. Few wild creatures were safe from them. Soon, in several lands, bands of the fugitives were moving on lakes and marshlands. And as they moved, their revenge was grim.

They slew promiscuously. At Lake Thingvallavatn, in Iceland, they had exterminated the population of waterfowl. In Norway and Sweden they had cleared streams of fish and killed wild mammals. In England they had marauded the Teign, the Avon and other streams, intent on massacre. They moved inexorably, revenge-takers, and they sought new valleys to terrorize.

At the core of the frost that night was silence. A round moon shone on the covert, its rays mirrored by the snow so that branch and twig, the least berry of winter, were conspicuous. Lanes were quiet. In thickest hawthorn, finches roosted: dark balls of puffed feather, rimed claw. In burrow and tree bole, rodents shivered. It was a quiet cold, silent as a lurcher, cruel, insidious. Such a cold stilled the sap, seized the weakened beast and froze the perched bird.

The weasel stepped briskly, with goblin energy. His place in the valley was traditional; his name, Kine, an English weasel name for centuries. Through history his family had hunted there. He knew the deep places, the fortress of the mole and the rabbit's stop. He could interpret a hundred signs, from the fox's print to the foiling of deer in grass. He was familiar with the hare's trod and the amber stain in the snow where it had nibbled the diuretic broom.

He knew the valley sounds. He knew the speech of the vixen in cover, the yickering of badgers at full moon. He knew, too, the yaffle of woodpeckers before rain and the piping of snipe when the winds of March died. And when the wild geese came trumpeting up the marsh in crazy harmony he would know his third summer had arrived, that lush days were back. Until then, Kine moved hungrily.

Near the covert, in dumpy thickets, grew blackthorn. He probed the thickets and ice-roofed hollows. Pausing, he scampered forward, then stopped again. A flock of redwings erupted from the blackthorn in startled flight. He cursed. All he could see between the thickets was virgin snow. It was the frost – that and the moon – which had unsettled the birds. It made them restless, like the hares on the marsh when food was scarce.

Straggling shadows marked the first trees. They were ash poles, enough space between the thin stark masts for a prowling owl, but devoid of life. No owl, no flitting bat, no creature of the wood's edge. Some, perhaps, had crept into the ivy on the oaks, or that which crowned withy pollard. Others, wrens and sparrows, had fled to farmyards, to the warmth of barns. '*Tchk-kkkk-chk.*' Kine chattered as he forayed. 'I am small,' he said, 'but formidable.'

'*Tchk-kkkk-chk.*' None, he thought, was more dashing, so light of foot. He explored the wood. It was both a familiar and a new world. Snow covered ash stump and willow, paths were hidden and glades transformed. Frost mantled old trees with new identities. Here, a sloping bough became by moonlight a glacis; there, branches grew frosty beards of stalactites. The ground was veiled, featureless. The weasel covered it with snake-like sinuousness, alternately low in profile then throwing a succession of leaps and bounds.

He was indeed small. Between questing snout and tip of tail stretched exactly ten and a half inches of russet topcoat and white vest. But he was whip-spare and moved with Will-o'-the-wisp agility. '*Tchk-kkkk-chk.* Let me teach you the steps of the dance of death.'

The shadows deepened. Great timbers engulfed the hunter, witches' caverns darkly furnished with moss-cankered stakes and boles. A frozen rill creaked. A bough groaned. Kine halted, his head raised, nostrils quivering. The air was freezing, the smell of rabbit strong on it. Swiftly he glided forward, nose to the throbbing scent. Thorns of briar and viperous bramble snatched at him. He soared over them. At each banking, dipping bound he seemed to volplane to earth and take off again. Then, ahead, a pool of light caused him to slacken pace.

A fallen tree spanned the glade, a rotting hulk in the flooding moon. Around, the snow had been trodden by feeding birds. Some now roosted in the boughs above the weasel. High on a finger of oak crouched a pigeon. And another. Lower, where the branches were thicker, perched a pheasant. Looking down, it saw the grey-lagged rabbit in the clearing – and Kine step lightly from the black trees.

And as lightly begin to dance. He performed with swaying elegance. It was an ancient ritual, and a deadly one. '*Tchk-kkkk-chk.*' Kine measured his step as the rabbit dithered. '*Tchk-chk.*' He judged the plunge to the neck. 'Stay,' invited Kine the hunter, 'behold my artistry!'

The scream of the rabbit filled the valley. Darkly, on the far ridge, the shape of a she-mink rose on its haunches, intently listening. Upright, the mink stood a foot and a half in height, the broomy tail another eight or nine inches of total length. It was a giant. Its tail alone could have flattened Kine. The shuffling flat-headed shape was black and trail-scarred. When its lip curled, the teeth which showed briefly were saw-edged. Then the creature shouldered forward and sat up again. Behind came more dark figures, eyes peering, glistening like pricks of blood.

Kine gorged where the roots of the Life Tree met the frosted pond. The old willow symbolized warmth for him. Country people, in the past, believed in trees with magic properties. English villagers had pinned locks of hair to them, hung possessions on them for health and luck. And should the Life Tree ail, bad days were prophesied. Kine believed no more than his senses taught him. For the weasel the Life Tree was what the name implied – he had been born in the womb of its living depths.

The hole, a foot or more above the ground, was just wide enough to admit a weasel. There, in their mother's nest, four weasel kittens had been suckled and grew fur, warm in the dry leaves which lined the niche. He remembered his mother vividly. She had been a fury of protectiveness. Imperilled, she would snatch her brood one by one in her mouth and race them to safety, or stand her ground with spitting fearlessness. She had been a red tempest. And a chatterer.

He remembered his first steps beyond the nursery, his hunting apprenticeship, her vituperative scoldings when he broke line. 'Single file, and no dallying!' Those were the warm days, when all had been colour and touched by sun. He remembered the blaze of butterflies on fennel, the hot breath of steers at the sward's edge. He had forgotten neither the thrill of following in undulating line along parched ditch, nor crouching in ambush by nettle patch.

Survival had depended on those lessons. Not only had Kine survived, he cut a dash with it. None, he reckoned, was more adroit in the dance of death, a finer hunter, or, when it suited him, more magnanimous. From time to time he met members of the family, but they prowled alone in weasel fashion and passed on. Alone, he gorged. And replete, his song was not a modest one. '*Tchk-kkkk-chk*. I am small, but I am Kine, and this is my land.'

Proclaiming the challenge, he swaggered on. At that cross of martyrs, the old keeper's gibbet, he paused in tribute. Stoats and weasels, perhaps a score, had been nailed to the moulding board. Time had withered many to mere strips; others hung in decomposing mummy-cloths, incisors yellowing on bald skulls. A few, the most recently crucified, retained portions of fur, no longer glossy but matted and turning black. The sight was salutary. It reminded him of the perils of trap and gun – and, since the keepers had gone, of his principal rival, the poaching man.

The scream in the night broke the man's dream. He had dreamed that his soul had left him through his open mouth as he slept by the fire, and that his soul had the form of a creeping mouse. The mouse had screamed as something pounced on it. Poacher did not exactly believe the fable of the soul-mouse, but, like the Life Tree, it haunted him. He had been weaned on the mysteries of the valley and, in the age of the combine harvester, was perhaps more pagan than miscreant.

There were stranger things on the wild side of nature, Poacher held, than in the visions of philosophers; and those who doubted should spend a night in the wood, or on the marsh below. Let them listen to the banshees of tree and hedgerow, the grunts and rustlings of the dark holes. Let them watch the white spectre that was the barn owl, or feel the breath of the bat's wing. Let them smirk at boggarts and sprites then.

After sundown the land was eerie, as full of rancour and mischief as a weasel's heart. By night the hedgehog scuffled, the rat squealed. In the darkness small solitary creatures prowled secret paths while whiskered legions marched and counter-marched. Then the clans of claw and talon gathered. Many tales were recorded in country history of travellers set on by bands of roving rodents, reckless as Highland troops with drink in them.

Poacher's bones ached. That winter the big white willow had lost a bough, since when the pains which beset him had been crippling. With a grimace he kicked the embers in the hearth and took his gun down. Rekindled flames glowed on the gunstock and the metal rims of the cartridges. The stock had come from a walnut by the cottage, seasoned and fashioned in his father's day. It had not the hard look of modern gunstocks, but a polish through which the grain curled like a girl's hair, alive and soft. Poacher stroked it. His hand trembled. Much more pain and the gun would be less use than the gawky youth now waiting for him outside in the gloom.

It was almost dawn as Kine watched the two approach. Peering from his billet he saw them dump the sack, its neck fastened, and their other gear close to it. Nets were the main part, a pile of them, yellow from exposure to soil and sand. Nearby, Poacher tossed his breakfast in a pouch, along with 'owlers' – the stout gloves used to turn thorn and bird-claw – and a billhook. They had also a narrow hollow-bladed spade of the type used on land-drains.

This the lad drove into the hard earth, its upright shaft a post to which he tethered Poacher's patch-eyed terrier.

'Right you are.'

''Tis cold, Poacher.'

'Still and clear. They'll bolt well, youth.'

They spoke laconically, the low voices reaching Kine as the nets were set. The track, powdered with fine snow, was little used, sarsen stones crumbling and over-grown. Across it, brambles and fallen branches lay undisturbed. Later purple orchis and bird's-foot lotus would flower there, and briar rose; now only thistles were stirring, flat-leafed, tentative. Occasionally, in banks thick with hawthorn, a neglected gateway intruded, its posts fungi-clad. At one such place, where rotting post abutted rabbit mound, Kine had dossed.

For a time they worked in silence, clearing brambles from the bury, laying nets across the holes, Poacher swearing as his back griped. Mumbling, he took the ferrets from the sack and contemplated them. The youth glanced at him. 'Still bad, then?'

'Aye.' Putting the ferrets to earth, Poacher straightened, agonized. 'But we'll manage – me and them.' The creatures sniffed the black chambers lazily. 'We're not leaving this wood to the vermin yet.'

Kine bristled. The smell of ferrets flattened the small

ears to his sharp head, and made his claws flex. He wanted to hop in the hideout, to bounce with rage. Instead he watched with contempt as the animals sluggishly went to work. He had no time for serfs, the slaves of Poacher, tame tunnellers toiling on the man's behalf. Let him suffer, he prayed, and may his ferrets shed tears for him.

'Here, youth, load the gun. We may be needing it.' The terrier was taut on its leash, trembling eagerly. 'And if you use it,' the man said, scowling, 'mind your damned aim.'

'Don't worry, Poacher.'

With a grin the lad dived for the earthen mound. The head of a rabbit had appeared behind the net at one of the holes, nostrils working as it puzzled the string mesh. Its inaction was momentary. Wild with fear as a ferret followed, the rabbit lunged, struck the net, and rolled entangled down the bank, where the youth pounced on it. There was a fleeting struggle before its captor, grasping the rabbit by the hind legs, cast it across his knee and wrenched its neck. 'They be coming,' he said, tossing the limp body to the track.

The ferret emerged and Poacher stooped to it. Above ground the animal moved bemusedly, robbed of scent, shaking earth from its fur in disgruntled spasms. It was put to another hole and disappeared. A second net filled. Poacher took the rabbit, pulling straining muscle until its back snapped and the body dangled lifeless. A flight of duck crossed the wood in loud, abrasive voice. 'Something's scared 'em,' the man declared, watching. 'Now what would that be?'

'Fox?' the youth said.

'Aye. Nothing else on the marsh.'

'Not at this hour.'

The trees dripped; the thaw had started. And, for a while, man and boy pursued their immemorial occupation, no more said than a volley of orders from Poacher's lips. 'Watch those nets! There's another! He's bolting – look smart! Cope forrard! Let the dog loose!'

It was time, reckoned Kine, to bestir himself. The youth had grasped the gun while the terrier, free at last, rampaged among the brambles by the old gate. Kine retreated. There was scant cover but, with most of the nets gone, the bury beckoned. Two leaps and the weasel gained the underworld. He knew the workings. Loam to clay, root to sub-root, he knew the earthy chambers, and soon left the yap of the dog behind.

He ran in the dark by scent and tactile instinct, a sixth sense, ears attentive to the sounds which swirled on clay-laden draughts. The engineering of the system was complex, abounding in escape lanes and cul-de-sacs. Grunts were audible. He could feel the vibration of scrambling feet. Jinking into a side-tunnel Kine avoided a bolting rabbit, then danced forward. It was damp now, mud clogging his pads and needle claws, the way deeper, roof and walls exuding a thick, peaty odour. Fibrous roots stroked his flanks. It was dead quiet. Then the path tilted: he was climbing, passing stones and flints as the level rose.

Near the end of the tunnel, light returned and the weasel stopped. Raising a long neck, Kine peered beadily from a grass-tufted opening. A wintry sun was shining, revealing the marsh in fresh colours as the frost thawed. He was on the fringe of the wood, above the levels. The yap of the dog was a distant bleat.

'Running from Poacher, Kine?' Another, rather smaller weasel was watching him.

Kine returned the scrutiny. Interlopers invited trouble, but Kia, being young and female, imposed on him. Why he let her, he sometimes wondered, for she chattered more relentlessly than had his mother, and possessed a sly tongue. He ignored her, tugging mud from his claws, regaining breath before, 'Kine runs from nobody,' he declared.

She eyed him sharply. 'You've a fine conceit.'

'Pride,' he corrected. There was a difference. Those who hunted alone, who pitted their wits against many and larger enemies, were sustained by pride. Modesty was for herbivores, nibblers of grass and berry-eaters. He said, 'Poacher is ailing. Soon, not even the rabbits will run from him.'

'You know a lot.' She watched as he cleaned himself.

'I know the signs of the wood and marsh.'

'All of them?'

He stretched complacently. The sun was quite warm. It was one of those mornings in January when the heavens surprise with a rehearsal of spring, and mid-winter's jurisdiction no longer holds. Doubly gratified, Kine tolerated her irony. 'Try me,' he responded equably.

'Tell me this . . .'

'Yes,' he encouraged.

Kia looked serious. 'Tell me what has webbed toes and fur, will climb a tree, smells more evil than the gibbet, and can kill a pike.' Her tail flicked. 'You don't know. You see, you don't know everything. But I saw it, and it frightened me. It was a demon, a water monster.' She chattered nervously. 'It came from the river with its billowing tail and atrocious jaws, half fish and half animal, and ate the pike. It climbed a tree, Kine. It climbed a tree and looked around, then returned to the stream, to the depths again.' She broke off, adding quietly after a moment, 'You'll run, Kine – you'll run, I promise, if you meet this thing.'

Kine followed the hedge to the flats, making his way then by the cut they called Mullen's dyke. Freed from its earlier stillness, the air wafted vapours of mist over patches of scrub, which they shrouded with milky haze. From cold barrenness the marsh came to life again. Mallard circled in celebration; flocks of dunlin dived like darts to the meadows. Beyond them, the plough-man's Massey Ferguson growled powerfully, seagulls gathering thick in its blue exhaust.

On thawing pasture lapwings stood motionless, tufts erect, like moored dinghies, prows to the light breeze. The hare, contrariwise, lay tail windward, the blind spot in her vision filled by the scents which blew down towards her. Kine's was one of them. Stirring, the black-eared doe quit her form, her lazy lope the mark of an old hand. Until her leverets were born she feared few enemies, for she was peerless at top speed.

Kine moved lightly to the river and watched it flow. There was snow where the sloping bank was still in shadow, and skirts of opaque ice. The water in winter had slight appeal for him. Later, when it warmed, he would swim in pursuit of voles and shrews, but he lacked the insulating fat of water denizens. Even so, he knew much of what happened there. He knew the shrewdness of the carp, the fox of the river; the stupidity of the roach. He knew the fierceness of the pike, and the greed of the perch, which ate its own kin.

Above all, he knew that when summer came the marsh frogs would squat by the stream in ceaseless gossip, and Kine had a taste for frogs.

Now, ranging the bank, he sniffed edgily. He felt less at home by the river than in the wood. It was a frontier. Across the stream, scrub willow, waterside sallow and osier, formed thin clumps in the bog grass that stretched to the far crest. To the ploughman in his glass cab it was just the reverse side of the valley, where a blue Fordson, toylike, was duplicating his own work. To the weasel it was uncharted country, taboo ground.

There was a rustle behind him and he spun round. It was a moorhen. The bird scrambled across the water on beating wings, leaving a chain of round ripples where its feet dipped. Kine relaxed. Floating weed was drifting downstream on a current muddy with slush draining off the land. Peering into it, Kine saw only the reflections of dead reeds and the pale distorted orb of the winter sun. He thought of Kia. Frothy races and eddies were conspicuous; water monsters, not so. He had tolerated too much chat from her.

Turning, he faced the wood and the home ridge. The limpid light cast the stems of the bare oaks in brown and purple, etching the Life Tree with silver strokes.

Brown-ribbed fields, south-angled to the sun, rose with tawny meadows to where Poacher's chimney coughed smoke from its sooty flu. Weasel country – Kine's heritage! Across the dykes a pair of harriers hunted, talons in readiness. He dismissed Kia's fantasy. There were dangers enough without inventing them.

CHAPTER TWO

WATER had a life of its own in Kine's country. It flowed and jabbered ceaselessly. As rainfall doused the high land, filling the pond in the wood and puddling Poacher's yard, it seeped through the top soil to the land-drains, was channelled downhill in the pipes, and disgorged into ditch and dyke. Cattle grazing on the slopes could hear it gabbling underground. Other water found its way along the surface, following runnels and tractor ruts, sluicing through gateways to the marsh and into the same troughs. Here the heron at siege was concealed by sedges, and shy long-billed wading birds probed the nutritious silt.

The water itself was still journeying. From lesser ditches and dykes it filled greater ones, major channels, these leading to pumps on the riverbank. At flood levels the water was pumped up to the river in gushing torrents, frothing eddies, to merge at length with the main stream and reach the sea. It was a perfect system for amphibious penetration, and now the scouting marauders travelled unseen. They were torpedoes, grim submersibles charged with malevolence.

Below Mullen's meadow, where the bend in the river caught the wind, the stream rippled, wavelets socking the bank with persistent plops. To the bustling shrew, who weighed a fraction of an ounce and was almost blown away beside the water, the waves were vast, oceanic in their squally force. Heaving and breaking, they drenched his pigmy body with scudding spume. The shrew was preoccupied. With a probable life-span of twelve months and an imperious appetite, he lived in a state of neurotic urgency, the tiny tapered snout snuffling for insects with frantic haste.

The moorhen on the stream bobbed elegantly. Riding the crests, intermittently obscured by them, she had in

23

the shrew's sight the grace of a schooner on a high sea. With each stroke of her yellow paddles the moorhen's tail flicked, revealing a dainty white underskirt, and the glossy fowl nodded her red cap. A flurry of rain blurred the image, then it returned. In the depths, the phosphorescent wakes of mink sped silently.

The brown-shaded snipe left the reeds with a shrill '*sceap*'. For the snipe the sludgy shallows were alive with food, the withered flags and dun grasses ideal camouflage. Rising from them, the snipe took no chances, shooting up with a dodging corkscrew burst calculated to deceive hawk and gun alike, then sweeping wide before descending to fresh ground.

A beetle stirred. The shrew crushed it between microscopic cusps and swallowed it. Shelves of wavelets drubbed the riverbank. There was a pulse to them, a repetitious sock-and-suck which matched the shrew's infinitesimal heartbeat. Across the stream a heron stabbed the water and caught an eel. And in the space of that stab the moorhen disappeared. The heron blinked. The eel writhing in its mandibles flailed the air. The moorhen had been there – then it was gone. For a moment the shrew searched the stream, but his eyesight was only moderate and he thought no more of the vanished fowl. The water, splashing and bobbing, had its own life.

Invisibly, the she-mink swirled through the depths, her spouse and lieutenant alongside. In her jaws the crumpled moorhen left a wash of red on the flood.

The man cut the sappy wand, trimming two pegs from it so that he had three lengths: the pegs a few inches long, the original member perhaps four feet. Bent in the drizzle, the scarecrow figure of Poacher looked wild and primitive. He worked with deft strokes of the clasp-knife, notching each peg so the notches coupled when placed together. Then to one peg he bound a cord, which he joined to the wand's tip. The result resembled a boy's home-made fishing rod, a peg dangling at the end of its short line; and a peg to spare.

He flexed his fingers. The pain in arm and shoulder made a trial of this simple task. Attaching a fine wire to the strung peg he formed a noose. He took the knife again. Determinedly he now sharpened an end of the second peg and drove this into the ground beside the run flattened by the rat which had lodged beneath his chicken house. He next sharpened the thicker end of the rod, embedding it a step back from the rat's run and bending it like a bow until the pegs notched, held in tension by the taut cord. Finally he stretched the delicate noose across the run itself.

The rat was artful. There had been a saying in Poacher's youth that a rat was not dead until killed twice, and the traditional gallows snare was designed to make sure of that. At a jerk of the noose, the pegs would part and the wand spring upright, garotting and hanging the victim at the same time. It was infallible. Satisfied, the man stood, hands at small of back, gaunt and grey in the thin rain. Grey, too, was the brooding cloud-rack, and the wings of the pigeons which raced under it. In the lane the Land Rovers approached through clotted mud.

At the sound of motors, Poacher limped to the hedge and glared malignantly. He spat as raw-boned beaters jumped from the vehicles and guns faced the covert on its east side. Twice each winter the shoot drew the wood for stray pheasants, a matter of an hour or two annually, every minute resented by the valley man. Kine was no less offended. While Poacher skulked, the weasel made for the Life Tree in savage humour. The wood was clammy. Moisture dripped from the big oaks to form globules where moles had cast fresh tilth. Holed up in the old weasel nursery, Kine smouldered. To be driven to cover by outsiders was a crass affront.

He lounged moodily. From afar he could hear knocking, the click of sticks, as beaters drove the undergrowth. A pheasant ran past the willow to the last of the trees before the lea, and crouched watching the still line of slanted guns. Another crept on damp leaves to the same thicket. Behind them the clamour of beaters swelled until the wood was wild with noise. Many creatures were in flight now, among them Kia, who dived into Kine's refuge, knocking the breath from him. Startled, he seized her neck. 'It's me,' she protested. 'Let go of me.'

Kine did so, and she panted her relief in subdued tones. 'Thank goodness you're here,' she said.

Kine snarled. The hollow of the Life Tree was sacrosanct, a place no other weasel entered. That she encroached on the wood itself was a liberty; that she invaded the willow was intolerable. It had been his mother's place and, since his mother moved on, the most private sanctuary of Kine alone. Apart from which, unlike this female, he derived no comfort from company which distracted and – in the confines of the hollow – constricted him.

'This,' said Kia in a small voice, 'is a safe place.'

The male weasel avoided the touch of her. The sound of the beaters was drawing closer, their shouts and knockings driving pheasants through the undershrub in frightened groups. Crouching, they ducked through thickets and round lichened boles, paused round-eyed to listen, then ran on. Almost black, a melanistic bird scuttled like a shadow among buff hens. Kine strained his hearing. Kia's presence diminished his alertness, and he scowled at her.

'It helps to share danger,' she tried again.

'It's not your danger. All you have to do is keep your head down.' For preference somewhere else, his scowl implied.

'It helps to talk,' she said.

To clack, he supposed she meant, like flock creatures who draw delusions of safety from their numbers, and he showed his teeth when he thought she was coming too close again. He said, 'The weasel lives alone. So it has always been.'

'When we were young we lived in families.'

'But were trained to be self-sufficient and hunt alone. Shut up and listen.'

26

He heard the men with the sticks draw abreast the tree, and pass on, shouting. Peering from the hole he saw the guns and, at the wood's edge, a host of wild birds and beasts ready to break cover. The hare truckled, black ears flattened. A squirrel, roused from slumber, scrambled out on a bough, then withdrew again. Now, where the badger's set steamed amid the massive roots of an aged oak, a white snout appeared, sniffing anxiously. Everywhere, it seemed, small creatures dithered. Kine watched scornfully. 'It's no virtue,' he growled, 'to die in company.'

'I don't like loneliness.'

He grunted. The first bird to break was a woodwale, closely followed by magpies, a pair of jays. They fled in silence, unmolested by the guns, the pheasant killers. 'To live in solitude,' Kia said with passion, 'would be terrible.'

'We live amid brigands and numskulls and go alone.'

'By what precedent?'

'By the sun and the moon, the mightiest. Don't the gods stride alone on their own paths?' Kine eyed the pheasants, gullible creatures, and pitied them. They kept to the ground in the brush, scrambling swiftly from the beaters to the fringe of the wood, where they rocketed out. The first to spring was a cock bird. It went with a screaming *whirr*, neck gleaming, tail floating – to jerk as the shot bit, then plunge to earth. A hen rose up, soaring in death, her throat haemorrhaged. More sprang as Kine watched. 'They follow like sheep,' he said.

But we aren't gods, the smaller weasel was thinking as the guns roared, and after a pause she went on, 'I don't believe we were meant to live forever alone, just for ourselves, Kine. I believe it's better together, to share our fears, defend each other.'

'Fears!' He snorted his contempt.

'They exist, even weasel fears, unless,' she told him acidly, 'your name is Kine, of course. Long ago our forefathers banded to protect themselves.'

'Long ago there were prodigies indeed!' He had heard

stories of weasel packs and war tribes, clans of what the gipsies called 'dandy hounds', but Kine was sceptical. Unlike Poacher, who happened to have seen a pack of the red midgets in his boyhood, Kine had no reason to believe in such freak events. If mobs of weasels had existed, they must, by his reckoning, had been aberrant, usurpers of the rights of individuals and their boundaries. He snarled impatiently, 'Two's a crowd.'

'I'd feel less frightened,' said Kia, 'if there were more of us.'

The shamelessness of her defeated him. Pheasants were running to the lea, springing forth to be met by fresh volleys as they gained height. The shot hissed; it broke wings and pierced feathers, to heart and lungs. Kia was a jibberer, but a grudging protectiveness came over him. 'Come on,' he said rather more gently. 'It's not us they're shooting at. You're not afraid, Kia.'

'Not of the guns, maybe.'

'Well?'

'The river – the thing I described to you.'

Kine had forgotten. 'Oh, that,' he responded dismissively.

'The *unknown*, Kine. Something evil is happening, I'm sure of it . . .'

Her certainty was obscured by the rising din. The whole line of guns was now in action, barrels blazing. The fever mounted, a wild delirium as rocketing birds filled the sky, smoke and drizzle intermingling over the sward. Pheasants side-slipped, rolled and fluttered, ran wounded, were blown asunder, collapsed in brown heaps. Then it was quieter, almost over, and '. . . our turn will come,' she was saying, 'but not from the guns. From the river, Kine. From the evil there.'

Kine despaired of her. When the guns had gone, he turned her from the hole and jumped out after her. The last female in the Life Tree had feared nothing. He thought of his mother, her dauntless never-say-die ferocity, and the inspiration she had been to him. He remembered her praise of the gibbet martyrs: 'They stood alone and unafraid, daring the owl and diving hawk, the man and the man's dog, against giants, and in our own trials we'll not forget. Alone in battle, we'll remember them.'

He looked at Kia and was unimpressed. 'One thing before you get on your way,' he said, the sharpness returning. 'The willow is not a common lodging place. It's sanctified, the tree and the hole, and in my custody. Goodbye, Kia.'

'I'm sorry.' She watched him go. 'I didn't realize. Wait for me . . .'

He loped off briskly, and the female, dodging the puddles, skipped after him until he showed his teeth. Then she said pleadingly, 'I've some news for you. I meant to tell you, Kine. Wait for me.'

It was raining hard now, the departing Land Rovers scarcely visible. The smell of gun-dogs lay low on the meadow – and of death, where small piles of feathers grew cold and damp. Eyes half closed against the downpour, Kia persevered. 'It's important, Kine. You'll want to hear this, you really will.'

She paused, shaking the rain from her coat, her eye gleaming slyly when she saw that his attention was fully caught. They had reached the woodpile by the midden, now disused, which adjoined the tithe barn near Poacher's place. The roof of the building sagged crazily above its obsolete threshing floors, water gushing and sloshing from unguttered eaves. 'I just thought,' Kia said, spinning it out, 'that you ought to know.'

Through gaping wagon doors the barn-owl watched from a high beam, the oaken rib of some bygone fighting ship. He was motionless. At night he prowled the valley on ghost-like wings, or threw his bloodcurdling challenge from the high ridge. Now, in the shadows of the roof, he drew his black-flecked cloak round white cuirass, and might have been carved from the beam itself. But every move of the weasels was seen by him.

Kine drew in by the stacked wood. 'You were right, I should know.'

'You don't always believe me.'

'This is different.'

'I can show you,' Kia agreed. 'There's no mistaking the rat's trail.'

Kine's neck bristled. This time he believed her gossip. Weasels were born to detect and abhor the rat, the traditional foe of their kind. 'You were right to tell me. It must be tackled before it's joined by more and they infest the place.'

Kia nodded. The prospect was a lot less chilling than her nightmare of the riverbank, but at least, she saw, it gained his interest, a novel prize in her experience. 'I didn't tell you,' she purred, enjoying her new importance, 'where the rat was. It's entrenched on Poacher's patch, beneath the chicken house.'

'Poacher's patch!'

'In Poacher's old orchard.'

'I see,' he said. He could not resist the fitness of the rat's choice. The unedifying Poacher and the detested rodent! They deserved each other, he reflected, and if the rat spawned its evil on Poacher, what should Kine, the detester of both, care? Did it matter? 'Why should I protect Poacher?' he asked aloud.

Kia considered it. 'Especially,' she said, 'as the rat is powerful with hunger at this season, and twice your weight. Why take foolish risks?'

'Risks?'

'The rat is clever and treacherous.'

'And Kine is twice as clever and valiant.' He had asked for an answer and received the one spur to action he could not resist. Indeed it mattered, for who was Poacher but a thief in Kine's dominion, and was not Poacher's patch on Kine's estate? 'You don't think,' he said, 'I'd let the rat stay? The rat must go.' He eyed the rain, stepping forward with brisk intent. 'I just mean that it isn't for Poacher's sake.'

'Suppose it won't go?'

'If it stays, it will witness the dance of death.'

'Then beware,' said Kia.

Skipping puddles in the track, they reached Poacher's gate. It was decrepit, a hinge loose. Kine peered under it. The weatherboard walls of the cottage were peeling from the beat of the sou'westerlies; the chimneys were streaked with the birdlime of many summers. In spring, jackdaws and starlings would return to nest in the sooty vaults. Now only sparrows, damp and bedraggled, hunched on the roof or took refuge on the ledges of windows, beside black panes. At one window a silver ball, the witch-repellent of country custom, gleamed dismally.

Kine's eye took in the weed-grown path, the row of slug-ravaged cabbages to one side. By the door, mud still clung to a besom where Poacher had wiped his boots, and a burdened wheelbarrow held wet logs. The smell of smoke, borne down by the rain, told that a fire burned.

'Poacher's in.' Kine eyed Kia askance. 'Where's the run? Let's see if the rat's at home.'

She led him by the hedge, through twisting ivy and dripping thorn, to the patch of scrubby orchard where the hens roamed. Gnarled apple and spindly trunks of wild damson loomed gloomily, the fingers of a centuries-old mulberry clawing them. The winter slime of neglect clung to everything. Suckers of damson spiked from rotting tufts of coarse grass and ossified stalks of dead cow-parsley. A mouldering hutch had moss on it, its slats strung with glistening spiders' webs. It was a dank place. At last, where part of the hedge had died and fallen, the she-weasel crouched and gave a low growl.

Kine saw the trail of trodden earth that had alerted her.

'There,' muttered Kia. 'We must take care.'

The male weasel's tail flicked. He smelled rat and the battle surged in him, the Blood Fury. He was trembling, shaking with hostility, his flanks twitching where the rain had slicked his red coat. 'Stay here,' he instructed. 'I'll see to it.'

'We'd best both go. The rat is big and canny and he'll fight hard.'

'Stay here.' The command was peremptory, and next moment Kine was snaking down the run, his nose to the scent, rump towards her. Watching, Kia was surprised by her anxiety for so bumptious and conceited an animal. He went in serpentine spurts, his undulating body swift and purposeful. Wet spurs of arum and vole-bored clods engulfed the trail, the festering tumours of root and stump. In places, the husks of massive apples rotted, windfalls Poacher had left ungathered. Through the frost they had kept many blackbirds and mice alive, the fruit now disembowelled and just the skins left. Kine was blind to them.

Obsessed with the glutinous odour of the rat's path, the weasel ran on scent, sight now secondary. He saw neither grass clumps nor the tree boles, and the hen house ahead scarcely registered. The arc of the bent wand eluded him. With each scampering spurt his momentum increased, his blood rose until, at full charge, he was singing his war-cry to the world at large. It was answered by an urgent warning from close behind. 'Stop!' shrilled Kia. 'The noose! Stop where you are, Kine!'

An inch from his nose the thread of the gallows snare gleamed lethally. He shuddered. His claws were buried where he had braked. As he did so, Poacher came from the cottage and Kine, turning, followed Kia's retreating tail through the scrub to the lane beyond. There, breathing deeply, they rested and looked back.

The rain had stopped and a watery brightness suffused the clouds. There was mud on Kine's coat and in his paws, and his head drooped. When he raised it, he did so slowly, avoiding Kia's gaze. 'The rat had a lucky escape,' he said.

'Yes,' Kia said.

By an effort of will he met her eye and held it awkwardly. 'Well?' he challenged.

She said composedly, 'I didn't say anything.'

CHAPTER THREE

I N February the rooks returned from their winter parishes to the old rookery in the wood, tumbling and squabbling in the wind, discordant in their overtures to procreation. The strengthening light of the season, shining iridescent on black wings, delayed dusk in the tangled thickets where the pigeons rifling ivy berries were as full as the rooks with brawling argument. There was an aggressive thrust afoot. On the marsh the polygamous buck hare had grown pugnacious, thumping violently. Tiny wren and tall missel-thrush staked their territories. Winter had not surrendered, yet the blades of change pushed up widely, corn and wild plant, flushing the ridge with soft greens.

Conspiracies of growth flourished. Insurgent nettles bristled where paws trod; thyme and colt's-foot remustered under dead leaves. In sheltered places troops of hovering gnats rehearsed their spring drills. Still the boughs of oak were naked, but not for long now. The sap was rising, and weasel fire burned in Kine's blood. Kia was missing. For a week she had been absent and, curiously, Kine was not gratified. Her chat was tedious but the vacuum which replaced it irked him no less. More vexing, the rat, avoiding snare and weasel alike, had made a fool of him.

Kine climbed into Poacher's hedge and settled edgily. Each evening he waited for the rat to make a false move. It must do so. Meanwhile the weasel watched his older foe through the windows of the parlour Poacher occupied. The room was gloomy, its furnishings dull with neglect and dust. Much there could have traced its origins to Kine's domain: boards of chestnut, the birch-wood box, the corded ash which cluttered the ingle and smouldered fitfully. The deal table beneath the window had once stood by the lane, a lofty evergreen. Now its striated surface was ingrained with dirt.

Poacher sat twisted in the chair he always used, sideways to the girl who had entered as Kine climbed the pinched thorn. The girl wore jeans and carried a shopping basket, her appraisal scarcely more approving than the man's scowl. She said, 'My dad told me you were poorly. I brought some things. My dad said I should get a proper meal for you.'

The other's face was as dark as Kine could remember it. The man said, 'I can take care of myself. The youth comes up with the wood. Don't need more help.' Nor deserved it, in Kine's opinion, but the frown of the ploughman's daughter was now solicitous. Resting the basket, she looked first at the plastic curtain which hid the scullery, then at the pot on the fire-jack. The pot was black. 'When,' she asked, 'did you last have a cooked meal?'

'I'm not hungry.'

She looked into the pot and made a sour mouth.

'Not hungry. Didn't ask to be disturbed, girl.'

This glanced off her, but her expression was grim as she surveyed the place. 'Well, let's see what I can do. God, the mess!' Her eyes narrowed. Crockery long unwashed was piled with gun rods and ammunition. A wooden spoon was thick with congealed fat. The room was a cave of cobwebbed shadows deepened by the brown stain of wood-smoke which, tarnishing the manteltree, spread to the ceiling beams, filling their interstices with umber grime. 'Have you been to a doctor? You ought to, Poacher.'

'Damn the doctor. Takes more'n doctors to cure ailments in old trees.'

The girl huffed. 'You should be in bed. You're not that old,' she said, stooping to the fire, 'you're just neglected. You live like an animal.' She crouched at the hearth, haunches smooth as a cat's, and stirred up the flames. They filled the fireplace with a glow which exposed the soot and tar of untold winters and brightened the drab walls. Rising, she went to the window and looked out. 'A wilderness! You should see how my dad keeps his garden. You take care of nothing, Poacher, but that old gun. Much use it will be when they bury you.' He pushed his chair back, and she said, rounding quickly, 'Sit still. I'm taking care of things.'

'Let me be, girl.'

'When I've got you a meal. God, this scullery!'

Dusk was thickening, and Kine, tired of waiting, scouted restlessly. At the back of the cottage the yard was desolate, closed off by a derelict wash-house and bristling hollies from adjoining land that was ploughed and clean. Kine listened. He could hear the clatter of pans as the girl worked inside, and distant tractor sounds. There was the usual evening flurry of sparrow argument. A tap on a stand-pipe dripped. It was an insalubrious corner, heavy with the stench of Poacher's refuse, and Kine regarded it fastidiously. For a moment he hesitated then, stepping forward, heard the shriek, and gained the holly in a single leap.

'*Aahee!*' An evil shape crossed the yard, brown and ponderous, and the shrill of the girl followed it. '*Aahee!* There's a rat here, Poacher, a great rat!'

'Damn the vermin.'

'Well you might! I don't wonder there's vermin in such a place.'

'Let the dog at it.'

Kine climbed higher in the holly, hissing softly, concealed yet watching through the spiked leaves. There was a lull in which the drip of the tap pronounced five measured beats, then a door opened and Poacher's terrier rent the dusk with its harsh yap. Kine's lip curled. Amid the dark glinting hollies he controlled his impatience as the dog searched. It searched rowdily. For several minutes it yowled into crannies, clawed at crevices, before, whining its frustration, it was recalled. Kine stretched cautiously. The North Star had risen; the yard was silent. Sharpening his claws, Kine crooned wickedly.

'The dog's a fool, weasel-dodger, but Kine isn't. All I
asked was one false move, one careless step, and you've
made it. You should have run, snare-evader. You
should've been gone before the dog came. Instead you
hid where the dog couldn't reach you. That was too
clever. That was your false move, your fatal move.'

Jumping from the holly he pranced swiftly round the
yard, chanting and bouncing, exulting in the war dance
of the weasel kind. Sparrows jabbered. From their
roosts in the eaves they looked down, and Kine, fired by
an audience, played up to them. Twilight burnished his
coat with a chestnut lustre. The white of his bib was
heightened by dusk; the eyes of the weasel were amber-
bright. Kine showed off, but as he cavorted, those eyes
were unswerving, never leaving the hole in the wash-
house wall. Near the stand-pipe a single brick had been
removed to provide a sluice, and there, as Kine was
aware, the rat had entered. It was in the wash-house. He
threw his song to it.

'*Tchk-chk.* The rat is smart but Kine is smarter. The
rat is large but Kine is swifter. The night is fine. Come,
weasel-dodger, and dance the dance of death!'

Low and sibilant the response came from the sluice-
hole: 'Come inside, Kine.'

Kine stopped by the pipe and gave a dry laugh. He
knew the wash-house – cramped and dark – and that the
rat had the advantage there. He pictured the rodent
crouched to corner him, to bring overwhelming weight
and power to bear. 'Kine fights in the open. Come out
and fight.'

The sparrows murmured. He wished Kia had been
there, not to help but to see with what style he con-
ducted things. Slowly he strutted the yard, head high, a
matador, raising his chant to the darkening sky. 'Test
your courage with the weasel, snare-dodger. Die with
credit. Only fear is served by postponing death.' That
drew no answer. He called again without result, then
directly into the hole, prepared to leap backwards
should the rat charge – but it did not. Ten minutes

passed and the sparrows, losing interest, grew somnolent. The tap dripped. The steady *plip-plap* irked Kine and it struck him that Kia's absence, after all, was maybe just as well. The rat was wily. With night gathering the rodent might yet have a trick to play.

Kine pondered. Two weasel instincts – astuteness and intrepidity – vied in him. One said, 'Beware the rat's ground, for the rat is a hole-in-corner expert, and a weasel doesn't oblige his enemies.' The other said, 'The fight goes to the daring, and the weasel is audacious.' Daring pointed to the sluice-hole and the rat's retreat.

He visualized the refuge as he remembered it. In one corner was an earthenware sink, cracked and littered with rubbish from the sparrows' nests. Near the sink, a small window would admit the slenderest of light, being choked with old spiders' webs and other filth. Poacher kept a collection of tools in the out-house – sickles, scythe, spades and forks – mostly little used, and a pile of sticks for the random drills of beans and peas he grew. It was a tight cell, a bare skip from wall to wall, the roof low-hung.

Somewhere inside, accustomed to the shadows as Kine was not, lurked the enemy. But where precisely?

Plip-plap. The tap seeped.

More stars were visible, beneath them the pale ghost that was the barn-owl, causing Kine to freeze as, bluntnosed, it swooped beyond the cottage like a great moth. Closer, a sparrow shifted from eaves to holly bush. That was curious. For the sparrow to leave the wash-house once dusk had set in was very curious, unless . . . Suppose the rat had clambered atop the wall, beneath the roof? That would be cunning. The descent from eaves to yard was not impossible, and if Kine entered the sluice, escape across the yard would be unchecked.

His spine tingled. The tap spluttered. Approaching the sluice, he sniffed cautiously. The bricks were green with dampness, and small tendrils of briar had rooted there. With a quick glance upwards he eased into the opening until concealed, then, twisting his body, faced the yard again. Prepared to sprint, he called loudly, 'I'm coming in!'

For a moment nothing happened. Kine quivered. Then a sound – a scratch of movement, a sliding on the wall – and abruptly the rat was in Poacher's yard. It was a mean and shaggy brute. Its brown-grey winter coat was coarse, the scaly tail obscenely thick-docked. Bare trunks of horny legs splayed from powerful hind-quarters and shoulders, their fingers hard-tipped, and when it spat, the long incisors which showed were chisel-edged. Kine's tremor was momentary. Such a brute could breed sixtyfold in twelve months. He sprang from the sluice with a cold heart.'

'We fight, weasel-dodger. There's no escape.'

'Stand aside,' rasped the rat, 'or I'll break your back.'

Fangs bared, it charged the weasel, its coat stiff, spine humped. It charged bull-like, heaving forward, shoulders labouring. Kine waited spring-heeled. Leaving his jump to the last moment, he danced to the rear of his adversary, obliging it to haul round. It came again, flattening the rank grass, its jaws agape. 'Faster,' mocked the weasel. 'Your dance is ponderous.' But he felt the breath of the rat, and was lucky to have skipped in time. In a maul his chance was negligible. He ducked sideways as the armoured tail lashed at him. Snarling, the rat came strongly, its speed deceptive, the stab of its neck treacherous. Kine gave ground. This time the rat attacked with a cumbrous bound that must have flattened the weasel had he stayed for it. Instead, he was at the flank, harrying.

Now the sparrows, roused again, peered from gutters, trembling fluffily. The battle filled the twilight. It was a miniature whirlwind, a tornado of dust and debris, of organic spin-off: fur, spittle, pellets of grit kicked up by hindfeet. Savagely the rat reared and lunged, crouched, lunged again. It was devious. It feigned disinterest then forayed suddenly. It drew back, then, erupting with fury, raked out a clawed arm. Weaving and bobbing, Kine stayed out of reach.

'Let me teach you,' he taunted, 'the finer steps.'

The rodent rushed. Anticipating evasion it swerved at the last moment, bowling over its slight antagonist, pouncing at him. Kine saw the fangs gleam; horny fingers reached for him. Rolling, he was on his paws like quicksilver, and away again. '*Tchk-kkkk . . .*' The rat, he knew, was most dangerous when desperate. 'You are tiring,' he purred. 'The froth of weariness rises. You grow heavier.'

'Come nearer, weasel.'

'Come to *me*.'

'Then beware!'

Earth flying, the rat stormed in yet again, and Kine, turning the umpteenth charge, measured the other with icy eyes.

Plip-plap dripped the tap. 'See,' breathed the sparrows, cosily horrified, 'how death approaches, how fresh the weasel is.'

Kine's eyes fixed on the neck of the rat. It was saliva-flecked. It strained and twisted and he knew the plunge must be immaculate, for the rat would not permit a second chance. He danced faster, seeming to hover above the ground. He rose from all four feet, a jack-in-a-box, touched down lightly, whirled away to one flank, then the other, churring his soft accompaniment: 'You are tiring. You are weary, weasel-dodger. Your lungs are painful. You must watch now, just rest and watch the weasel's elegance.'

Despairingly the rat lumbered forward, nostrils flaring. The lunge surprised the weasel, the yellow chisels so close he felt the fur wrenched from his body, and jumped back swearing. The rat raged at him. Its strength was dredged from the depths, forcing Kine to leap vertically to save himself. He soared mightily. As he did so he knew intuitively the time had come, and, twisting mid-air, landed facing the rat, behind its back. He nerved himself. Slowly the coarse brown hull was turning beam-on to him. With all his force Kine plunged at the meaty neck.

The rat heaved. The weasel's jaws locked. It was crucial to hang on at all costs. He felt himself lifted bodily as the rat reared, knocked breathless as it came down on him. He was being swung in circles and his head swam. He had no idea which way up he was, but the death-lock of the weasel was inflexible and life was ebbing from the threshing hulk. He was exultant – bruised and dizzy but exultant – and his eyes popped.

Other eyes were distended in disbelief. In Poacher's scullery the ploughman's daughter wiped steam from the window with a flat palm. Her voice was resonant. 'It's a weasel! Heavens, Poacher, there's a weasel killing that rat I saw!'

The intoxication of victory was in his step. Rooks slumbered. Badgers roamed. Few creatures foraged with less finesse than badgers, and their rumpus was conspicuous. They snorted, grunted, snapped twigs and scuffed leaves. A fox would pace the wood's length without sound. A badger could not move a yard without blundering. Kine galumphed, heedless of badger noise, big with victory. The rat was dead. It was the largest rat he had ever killed.

At the gibbet he paid a conqueror's tribute to fallen heroes. Low and full, the moon silvered the marsh, touching the land beyond the river with chimeras. The gibbet was black, its withered relics silhouetted, ancient warriors whose spirit filled Kine with weasel pride. He had kept faith. He had purged Kine country, and stood tall in the hallowed place. He 'remembered' them.

'Time,' piped the shrew, falling in with him, 'is short. We'll all be relics soon.'

The weasel scarcely heard the pigmy, or the badger's noise. He was reliving the epic of Poacher's yard, savouring triumph: the clue of the sparrow, the sluice-hole ruse, the sublime dance. How he had danced! If he said it himself, how cool his strategy, and in execution how masterful! The rat had proved formidable, yet Kine had out-thought and out-fought the rat. It was a fight to be savoured and sung afield.

'Time is short,' piped the shrew, 'and comes the reckoning.'

'Rejoice, shrew!'

'The end is near.' The brief-lived shrew shrilled his woes unheeded in wood and marsh. It was the ploughman's daughter – who had cupped him in her hands and put him out when sometimes he bumbled under the cottage door – who had named him Scrat, a house-sprite of country fable in those parts. He was, in Kine's view, ludicrous: a snuffling atom and a ball of nerves. So highly strung were some shrews that Kine had known them to die in thunderstorms. Scrat's piping litany of doom aggravated him. Had pride permitted, the weasel might have hastened the prophet's end. Instead, he said with ebullience, 'The rat is dead!'

'Death . . .' Scrat paused, peering up from his dwarfish brows. 'It stalks all of us, for I've seen the moorhen dive and not come up, Kine. I've seen the mallard stricken, blood wet on it, and the fish which lie headless on the riverbank. I've seen the mark of the terror which strikes invisibly, and the truth is plain, weasel – the vale is doomed.' He snatched a bug from the night and chomped nervously.

'The rat-slayer stands before you. Rejoice, Scrat!'

The shrew whined.

'The vale,' cried Kine, 'will resound with acclaim when the news spreads.' When it was told how the rat had been outwitted and brought to battle, how the duel by twilight had swayed and raged – that final vault, with its inspired contortion and consummate landing, would live in the annals of Kine territory. Kine swaggered. He said, 'You're a fool, Scrat. You peddle nightmares to the bringer of death himself.'

'Not you – you wouldn't . . .'

Kine laughed. 'Be glad I'm charitable.'

Then he went to the Moon Pond and thought of Kia. When the moon swam in the pond, all thoughts were possible. It was a sequestered place deep in the wood, bowery at the banks, where the roots of the Life Tree burrowed, and glassy where it brimmed free of canopy. At the pond's edge a line of willows had linked arms as if to hold back the surrounding oaks. Reedy grasses thrived there, and water-plantains. Belladonna grew in tangled skeins. There were tall-fronded inlets for paddling birds, and bights which were clear to the bank itself.

Kine liked to drink from the ledge by the white willow. Here the pond was a foot or two deep, so pure he could see caddis-worms on the bottom, or watch water beetles in gliding motion. Occasionally a curling tail would betray the form of a resting fish. But in dry times, when the pond was lower by several inches, the ledge dropped to the surface in a small bluff, compelling him to quench his thirst among the reeds, where his feet blotched the water with swirls of sludge.

In summer, ducks built their nests beneath the bluff, and dragonflies gleamed above the Moon Pond. Warmed by the sun, an emerald quilt of floating weed spread from the banks, while small fry broke the surface in flashing arcs. Warblers sang there; crested newts paddled lazily. It was, relatively speaking, a safe place, the dour square-hulled coot patrolling with such vigilance that the other fowl were reassured. It was Kine's place.

From the Life Tree his first view of the world had been the pond. Peering from the lip of the nest that warm night, he had seen the moon beneath him in the pool, the shadows thrown by the treetops reaching down to it. For a while, deep in the hole, things had seemed that way up to him. Later, when the world was established in reality, he could still peer into the pond on a moonlit night and see what might have been – another Kine peering back from the water, the stars under him. At times he imagined he saw different reflections there: his mother, his brothers. Once, a strange grey-muzzled weasel had peered up from the pond, with a single eye, the second missing, then dissolved – perhaps some unconscious memory of infancy.

The pool was a place of spells. Kine indulged his fantasies on its banks, entranced by the place but not deceived by it. It was Kia who confused the two worlds, whose romances and nightmares seemed true to her. And Kia he missed now, for he could not boast of victory to a pond, and Kine was bursting to recount the tale. All he saw in the Moon Pond was himself. The fronds shivered. He looked again.

'Hello, Kine, I've come back to the wood,' she said.

He turned, startled.

'You look surprised, Kine.'

'Where've you been?' It was more brusque than he wished, and he regretted it.

Kia said, 'Prowling alone, as you directed.' Then, with a purr of admiration, 'I've heard the news. I'm thrilled and proud of you. You've lost some fur. I must know all of it.'

'It'll take time . . .'

CHAPTER FOUR

THE wind howled, and in its eye the she-mink towered from the river and climbed the bank. The wind swept fear up the valley, confusing the defences of its creatures, their smell and hearing. It hampered vigilance. Gusting and roaring, the final gales of winter chafed the nerves, making cowards of otherwise calm beasts. The blackbird, ripe already with egg, held to the ditches. Rabbits sat near their burrows. They had begun to couple by February, and would not stop through summer, the cycle continuous since doe could not suckle till at buck again.

Above the wood, rooks swirled in the fierce draughts like charred paper, some dropping to leeward of the trees where they sheltered, stabbing for ants whose formic acid they applied against parasites. Lapwings, swept on the currents, dived screaming to marshy hollows and the quieter coombs.

The she-mink shed water. When her consort had joined her from the stream, she shuffled to the pump-house and examined it. On one side, sloping concrete shoulders flanked the great spinner – the thirty-foot Archimedean screw which hoisted water to the river from Mullen's dyke. On the other side, a hinged iron cap, set in the outlet embrasure, prevented backflow.

Astride these elements, a plain brick box – windowless, though with a door – housed the motor which powered the screw. Operation was automatic. When the dyke rose, electrodes called for power and the pump churned, switching off when the water level fell again. Such pumps were common along the river, and the mink approached with familiarity. Neck extended, she inspected the base of the brick house. Buds were swelling on the verdure of celandine, and the grass was lush.

But round the building the earth had constricted, leaving dark rifts.

For a moment the she-mink nosed the cracks, then pushed into one. It was murky there. Dust clung to her coat. She was in the foundations, amid abutments of rough cement and metal joists. She knew the labyrinth. At its heart, a concrete-walled bunker, the wind was lost. The creature grunted. Circumscribing the clay floor, she made a shallow scrape, a proprietary mark. Her lip curled. It was a nice irony, she thought, that the persecutors of her forebears had designed the perfect base for her onslaught of the land around.

The male watched her emerge from the labyrinth. She was, even in his own eyes, a sombre brute. There was no value to men in her coarse skin. Fur dealers looked for finer stuff. In the compounds where captives had languished were colour mutants: mink with names such as Pastel, Pearl and Platinum. But escaped strains reverted in a few generations to their wild coats and, in the genealogy of the she-mink, ranch-bred Topaz had begotten the plainer Dun and the common Brown.

It was a brown pillager, loury as thunder, who had sired the female, and she had run with his gang of plunderers. No mink was more voracious, so insatiable. On the leader's death she had ripped the throat from his lieutenant, proclaimed her succession, and led the brigands. She had killed with hate, with a lust beyond hunger, and for greater power. Now she staked her stronghold for a new campaign.

The violence of the pump, when it churned, fascinated her. It sucked in water as she sucked blood, slaking its thirst in muddy draughts which boiled and sloshed until the dykes drained. The force was demonic at the outlet valve. It hammered the iron cap with pulsating thrusts which created writhing and macabre scums. And the turmoil bore its own fruits.

Carrying edible fragments from the land, it attracted fish – gudgeon, barbel, bream, sluggish tench – which the mink relished. When the monster spawned her brood, there would be nursery meat. She eyed the rich slopes, the woods for plundering. Ploughlands blanched in the wind. Her head turned. For a while, in silence, she viewed the vale, before she spoke at last.

'Here,' declared the she-mink, 'shall be my stronghold, and all the land to the ridge shall belong to me. The pond shall be mine, and the oak wood. And those who dwell there shall dread the plunderers.'

'Did you miss me?'

'I noticed you'd gone.'

'I went to the river,' said Kia, 'to lay old fears.'

Kine watched the Massey Ferguson grow bigger and bigger until, dwarfing them, it wheeled the rollers behind it in a half-circle, powering back across the field. The earth vibrated. As the towering machine turned, the sound of music blared from the cab radio. In the wake of the rollers a swath of small corrugations showed where the rims had been. The weasels resumed their way, crimson tassels of poplars blowing down on them. 'Were you unafraid?'

'I was bold, Kine.'

'And saw nothing?'

She hesitated and the tractor returned, the girl's father spinning the wheel, glancing back at the rollers as they slewed round. Music wailed, drowning the lament of the velvet pigmy who fell into Kine's path.

'The end's near,' screamed Scrat. 'The end's revealed to me.'

Kine tumbled him.

'Let him be,' Kia entreated. 'Let him go, Kine.'

'And have to listen to *that* until he drops dead?'

'Let him be.'

Assenting with a shrug, Kine went on with her. She eyed him artfully. 'Sometimes,' Kia proposed, 'it pays to listen – before your head's in a gallows snare, for instance. He's small but useful. He sees things without being noticed, then reports on them.' She paused again,

46

continuing seriously, 'There's something you must know, Kine.'

They reached the marsh gate, the wind still gusting, bending poplars, twitching yellow gorse beside the field where the tractor moved. Broad clouds shoved nor'east. They darkened and brightened the sky by turns, and Kine, keyed to their restlessness, felt vigorous. 'Go on,' he said.

'Beyond the river – have you ever been to the other land?'

'The devil's wilderness?'

'You might be surprised.'

'It's taboo,' he said sharply. 'It always was. It's not weasel land.'

'That's the point,' she said.

Her gaze was distant. They sauntered by the dyke, overhung by sedges and dead flags, treading the strand left by the drained flood. The pump had stopped, and the lowered levels of the channels brought in the birds. Sandpipers foraged; buntings buzzed them in dipping flight. A wall-eyed ewe stared bleakly where a little cliff was drilled with martins' holes. Kine, stopping where mussels wallowed, demanded, 'What point?'

'That we're wrong. There are weasels across the river as well,' said Kia. 'I saw one.'

'In the other land!'

'Large as life, on the far bank. That's what kept me. I swam across to him.'

'I see.' Kine looked black. So much for her fears; they had been short-lived. He was not sure he preferred the emboldened Kia. For a moment he glared across the marsh to the land of sallows and boggy wilderness sprawling to the far heights. None save the birds, who were safe in flight, crossed the frontier to that obscure world. Dependable sources told of beasts who had fled there to escape pursuit, breasting the water to questionable safety, but he had never discovered one who came back. Until now. 'And what manner of weasel lives in such a mire?'

'He's young – younger than you – and just as assertive.' Kia twinkled. 'The point is,' she said with greater earnest, 'his belief was the same as ours. He never dreamed there were weasels across the stream. Like you he saw the river as a frontier to forbidden country.'

'As, by the gods, he'll find it if he dares to cross.'

'That's what he said of you, Kine. How typical! Don't you have enough enemies? Think of the opportunity. There you both are, clinging to silly boundaries, when you could unite and be twice as strong. He's quick and stalwart, a lusty animal. You'd make a good alliance in dangerous times.'

'*Tchk!*' Kine turned his back. He looked round angrily. 'If he's so impressive, how is it you didn't stay with him?'

'Maybe he was too insistent I did so,' Kia tossed at him.

He retraced his steps and she followed moodily. At the edge of the wood the rookery look-out peered down crustily. The Watchman, as Poacher called him, was not impressed by their red backs. A fox or owl might have precipitated the streaming flight of the colony – the Dread, in valley language – but the Watchman merely blinked now and hunched his neck.

His eye was caustic, his face grey and bare of plumes. There was a bitter edge to the raked beak. Across the oak crowns the rest of the rooks held noisy parliament. The Watchman viewed them acidly. Age had diminished his taste for endless and brash debates which, he concluded, established little but the garrulity of his kind. The season would run its course. Debate or no, there would be matings, births, deaths, infidelities. Scandals would bring longer arguments, disputes would be clamorous – and as usual, the Watchman supposed, his libidinous mate would make free again. Already one lewd bachelor was courting her.

In the end it was all the same. He watched his spouse fanning and flirting on a far bough. The old rook had been cuckolded more times than he remembered, and still she built him the best nest in the rookery, as she would while they both survived. It was a rich nest, twiggy and packed with soil, a solid lump of the valley atop a tree. No other nest was such a garden of earthy life. By summer it would bulge with grass roots, sprouting potatoes, slugs, dozens of earthworms, woodlice, centipedes. Such a home would make up for much else in the Watchman's life.

He stiffened and was suddenly loud with warning. What he saw was not weasels but an old foe of the rooks, and the commune stirred. One by one its members were airborne on thrusting wings, beating south with deceptively steady strokes, like some old-time galley in full flight. Kia looked up and saw the straggling black tide of rooks.

'Kine, it's the Dread!' She could see him ahead, nose down, preoccupied. 'Be careful, the rooks have been warned, Kine!'

The shrew was hiding. She saw Scrat tremble, and the owl come round the wood with sullen majesty. He prowled low, increasingly a daylight hunter since spring approached. He lurked quietly, flapping with lazy insolence, eyes sharpened by end-of-winter appetite. Kia saw the great eyes in the visored face, the broad white breastplate, black talons unfurling as the owl swooped. From Kia's perspective the talons seemed as large as the owl himself, just missing her as they drove down at Kine, and she screamed his name.

'Kine!'

He had begun to turn as the claws struck. Kia saw a flurry of dust, and the owl straining for height, his victim dangling. To Kine it was as if the heavens had collapsed on him; as if something had ripped open his back, tearing the flesh down across his ribs. The vice which gripped him had the force of a spring trap. Stunned, he imagined himself vaulting the rat in Poacher's yard, yet he could not be, for the ground was too distant and the pain was unique in his experience.

It paralyzed, shrieked for oblivion. At all costs, he was aware, he must not pass out.

The owl flew silently. He had ventured dangerously in tackling a weasel, and scored faultlessly. He winged for his eyrie in the barn roof. Rhythmically the great hull above the weasel lifted and plunged its wings, intermittently expunging and exposing the sky to Kine. The earth tilted. Trunks of trees were passing hazily, Kine's mind clouding, and all the will in the weasel was directed to rekindling clarity. He must stay conscious. No owl, he told himself, took a weasel with immunity. Defiance burned in him.

The wood scudded by. He saw the weather side of trees, green tinted; then the leeward side, grey-barked. Tractor, gibbet and woodpile passed under him. On the lea, a red streak, the lean body that was Kia, followed breathlessly. His vision drifted. He saw Poacher's chimney, blurred and tilting, and the ribbon of the lane on the ridge between ploughed fields. Lichened tiles loomed. With sudden clearness Kine saw a wattled hole where daub had crumbled, and the gape of the barn doors, then he was whirling into the maw of the owl's retreat.

The barn was shadowy. Thick odours hung where bales of straw lay under timbers of massive girth. A flock of small birds fled from the threshing floor. It was a musty cathedral of dark deeds, and stark urgency impelled action if Kine were not to find himself on the butcher's block of its soaring beams. He called the gods to him. He summoned the martyrs and his mother's strength. From the depths of him he mustered weasel defiance and made his bid. Twisting wildly, he clamped the needles of his forepaws in the owl's leg and heaved until he seemed to be pulling himself apart.

In blinding pain from the clamping talons, he stretched his neck. He stretched it until every fibre protested; then, as far up the feathered limb as he could reach, he applied his jaws and bit ferociously. The reflex was simultaneous. For an instant the bands enwrapping him relaxed, and he jerked free. Next moment he was semi-senseless in straw, and wings were beating somewhere in the gloom above.

Instinctively Kine bared his teeth. The owl was banking, swooping to the bales, and the weasel could not move for cramp and injury. His eyes were opaque with glaze. A yard from him the helmeted predator perched and prepared to strike.

It was to such a scene that Kia arrived. Spitting and bristling, she erupted from the straw, her voice furious. *'Tchk-kkkk!'* She spoke five words. She said, 'Touch him and you die,' and the owl, in little doubt, rose prudently to the safety of his high vault. Smouldering, he watched her snatch the limp weasel by the scruff, as if Kine were a kitten, and make off with him. The strength in her slight frame was staggering. Weasels had been known to haul grown rabbits across roads, and Kia went off with her burden at a surging lope. Only on reaching the shelter of the woodpile did she stop at last.

The air was still, the Dread expended. Small eyes peered with curiosity, noses twitched. There was a morbid interest among woodland creatures in spilled blood, and news spread rapidly. Not even the rook could forebear a concerned squint. 'He looks dead,' the Watchman said.

Scrat said, 'He *is* dead.'

'Dead or insensate.'

'Dead,' the shrew said.

'He is not dead,' Kia snarled, resuming her attendance of the torn shape, licking the talon wounds. Her tongue was tender but her temper was savage, and Scrat held back. 'Watch that path,' Kia snapped as she worked. 'I can't do everything. And you' – she looked up at the rook – 'watch the other way.'

'I gave the warning . . .'

'Just look out.'

'If he'd listened,' huffed the Watchman.

'Listened!' Scrat said.

'He'd not be hurt,' said the Watchman.

'He *never* listened,' said Scrat. 'Ask anyone.'

Kia interrupted commandingly. 'I must get him to the Life Tree. I want to know if the path's safe. Fly ahead, Watchman, and see for me.' The rook hesitated. It was none of his business, but her loyalty touched him and, somewhat gracelessly, he obeyed. The she-weasel advanced in determined spurts, resting her burden where there was cover, scouting cautiously, then toiling on again. The bird flew over her until, her task accomplished, she emerged from the willow – when he asked almost caringly, 'Is he all right?'

Kia nodded. 'He's coming round. A rest – he'll be his old unheeding, stubborn self again.'

Violence, generally speaking, was conspicuous. It attracted attention, and one might have been excused for believing it the dominant mood of wood and marsh. This was not so. Peacefully occupied, the inhabitants of the valley were less likely to catch the eye, yet concord, even between hunters and those on whom they preyed, was more usual than disharmony. Most mornings the vixen might be seen strolling amid browsing rabbits, with disinterest on both sides; the stoat be seen at rest while meaty voles passed beneath his nose. Like the herds of exotic places which have no fear of a sated lion, the cautious creatures of Kine's country had a way of knowing the intent of neighbours.

When Poacher walked with his gun the rooks clamoured; when empty-handed, they scarcely looked twice at him. The stick he now carried did not bother them, for they knew the difference between a stick and a gun at a hundred yards. They sensed, too, his infirmity, the dragging step which reassured bird and beast as, leaning on the stick, he took the pond path.

For a man it was the best time of year to broach the wood's depths. The loam was drying, and growth had yet to hide the pitfalls. Soon brambles would lay ambush to all approaches, while nettles and thistles rose forbiddingly. Then skulking burdock would smother clothes

52

in its sticky seeds; mosquitoes plant venom in human flesh. Meanwhile the path was free, the hint of luxuriance delicate. The smell of sap and the first fragrance of primroses mingled with the perfume of fertile clod. There was a russet tinge to the oaks now, a green fuzz on thickets. The hazel catkins were tipped with red stars.

The bent figure with the stick was not blind to them. Poacher had learned the ways of the wild in that same vale, stalking rabbits in warm hedgerows while still a child, cudgel in small fists; slaying his first cock pheasant with a catapult. His understanding was not as subtle as a weasel's, but he was informed where most were ignorant. He saw the fleck of fur by the path and knew the rabbit had her litter near. The doe had plucked her fur there to line the stop. He saw the mutes of the kestrel and, looking up, knew its nest from the pigeon's or the squirrel's drey.

He knew the sounds of chaffinch and yellowhammer, and the soft double note of the chiffchaff which began in March. There was not a great deal Poacher missed, whether the first flash of the kingfisher by the river, the arrival of the willow-wrens, or the debut on the lea of the brimstone butterfly. But the sights and sounds did not solace him. He was too cursed in his joints now to use the gun, and without it Poacher was unmanned. He watched the hare run towards him, sniff with perception, depart unhurriedly. That was the measure of his impotence.

He could feel his finger on the trigger, see the glint of the barrels, feel the stock where his hands had worn the old wood. But all he had in his fist was a briar stick. Even that had been a tax on his fingers for the past week. 'You're worse,' the girl had told him. 'Don't lie to me.' A wood pigeon took flight with a clap of wings, passing overhead with casual insolence. His eye followed, allowing for speed, timing the ghost shot – watching powerlessly. Something evil was happening. The hares were fearless. Pigeons scorned him.

Something was happening to the crooked old hunting man.

An adder stirred. Roused by footfalls from its fastness in a birch bole, the snake slipped quietly through the ivy and disappeared. Poacher prodded the ivy with his stick. The sombre leaves embraced dead wood, berries darkening, a funereal note amid quickening life, and his scowl deepened. A burst of drumming, like the Spandau gun-fire he remembered in a French copse, was followed by wild laughter as the woodpecker flew off. Skirting an uprooted pole, Poacher reached the pond's edge and stopped, eyes narrowing.

Fleetingly, where the toad slept under the bank, he saw a weasel, then it was gone and only tree roots figured the small bluff. 'Aye,' he said aloud, 'I seen you, you red beggar. I'll have you presently . . .'

It was some time since he had penetrated to that place and, for a moment, he lingered uncertainly. A heron rose. Poacher scanned the willows for the Life Tree. The crippled bough caught his gaze and he moved, heavy with apprehension, towards the gloomy trunk. Stretching an arm, he hesitated, fingers near the bark, then withdrew the hand, raising his sight instead to the stricken limb. His neck stiffened. There were no signs. It was, perhaps, too early for any sign, but Poacher kept looking for rejuvenation above him on the stark branch.

CHAPTER FIVE

KINE carried the scars of his lesions for a week or so. They marred the perfection of his raiment, but if the cosmetic flaw irked the weasel, he was more than compensated by that side of vanity which relished the symbolism of battle wounds. How many, after all, had lived with the mark of the owl on them? None in Kine's territory. The scars were eloquent. They read: 'Molest the weasel at your own risk.'

Poacher would have envied his recovery. There was little time in Kine's world for convalescence; either the injured kept going or they were overcome. Their capacity to 'soldier on', as Poacher termed it, was remarkable. Creatures had been known to leave legs in traps and only hours later be foraging on the three limbs which remained and a raw stump. The sheer will to survive was their healer.

'You're as good as new, Kine.'

'Fighting fit,' he said stoutly, his beam for Kia luminous. There was now no aversion to her closeness as they sheltered where the snake had left the ivy bower. April, in a characteristic tantrum, was hurling hail, and they had scuttled for cover as the stones bounced. Amid the flurry, blackthorn blossom, white as the shots of ice, signalled spring, and Kia was conscious of a growing attachment to the wood; not as Kine was attached to it, by the past, but by a prescient awareness of the need to settle and choose a home.

To the rook, who had taken refuge from the squall in the thorn, the pair had a mawkish look. In the Watchman's view it was the first sign of approaching madness, that seasonal affliction which made fools of the sane, wantons of maidens, and a flagrant scandal of his own mate. He recalled his younger, impassioned days.

'Imbecile,' he muttered, transfixing the weasels with a blighting gaze.

Kia purred. 'You never looked better, Kine.'

'Last time I saw him,' said the Watchman, 'he looked a poor fish.'

'Not for long. Kine's resilient.'

'Bah.' The rook drew back from the hailstones. 'Lucky, I'd say. There's some who listen . . .'

'And some,' Kine crooned, 'who bolt from the treetops when the owl prowls. Each to his nature: the rook to the Dread. I'll take the battle scars.'

'You see,' Kia said diplomatically, 'he has his duties, Watchman, as you have. He must be bold, defiant of enemies. Who else would have fought and destroyed the rat?'

'And who,' said Kine, 'would have braved the owl's mansion but a weasel? Kia is daring and swift, a true weasel . . .'

'Because,' she put in, her voice silky, 'I've learned from Kine.'

They continued for some while as fulsomely, and the rook, nauseated by their mutual admiration, ruffled his nape, reflecting on the virtue of dispassion acquired with age. What was this so-called season of blossoming? The blackbird summed it up for him, hurling notes in a combative outburst at the brisk hail. Covetousness, jealousy, aggression – the joys of spring! In spring the shy moorhen flashed spurs and drowned his rival in the calm pond. In spring the pacific hare punched and kicked his brothers with demon vehemence. In spring, ditch and verge reverberated with violence as tiny sex-possessed creatures fought like tigers, forgetful of their timidity at other times.

In the crabbed view of the Watchman the weasels would do well to beware of spring and its fevered blood.

Kine was asking, 'You've not been back to the river, Kia? Since I was injured you've not met the weasel from the other land?' It was the corollary of mushy senti-ment, the jealous doubt which, like hail in April, stabbed from blue skies. Head cocked, the Watchman listened cynically. They would croon and bicker, doubt and croon again. The early stages of spring fever were as predictable as they were fatuous.

'I'm here now. Would it matter,' teased Kia, 'if I'd been back?'

'I shouldn't like it.' Kine had dwelt on the subject while recovering, haunted by the thought of the other weasel, even conjuring him faceless in the Moon Pond, muscles rippling. They called the tractor in the other land Fordson, son of Ford, a blue monster, and Kine, in the first delirium of injury, had imagined Ford a uniquely powerful weasel with a lust for Kia. 'I shouldn't want you to see Ford – that is, *him* again.'

'I've not been back, Kine. I've been preoccupied with an invalid. He's mended, but he's still inclined to a sore head.'

'It's for your own good.'

'Is it?' she twinkled.

'I'll say no more.' He eyed the ice drops. 'I just don't want you to see him again,' he said.

The rook despaired. Dear, oh dear, what fools it made of them! How naive was the dashing Kine in the game of spring. The old bird shook his head and watched the female give her hero a cool glance. 'You've no right,' she told him. 'I admire you, but you've no right to decide who I see, Kine. You can advise me; orders I'll not accept. We don't possess each other just because we're friends. You always say: a weasel belongs to no one.'

'Maybe . . .'

'Then be consistent. There's no cause for jealousy.'

'Jealousy!' He packed the word with outrage. 'Kine, jealous?' He would make quite sure no outsider, no faceless Ford, came sniffing around her.

'I'm fond of you, Kine.' Her tone was soft and she nudged him, amused by his spleen. 'I don't know why,' she laughed, 'but I really am.'

And would possess him, thought the Watchman, as a spider a fly despite the dewy hypocrisy of innocence. He could have dictated the scenario. The squall was now passing and the sun shone. They would make up, they would bicker some more, and make up again. There was no escape from creation's oldest malady, the complaint of the bawling blackbird, the dementia of Watchman's own youth. Only age brought release, and that uncertainly. Rising to a clearing sky, the old rook saw his mate's paramour, their young neighbour, complacently preening on a damp bough. Below, the lanes were white with hail and blossom. Perhaps it was the blossom – thorn, wild cherry, damson – or merely the smugness of the younger bird, he did not know, but an almost forgotten urge rose in him, a fleeting lunacy.

Flipping over, the Watchman closed his wings and, issuing an exultant cry, swooped like a hawk at the Lothario. Racing by, he snatched a prime feather from the other's tail, flew to the nest and presented the gift to his astonished spouse.

The marsh-dwellers knew Kine had recovered by his war chant. He sang it ranging the riverbank in darting bounds, throwing his challenge across stream to the weasel Ford, to the wilderness and Castle Mound. For a while his cries hung over the water then, dying, seemed to drop to the current and float away. Near the banks the flow was lazy but midstream it was faster, sweeping twigs and other flotsam in bouncing convoys, dispersing his unanswered jabbering. As he thought, his reputation was enough to deter trespassers.

It was warm and Kine felt sticky. Entering the water, he freshened, feet on the bottom, dunking his head at the stream's edge and flicking droplets from his whiskers so they shimmered and sparkled in the sun's rays. The day had a fresh morning smell to it. Behind him, on the marsh, lapwings were fussing over nesting sites. Some already had eggs on the moist ground, and a crow was mobbed as it prowled overhead. The crow jinked clumsily, flustered by harassment.

But the river was quiet and the bank calm. A wagtail

on a boulder had a lonely look. Sometimes a creature could sit on the bank so long without company that a drifting log seemed companionable. Other times it was lively there. You could not tell, Kine reflected, at the water's edge. You might come down and find a froth of writhing elvers in a small creek, a regatta of fowl, frogs sunning themselves along the whole bank.

There were bank voles, velvet sausages of nutriment, which took to the water when Kine harried them. He would swim after them. They swam with a running motion of stubby legs, like diminutive scows, submerging when hard pressed, and he would grab them in the green tide. Sometimes rabbits would bask in clumps of reed beside the river. He had caught them unawares there, and once taken a half-grown rat which had come to water where the stream crooked.

Now Kine was alone beside the broad reach. Skipping from the shallows he shook, and eyed the far shore. It held no appeal for him, backed by bog grass and oozy swamps, and he mused on Kia's visit with mixed sentiments. Foolish it may have been, the bravado of immaturity, but he had to admit it had taken nerve, as had her timely appearance in the tithe barn. The old she-weasel of the willow would have approved. Kia had spirit. She had the makings, he thought with pleasure, of a weasel in his mother's mould.

He snuffled absently for food, but it was too early in the season for marsh frogs, the level of the stream too recently dropped for voles to have settled in. The warmth tempted him to loll amid some fronds and simply worship the sun a while. Indolence was not always unprofitable. Meals had a way of delivering themselves if you kept low, and Kine, like all weasels, was adept at drowsing watchfully.

The lonesomeness of the lazing river was soporific. Below him a little beach was freckled with shadows from reeds, now and then agitated by a ripply breeze. Minnows fanned where the water was slight in depth. Kine watched them with an idle nostalgia for the days when he would stalk small fry with all the zest and futility of stripling enterprise. Midstream, a boiling circle spread and vanished, marking larger game. A floating bottle passed briefly through consciousness.

Kine's gaze drifted. Cuckoo-flower already blossomed, lance-shaped leaves skirting pale mauve inflorescences. High above, the heron soared on a thermal in spiral flight, until he dwindled to lark dimensions in a blue haze. There was no sound, yet a sixth sense told Kine he was no longer alone, and he flexed warily. There was no scent. The off-land breeze was innocuous. Yet the presence of something hostile registered. Could the other-land weasel have heard his call? Slowly Kine eased his view towards the stream through the tall fronds.

The stream flowed harmlessly. Only the breeze broke its surface, barely dimpling the water where the course turned. It was deserted. Even the wagtail had left its rock. There was an empty air to the far bank, the straggling sallows, the tree-clad mound. For as far as Kine could see, to the mist which dissolved the skyline, there was no sign of beast or man. The marsh sheep grazed elsewhere, their attendant starlings with them. Far off a low rumble might have been spring thunder, or the blasting of tree stumps with dynamite. The distant sound merely emphasized the peacefulness.

Kine swivelled his head on his lean neck. Below him, where the minnows had flashed, the dappled strand formed the floor of a small cove – and the creature sat there. Kine goggled. His hackles tingled. It was a grim brute. It was no weasel. For a moment he thought it was a black cat, but neither was it a cat nor, he knew with chilly certainty, any beast he had ever come across. He recalled Kia's description: 'a river monster'. This was indeed monstrous, and he peered at it from the fronds with appalled gaze. 'You'll run, Kine – you'll run, I promise, if you meet this thing.'

But curiosity held him, the perverse weasel impulse, and the greater compulsion to prove her wrong.

She was not entirely right about the feet, which Kia had described as webbed. They were only partly so, the rest of the toes free to grip, which was consistent with her statement that the brute had climbed a tree. The dark coat of the monster was formidable, underfur dense and matted, longer hairs stiff with a glossy finish. Only the feet lacked the long hairs conspicuous in the tail, a great bush accounting for a third of the creature's length. It sat with a hunched posture, its coat stark, giving slight indication of its supple power in water. But it was ugly, and when the breeze dropped, an evil scent stifled Kine.

The she-mink glared at the river, gaping murderous jaws at the world at large. These tools of carnage appalled the weasel. Though far from squeamish, Kine shuddered at such armament. The patch-eyed terrier would flinch from it, the fox recoil, the hawk tremble. No creature of the valley would molest the mink.

The monster moved. Tail dragging, it shuffled to the water and, scarcely crinkling the surface, it submerged. Kine stared at the empty strand. But for the part-webbed footprints, he would not have accepted what his eyes had seen. He stretched cautiously. Sniffing the beach, he followed the indentations to the stream, entered and, pausing prudently, dived under. The blue-green world of the fish was cool and languorous. He scanned it charily.

Spinneys of tall weed rumba-ed, drowned thickets swayed, green fingers trembling in the undertow. Pouches of jelly couched the eggs of the watersnail. Trailing blebs of air, Kine slid in search of the bigger animal. The depths teemed with midget life. He passed wandering beetles and waterfleas, hymenoptera using their wings as paddles, nymphs with voracious masks and exquisite tails. A spider watched through the wall of its silken air-bell. But the monster had disappeared. Surfacing, the weasel gulped for breath and went down again.

The sensation of weightlessness was pleasurable. He

banked, let the current take him, then oared languidly. The limpid fluid remained undisturbed. Above him the shadow of a hawking demoiselle blotched the marble of refracted light. He saw no fish, no big submersible. Perhaps, thought Kine, the creature was less fearsome than it looked – a shy monster. Size and aggression were not inseparable; in the flow of the translucent tide the tiny stickleback was incomparably more pugnacious than the largest roach. Kine turned in the current and was nosing upwards when he saw the black shape.

At first he did not connect it with the humped brute. This was streamlined, a piscine form. It came like a streak through the water, like a pike, a gliding bolt growing larger with frightening speed. The transformation was incredible. The shuffling creature of the beach had become a deadly missile, sleek and swift with a lancing wake of opaque turbulence. It seemed to Kine he was motionless, suspended in swim by the sheer velocity of the mink's approach. And as he watched, the she-mink's consort loomed beside her, racing parallel.

In the splitting of a second, Kine's folly bore on him: the folly of invading the mink's element. On land he sparkled, but he was nobody in water, a nonentity. The humble newt was a better swimmer. Speeding images filled his eye, and as they did so the weasel somersaulted through a liquid nightmare, diving for the bottom with bursting lungs.

It was a tactic of despair, a plunge to a graveyard of mud and slime, where the lowest of orders lurked. Flat eroded stones met his vision, with leeches glued to them. A crayfish ogled in fear from a drowned burrow. Kine's head hammered. He needed air, but the jaws were behind him, and he pressed down. It was vital to reach the bottom, the grey silt where the dull-shelled mussel ploughed its trench. He steered for the mussel, concentrating on the circles of its muddy case. They signified survival, the consuming imperative in Kine's mind.

Hitting the silt, the weasel threshed with his legs

until it billowed, drifting up towards the surface in a dense pall. His breath was gone and he thought his chest would collapse on the vacuum in him. Blinded by the mud cloud, Kine rose concealed at its centre until his head met fresh air then, snorting water, struck wildly for the near bank. For several seconds he lay gasping where he dropped on the earthy ledge. From above, the stream looked placid and the drama of the depths could have been a fantasy.

But the fluid he was disgorging was real, and he felt terrible. The muddy slick on the current dispersed. The river shimmered. He was beginning to revive when the water heaved, and the black monster surfaced in a wash of foam. The drenched skull of the she-mink cranked round viciously. She was no more than a spit from the weasel, and he thought of Kia. 'You'll run, I promise, when you see the thing.' He had not run. He had followed, observed and outwitted it. But he ran now, retreating unashamedly from the bank.

An hour later he was still jabbering with outrage at the wood's hem. He bounced with passion. 'It's no good,' Kia told him, 'you can't fight them. They'd dismember you.'

'Brutes like that on the frontier! I'll die first. I'll die with my teeth into one of them.'

A pair of swans flew towards them. The throbbing rhythm of their flight could be heard a mile off, a droning like swarming bees, growing louder as they approached overhead, until it might have been steers stampeding for the noise they made. In sudden silence they planed down to the marsh from the wood above. Kine glared at the dykes on the valley's floor. 'I should have believed you in the first place,' he told Kia.

'I'd stopped believing myself. It wouldn't have made any difference: they'd still be here, Kine.'

'By the gods!' He could see the reach below, sun-burnished, and he bristled at the thought of the invaders, the monsters there. They would dominate the water and the riverbank. They were brigands, monstrous aliens, and they threatened time-honoured valley laws. He said, 'By the gods, I'll die before they stop on this territory!'

'Maybe,' Kia said, attempting to calm him, 'they'll move on.'

'Yes, to the marsh, more than likely, then what happens?' It was unthinkable. The gods of storm and lightning enacted such themes in passing dramas, but what if the mink were not passing? What if they stayed to conquer, to tyrannize? Scrat's predictions might after all be realized. A balance of nature evolved through centuries in the vale could be demolished. The fish could go, and the otter with them. Fowl could be routed. By decimating the prey of fox and weasel, the mink could impoverish fellow predators, bringing hunger, emigration, plundering. The gibbet heroes had never faced such a threat.

Gracefully the swans touched down on the marsh, arching powerful necks. They seemed somehow unreal in the circumstances, a tableau of harmony at the heartland of the problem, and Kine envied them. A swan could kill a dog. It had little to fear from the invaders, nor was it motivated against them unless molested. Indifferent to the strife of lesser mortals, the great birds floated with white magnificence. Necks twined, they whispered huskily, half-raised wings making baskets above their backs.

'Don't worry,' said Kia. 'The monsters move by water. They won't go far from the river and the marsh dykes.'

'That's far enough.' He seethed as he viewed the levels. The region was webbed with waterways, reedy cuttings in square geometry, threaded by the river, the central artery. In the sun the system shimmered. There were no fences or hedges on the marshlands, simply moats to constrain grazing animals. From the flat, sheep and bullocks appeared to range unhindered, but from above it could be seen that flocks and herds were in fact divided by water barriers, the marsh a patchwork of meadows reached by bridges across the dykes. 'More than enough,' he reconsidered, 'by the gods it is! That's half my country. I'll die defending my right to it.'

He watched the cob swan drive a rival from the female, busking violently, ploughing forward in hostile bursts, wings and scapulars elevated. Kine, stirred by the performance, said savagely, 'The weasel is small but he is dangerous. He has the heart of the swan, and greater cunning. Let the brigands beware, for they will hear from him.'

Kia said soothingly, 'You must wait, Kine.' His blood was rising, and if the Blood Fury gripped him he would pay for it. She must save him, she knew, from himself, for a weasel in the throes of the Blood Fury saw no danger, flew at anything. 'You must think. It's a new situation. You'll think of something, but take your time. Given time, many problems resolve themselves. Consider Poacher – how you've had to wait, outwit him step by step. Poacher was more fearsome than any beast, yet he has weakened at last, and you are strong. You bested him.'

'That's true.' Kine felt calmer. 'The man was smart and I outsmarted him. You're right, we must be canny.' The 'we' now came naturally. 'All things in time. We must take their measure, then they'll learn that this is Kine's land.'

'An ancient country.'

'And not for ravaging.'

Part Two

KIA

CHAPTER SIX

THE girl was leaning on the gate by the wood when a yellow pick-up approached along the marsh track. It had in that wild place the incongruity of a Martian vehicle, spick and span, chrome shining, the legend *River Board Engineers* inscribed on it. Though she affected indifference as it drew near, she was a creature of the land and did not miss much. The young man at the wheel was in shirtsleeves, and smiled as he braked the van. 'Seen the old chap from the cottage?' he asked amiably.

'If you mean Poacher,' the ploughman's daughter answered, 'he's not well. He's been sickly a while. I'm anxious for him.'

'I'm sorry.' He took in her sturdy figure and the gate which creaked quietly beneath her weight. Her jeans were pale against the deep sea of bluebells which lapped the oak boles. She wore a T-shirt, jacket over it, and looked away when he asked, 'Are you family?'

'Hardly.' Her tilt of head was stand-offish as a farm cat's. 'I'm a neighbour. There's no family. That's why I drop by. He needs caring for; he neglects himself.'

'That's not good.' The vanman frowned, getting out of the vehicle. Backside to bonnet, he regarded her. His face, she thought, was not unpleasant, his figure well-coupled and quite tall. He said eventually, gaze reflective, 'I haven't seen you before, but then I don't come here often. I service the pumps along the river-bank.'

'I see.' It was sardonic, her eyes on the slogan across the van door.

'It's quiet here, isn't it?'

'I suppose.'

'Saw a weasel down the track.' He surveyed the

69

valley. 'And a mink by the river, a big one. D'you get many mink here?'

'I've seen none,' she said shrugging. 'Poacher might have.'

'Reckon you will,' he told her. 'There's a lot upstream. They'll find their way here. Marshland, see – just the place for them. Find a place they like, they take over. Ruthless, mink are. Kill on land or in water, they're not particular.' He looked serious. 'You won't believe this – the Swedes destroy twenty thousand mink a year, the Norwegians fifteen thousand, and those numbers are a fraction of the total running wild there. All because a few escaped from fur farms. You see how bad it could get here.'

'You know a lot.'

'Just what I've read. And working on the pumps you get to hear a bit.'

'Pity Poacher's unwell. You could talk to him.'

The vanman grinned. 'I'd as soon talk to you,' he said, adding when she declined to respond, 'Aye, he knows about animals, the old man.'

'He lives like one.' The girl grimaced, but her tone was more caring than derogatory. 'He's a scruffy, ungrateful pagan, but he knows things: he knows secrets of the valley no one else knows. My dad says Poacher's people always lived here and knew everything. He knows every pheasant's nest. He knows where mushrooms grow, and wild strawberries, when others search fruitlessly. He can tell mysteries. That is,' she said, tossing her head, 'if he wishes to.'

'I've read of people like that. It's like the gipsies,' the young man reflected, 'in Borrow's day.'

'He can call the cuckoo from a tree, my dad reckons, and answer the vixen's bark.'

'Like the primitives.'

'He's *that* all right.' She smiled at last. 'The way he *lives*! When we were small we thought the world of him. He would take us to see the kingfisher; show us the blindworm and the wren's nest. He used to say the nightingale never slept because she had got her eyes from the blindworm, and if the blindworm found her asleep he would take them back. That's why the nightingale sings through the dark hours! We thought Poacher was a king,' she said. 'Now look at him!'

'He promised me some rabbits.'

'He won't see a doctor. I nag at him.'

'It's not *your* job.' The young man admired her freshness, her country tan. 'You must have better to do with your spare time. For instance, going to town. D'you like the cinema?'

'Do you?'

'Aye,' he told her.

'I might,' she said.

At which point the rook, who had marked them from his perch, concluded they were harmless and yawned drowsily. It had been a morning of alarms, and the Watchman was ready to feed and rest. He had little to learn of humankind. Rooks had looked down from that same wood when the forerunners of the girl had huddled in hummocky camps and used flint tools. Ancestors of the Watchman had known the valley when the marsh was an estuary. Galleys of swart Romans, the raven banner of Viking longships, had met their gaze. Then the sea had receded and the marsh evolved.

In humid weather the thick ground mists which lay on the flats still showed where tides once lapped and earls had flown their pennons on ancient fleets. Now the topgallants above the vapour on such a morning were the brows of spiky bushes. And as the sun burned off the mist, more scrub showed. Gradually the dark tassels of sedges and the tapers of rushes could be seen, the vapour retreating to the long dykes. Even there, warming rays at last followed and vanquished it.

With the mist gone, spring's new crop of flags and reeds was visible. Growth was slow while the nights were cold, but soon they would flourish, along with plantains, comfrey and, later, arrowheads. Close to the water, clusters of green stuff were pushing through last year's dead leaves and stems. More was exposed as the sun rose.

Already some creatures had brought young into the marsh world. Caught by the sun on a stony track, the infant lapwing lay motionless, its blotchy down a natural camouflage. Only the beady eye which sought its parent was conspicuous, a jewel of agate brilliance. The new-born leveret huddled in tufty grass. Unlike the rabbit, whose young were naked and blind at birth, the progeny of the hare had passed from womb to mist that dawn complete with sight and fur, able to scuttle about almost immediately. Now the doe was suckling her other leveret across the marsh, her young being hidden separately.

The mallard moved stealthily along a dry ditch, shepherding her brood towards Mullen's dyke. Her quiet warnings were anxious, keying the grey ducklings for the alarm that would bring them beneath her wings. There were five young, a few days old. The mottled brown mallard was the first of the marsh fowl with poots at the winter's end. Her young scrambled fluffily to water, exploring jerkily.

The dyke was smooth and long-legged skater insects danced on it. Near the screw the banks were earthy, pocked by the mouths of rabbit tunnels which bored deep by the pump-house in pale-coloured soil. A metal grill spanned the intake to the cylinder. When the screw churned, water would be sucked through the grill in a swirling flood, but now it rested, the dyke in a tranquil mood.

Atop the banks the grass was inert, heads of old sedges motionless. The swans flipped black paddles, their necks elegant. Momentarily the severe eye of the cob fixed on a tiny cascade of earth, then returned to the preening female. Scrat, tumbling down the bank in a shrew-sized avalanche, snatched a stranded worm and climbed up again. Chomping hungrily, he blinked

72

down from the grass at the reedy channel. His view was excellent. In a minute he saw the head of the mallard peer cautiously from the growth, withdraw then reappear. Satisfied, the fowl took to the water and called her brood. They swam with eratic zest, like the skating insects, skittering all ways, some close to their parent, some more adventurous.

The shrew twitched and scratched his belly, the sun warm on him. A large blue fly was droning at one of the rabbit tunnels, and Scrat weighed the chances of its settling. The fly was hesitant. For a while it hovered, then no sooner landed than it fled from the opening. Scrat was curious. The insect's interest had been strong, its flight sudden. Both were explained by the eyes which appeared at the tunnel's mouth: fierce eyes, not the eyes of a rabbit but small and menacing. Fascinated, the shrew saw similar eyes in other holes.

Trembling, he watched the monsters come from the rabbits' burrow. It seemed to Scrat they were everywhere, hard-faced, jaws grim, and not a rabbit apparent in any shaft. It was as if an evil spell had transformed the occupants. Then, where the pumphouse loomed beside the tunnels, the she-mink came from her bunker with thunderous gaze. Her signal was unambiguous. 'Kill,' it ordered, and as the foray began, 'Kill and kill again . . .'

The young creatures by the water had little chance. A single snap obliterated the lapwing chick. The hare had not returned and, near the dyke, her leveret stared innocently at the slavering head which reared alongside. For a moment the mink relished the sight of the softly palpitating infant, then struck down at it. The leveret's squeal was the first and last of its brief life. Scrat shuddered. He saw a dun brute emerge from a hole and crouch balefully. It was not as big as the black matriarch but the shrew, awed by its proportions, was petrified. It raised a pink nose and was sniffing the dyke, when its twin appeared.

They were like great sandy ferrets, their eyes crimson. Diving suddenly, they converged on the ducklings with deadly purpose.

The mallard's cry to her young was desperate. Sheering between her small brood and the killers she deployed the only manoeuvre open to her. She spread her wings as though to fly, pitched sideways and, with an anguished screech, writhed and flapped on the water as if in agony. It was an inspired and despairing act, so realistic Scrat was convinced her wing was broken, and that the duck must fall to the speeding mink. And a brave act. For, as she threshed and limped across the channel, she barely outpaced her enemies.

At the same time the ducklings, on inborn impulse, dived and were gone from sight. Finally, when the duck seemed lost, she rose reluctantly from the dyke, flew low round the marsh and slipped back behind the sedges to thick grass. Minutes passed. Then, unable to contain herself, she inched nervously to the reeds, a tremulous summons in her brown throat.

Scrat saw one grey infant scuttle from the water to find the mallard. A second followed. He saw no more. For a long time the duck called, but the mink, discovering her deception, had scoured the dyke, and three of the ducklings had been seized. Scrat waited no longer; he had seen enough.

The man said, 'Who's that?'

'The River Board engineer.'

Poacher had turned stiffly at the sound of the departing pick-up, and the girl, leaving the door open to air the cottage, watched him cleaning the gun for the umpteenth time since he had used it weeks ago. It struck her as a sorry sight, though Kine, concealed in the thorn outside the window, would have disagreed. The half-smile on the girl's freckled features was slyly smug. 'He's been to service the pump,' she purred.

'I suppose he wanted rabbits.' The man broke the breech of the shotgun awkwardly. 'I've got none,' he growled, squinting up the barrels. 'Won't have until I can work again.'

'Work?' the girl said. 'Since when did you ever work? You won't be shifting till you see a doctor, you stubborn idiot.'

'Damn the doctors. Quit nagging, girl. Damned if I need a chit of a girl keep on nagging me.'

Kine climbed higher, improving his view of the room, and of the distant lea. Outside he could see rabbits gorging sowthistle, dandelion; inside, their crippled foe languished helplessly. The sight was heartening and Kia, he thought, had been right: some wars were of attrition, best fought with patience, not impulsiveness. Poacher was incapable. His garden, always rough, had become a jungle of docks and quitch. The grass had overtaken faded daffodils, providing cover for the long-tailed field-mice which attracted Kine.

Even Poacher's terrier was demoralized. It growled up at the thicket where Kine, aware it could not reach him, spat back at it. For a while the dog took the insult then, frustrated, turned its interest to the hedgehog which dossed beneath the holly in Poacher's yard. The hedgehog, well protected, was unimpressed. The dog snarled and, still snarling, slouched off to scratch dismally.

'Some men,' the girl was saying crisply, 'are pleased to be with me. *He* was.'

'Young beggars,' huffed Poacher. 'Where's my gun oil?'

Unlike the garden, the parlour had much improved. The girl's attention showed. Poacher's sticks of furniture had a fresh gleam and the smell of beeswax infused the room. The hearth was tidy, the heavy iron fireback scraped clean of tar. Rude mats had been beaten, floor-bricks scrubbed and stained. The ploughman's daughter had been reared to hard work, and there were now many signs of her influence. Poacher's tarnished campaign medals had been polished and

75

shone in the cabinet, while wild flowers graced the table in a pretty pot. Poacher's grumbling was less convincing than it once seemed.

'He's asked me out, the engineer. I like him, Poacher.'

'Young beggars. Don't trust 'em, girl.'

'I don't trust you, you evil heathen, I've known you too long. He's a nice fellow.'

Poacher scowled. 'You beware of them.'

He eyed her darkly, full of memory. He was recalling a time many years ago, though it seemed like yesterday: the youth in uniform, the girl so similar to this one, so self-contained. He could smell the wood – it had barely changed – and hear her laughter pealing through the still trees. It had been another bluebell time; the ground was moist. He had been strong then, strong for the girl and the Normandy beaches a few weeks afterwards. And she sensible, for she had married the ploughman, a steady man, while Poacher had crossed the Rhine to another wood, the Diersfordter Wald.

'Aye, you beware of them.'

'Get away!' She titivated the flowers, her eyes mischievous. 'He's got sense,' she told the cripple, 'more'n you have.' A head for facts, she was thinking, the sense to read books, and a good trade. An engineer, she concluded, was somebody. They did not send *anyone* out to service river pumps. She had liked the young man's face and his leanness, and the fact that he was taller than her by maybe half a foot. When he grinned it had been appealing, with just enough impudence and no more. 'Anyway,' she reasserted, 'I'm going out with him.'

Poacher closed the breech of the gun with a sudden snap. 'Reckon I shan't see you, then, that evening. I'll be sat here alone while you go capering.'

'Right. You won't have a chit of a girl to trouble you.' She chuckled then, catching his glare, hooted lustily. 'You hypocrite, Poacher. You rotten hypocrite!'

'I'm not bothered.' He stroked the gun, caressing

stock and chased finger-guard, his face downcast. 'I'll not expect to see much of you from now on, but I can mind myself.'

'Like a baby!'

She stopped laughing and sighed, saying at length, 'What a fool you are – worse than a lover. I'm not deserting you. I haven't tidied this cottage just to see it a sty again.' From the scullery, where she went to fill the kettle, she called to him, 'By the way, I meant to tell you. He saw a mink by the river. It was a big mink.'

Poacher grunted. For a while he clasped the shotgun, his knuckles white, then said savagely, 'Can't turn your back but there's devilment, vermin everywhere. Weasels footloose. Now mink. Just wait . . .' There was silence. Then he said, voice trailing again, 'I'll have 'em, just wait . . .'

Kine jumped down from the thicket as Scrat wailed. The shrew was running; Scrat had not stopped running. On the marsh, osiers and withies had engulfed him, twisted trunks mocked him with grotesque masks. The sun had gone and he ran with tears in his eyes and a pounding heart, at length spotting the weasel by Poacher's cottage. 'Kine! I've seen the faces of doom – of the reckoning!' He stood gasping, blurting feebly, 'By Mullen's dyke. They took the young of the lapwing, the hare and mallard. There's a pack of them.'

The weasel stopped. Forgetting Poacher and the girl, he calmed the midget. 'Take it easy. Catch your breath,' he said, no longer dismissive of Scrat's fears. 'I've seen the brutes, too. Steady up, Scrat.'

'They're on the marshbanks – the agents of doom itself.'

'Many?'

'Many, Kine, and their leader, a black giant.'

'I've seen her.' He recalled the monster on the strand, the shuffling she-mink who became in the river a lethal bolt. And he dwelt on Kia's wisdom,

77

her stable influence. Kia had steadied him. 'I out-smarted the giant, Scrat. It's not the end of the world yet.'

'The time's near.'

'Nonsense.' He pondered the greening ditch. A blighted teazle, dead a couple of seasons, was still erect where old stems of burdock had rotted and lay in a tangle with coiling briar. The defiance of the teazle, strong beyond life, recalled the heroes of the gibbet, and Kine growled, 'I'll teach the monsters. Weasels have always defied intruders. It won't, perhaps, be a quick task – it calls for scheming – but those who challenge the weasel come off second-best. Think of the rat. Think of the owl, Scrat. Use your intelligence.'

Scrat moaned, his pessimism rooted in shrew history. He was, Kine reflected, a vulnerable and maligned mite. For a long time humankind had believed the shrew caused sickness in beasts by crawling over them. The cure for a so-called shrew-struck cow had been the touch of a shrew-ash, part of a tree into whose trunk a live shrew had been plugged and left to die. There was an ancient shrew-ash in the valley, its wands once sought by Poacher's shambling forebears when their cattle ailed.

True, such persecution belonged to a former age, but shrews, in Kine's opinion, were haunted creatures, born despondent and highly-strung. Short-lived and neurotic, they lacked destiny. 'It's all right for a weasel,' Scrat protested, 'but the shrew is insignificant. The end is imminent.'

'I'll give you a role,' Kine encouraged, 'an important one.' He eyed the midget. 'Insignificance is the ideal attribute for a spy – you can spy for us. Watch the mink. Report on their movements and dispositions. The first thing is to *know* the enemy, his strengths and weak-nesses. You could do it, Scrat. It would give you con-fidence.'

'If I survived. If any of us live long enough.'

'You'll survive.'

'I don't know.'

'Come on, Scrat.'

'Well, maybe . . .' His voice was timid but his tail had gone up and he described a small circle on clockwork legs, as if testing his intrepidity. Enjoying the sensation he strutted dwarfishly. 'I'd be someone,' he pondered, 'someone to reckon in these parts.'

CHAPTER SEVEN

ONE and a half millennia earlier a great storm had transformed the valley, upending trees in the lower woods, bulldozing debris in a soupy flood to the estuary, where it had formed the foundations of the present marsh. Legend told how the survivor from a stricken boat, a lumpish Jute or Saxon figure, some kinsman of Hengist perhaps, had stumbled up the slope to the ridge, where a bolt of lightning had rooted him.

Stranger prodigies might have been believed when thunder crashed and jagged flashes filled the country with blinding light. Some of the fiercest storms occurred at springtime in skies of umber violence over cowering fields. Then the ploughman, whose wife had hated thunder, was grateful at least her fear had died with her. He flicked the wiper on the tractor's cab to full revs. The rain was pelting, lightning sizzling.

Sweat moistened the ruddy-cheeked widower. Most years lightning killed one or two valley beasts. A bolt had slaughtered four of Mullen's steers at a stroke, and the metal frame of the tractor was not comforting. Foot on throttle, he powered in search of shelter until the storm cleared. The air was sulphurous. Trees flinched. It was an unnerving place when the volts mustered, and he hoped his daughter was indoors.

Others took refuge as best they could. Amid drenched fronds the heron hunched so his head and body appeared one, eyes closed to the glare which streaked from heavy clouds. Cattle sought thickets, rumps turned windward, trembling jumpily. The drama was spectacular. Lightning forked, ribboned and sheeted, throwing the ridge into sharp relief. The sky exploded. One bolt, leaping horizontally, bathed the river in white brilliance. Simultaneously, a soused creature clambered from the water on to the bank.

The weasel they would come to know as Ford shook his tousled coat. He seemed to shrug off thunder with indifference, gulping the thick air in easy draughts. Water sluiced from him. Casually he sniffed the strange shore, exploring with bustling confidence, then, lifting his head, laughed in the teeth of the deluge, as if inured to all discomfort by the rigours of his native bog. A brawny specimen, coarse of countenance, he advanced with the dauntless hustle of a bull-terrier.

Slowly the storm rolled downstream to blast the sea. The vale had brightened, sun slanting, as Ford charged from the marsh and paused admiringly. Ahead, the slopes steamed. Land-drains gurgled. Rain-washed, the scene before him of lush fertility was so alien after the bog that he lingered to savour it. The land was firm, hedges burgeoned, crops sprang sturdily. A rook sat on a paling, eyes inscrutable.

'So this is Kia's patch,' the weasel said.

He looked back towards the river and the other land. Across the stream, through scrub willow, the tufty wilderness spread hazily. It was a rough place; neither crops nor hedges favoured it. It was a grim swamp, in which an animal could get bogged, sucked down between the clumps of spiky grass, if it strayed from the worn trails. For generations sheep had picked their way in single file through the morass, treading narrow avenues. Even these were dangerous. Harriers claimed a heavy toll on the bog paths.

He said, 'This is honey – just look at it!'

Even the marsh was drained. On his own bank – leave aside Castle Mound – there was an endless trek through bog and scrub to reach the higher ground, whereas the slopes here came almost to the riverside. And what slopes! He let his gaze roam. Broad rook-dotted acres were green with corn; sheep grazed in tilted meadows; noble woods provided shelter and concealment for untold denizens. It was a vision almost too rich for the bog-weasel. 'You don't know your luck in this territory.'

The rook wheezed.

'Take my word.'

The bird showed him a jaundiced eye. Nearby, a bird-scarer echoed the bangs of the departed storm. With each explosion something rose swiftly, fluttering back to earth. The machine comprised a cylinder of propane gas, a combustion chamber and a tall rod. Filtering from the cylinder, the gas filled the chamber until an electric spark exploded it. The result was a sharp report accompanied by the propulsion of a plastic 'hawk' up the rod, where it hovered briefly then tumbled back. Birds unused to the contraption fled, but to the Watchman all scarecrows, turnip-headed or gas-consuming, were frauds, and he had fed undisturbed until the stranger passed.

He said, 'You're trespassing.'

Ford laughed. It was brazen, and the Watchman blinked wearily. Weasels were much the same, this one bigger than most, an uncouth brawler, less astute perhaps than Kine, but there was little to choose – bouncers and swaggerers. He knew what the weasel wanted, and when the stranger confirmed it he groaned inwardly.

'I'm looking for Kia. She told me she lived here, and I've come for her. We met in the winter, by the river. When the time came, I promised, I would find her, take her home with me.'

'To the bog? A treat for her.'

'Kia will thrive, she's got the spirit. She'll hold her own. It's plain to see in her: she'll fit into my life, raise fighting kittens. I'll be proud of such a mate and make much of her.' The bog-weasel's face shone almost tenderly. There would be good times. It was hard beyond the river but, in Ford's estimation, rewarding too. He thought of the mole cantonments in the wilderness, muddy mines to be plundered for blind tunnellers. He thought of lying in soggy ambush for marsh frogs. And there was Castle Mound in bleak magnificence, its sweeping views and, in summer, its leafy canopy. To run there with so sleek a spouse as the dainty Kia would make him the envy of the other land. 'Kia is the prize of the valley; you've just to look at her.'

And just to listen, thought the rook, to such drivel to diagnose the spring complaint. It was the season of lust, and sex was everywhere – stags at rut, does to buck, foxes clicketing – the whole valley alive to it. The veteran squinted at the ewes in the adjacent field. The thick-browed ram in their midst drooled mindlessly. He wore harness and ruddle block to mark the females he covered, who could then be tallied when the shepherd came. So much for the muse of romantic spring!

The rook cogitated his own luck: wanton spouse, cuckolding neighbour, the insatiable fruits of passion soon to break their shells. Feeding them and his brooding partner would cripple him. Young rooks required the moist protein of earthworms and leatherjackets; finding them would mean toiling without break from dawn to dusk. He was, he told himself, too old for parenthood – and for humouring strangers of the weasel kind.

'What makes you think she'll want *you*?' he asked testily. 'Kia runs with Kine. It's his territory.'

'I'll deal with that. What sort of weasel is this Kine of yours?'

'A bit of a ruffian, like yourself. A bit of an uppity, cocksure type.' The Watchman enjoyed it. 'He likes a scrap.'

'He'll get a skinning. You don't know what a fight is on this side. Bog-weasels are born battling. I was reared by die-hards of the bog clan, hardened by the struggles of the frontier lands. I'll fight anything, any time, anywhere. I'll demolish your Kine. She'll be rid of him.'

'She may not thank you for that; she likes the idiot. I'd say their condition was getting serious.'

'You'd say that?' Ford derided. 'I'd say this, rook – I'd say she'll go with the victor and bless her fortune. When I've finished with Kine he'll be no good to anybody, least of all Kia. You'll see, she'll be proud of me.'

'Perhaps.' The rook doubted it. Still, the prospect of the skirmish enlivened him. He had no objection to any number of weasels raising hell with each other. He had watched weasels fight, and even the winners were diminished in bumptiousness. Nothing would part them when they duelled for mates or territories. A human could walk up to brawling weasels and they would take no notice in their blind rage.

But it was not Kia's sport. Her dream was weasel unity, a concept as unlikely as mink charity, yet dear to her. 'Kia has a mind of her own,' said the rook. 'You can't dictate to her.'

'Kia's wonderful. No she-weasel is as delicate yet so hardy, so gentle and yet spirited. No other is as superbly sinuous. I've seen them, roaming females you couldn't compare with her. She's a dancing beauty, a red flame. She's unique,' Ford asserted with passion. 'That's why I'll kill for her. I'll flay Kine, rip the heart from his breast and let the crows feast.' He breathed confidence. The storm was a far-off smudge; the bang of the bird-scarer, desultory. Inhaling with relish, he snarled, 'I'll butcher him.'

'That's love,' said the Watchman. He had heard the cuckoo. It was spring all right. 'Always assuming you're invincible.'

The bog-weasel laughed. It was a crude laugh, as harsh as the other land.

The Moon Pond was calm, the sky luminous. Kia was hunting, and Kine, restless in her absence, watched the birds roost. They came to the wood in their different fashions, some flying swiftly to perch, some pausing in the last light to stuff their craws. The green woodpecker pitched to the lea, where he drilled for grubs before winging like a shot to the nearby trees. A flight of rooks drifted duskily to the crowns and their brooding mates. Pigeons clattered, fidgeting and mewling until comfortable. Large and small, they filled the covert, but it was

Kia whom the restless Kine awaited, mooching aimlessly.

If she killed promptly she would drink at the pond and chatter with him, a habit he had come to enjoy – or miss, should she not arrive. Of all hours the hour of dusk most reminded Kine of the female weasel, especially the twilight of early spring. Then the air was dry and sweet, the stars sharp-edged, and the song of the thrush throbbed with mystery. At such times, it seemed to Kine, the valley was made for Kia, the moon soft – not hard and devouring as in the frosts, but a gentle explorer of bower and brake.

By meadow and at woodside, pale blooms shone in the gloaming like small planets. The great mass of spring blossom had yet to open, but clusters of petal, some furled by evening, were bright even where the slightest of light probed. Constellations of stitchwort starred shadowy ditches roofed with wild rose. Elsewhere, buds of May, tightly knotted, glowed whitish-green; the first cow-parsley in bloom forming creamy lamps. Later, the smell of night-scented flowers would drench the wood; now the fragrance was subtle, as much of leaf and stem as of bloom itself. Moths reeled in the half-light like dancing ghosts.

Kine went into the Life Tree, but could not settle. Absurd as it seemed, the female consumed his thoughts. Leaving the hole, he moved lightly through the trees and surveyed the lea. At dusk it was a promenade for rabbits, and the dumpy shapes had begun to congregate. At first they kept close to the thickets, heads turned to their burrows, prepared to reach cover with a single bound. After a while they grew venturesome. Some of the does had nests beyond the wood, where the tilth was soft, false tunnels abounding to confuse predators. The fox would dig for young rabbits; Kine disdained such work.

Shifting his gaze he saw a blur of white a few feet off the ground at the wood's fringe. It swept silently through the shadows, turned away round the hedge and came back to the covert at the far end, scattering the rabbits who spotted it. Kine bristled but the barn-owl passed him without a glance. The bird, Kine thought smugly, had learned respect. He crowed inwardly, but satisfaction was fleeting and, returning to the pond, he paced impatiently. She was not coming that evening, he told himself.

The thrush sang late, finally muted as the air cooled. It was quiet now, and Kine watched moth wings, amputated in flight by a hunting bat, fall like tears to dewy earth. So still, so deep was the hush before long that the chomping of mice among the bluebells was clearly audible. Another time Kine would have stalked the woodmice, but he was oddly unhungry in Kia's absence. Neither mice nor rabbits tempted him. It was not loneliness, for the weasel spent most of his life alone. There was more to his unrest – a nagging possessiveness, a fierce jealousy for her, quite strange to him.

His mind was disturbed, he feared. More than once, to no purpose, he prowled the pond's edge. The moon was crescent, a shard in the dusk above the spinney where, as if to mock him, the vixen howled. Far sounds echoed. On the road beyond the ridge a late-returning lorry laboured uphill, its vibrations shaking cottages. Badgers grunted. Kine watched the flitting bats above the Moon Pond. It took a keen ear to catch their voices. The weasel heard them; heard, too, the hum of wing-membranes as they dived and jinked. But he heard with ragged interest. Halting at the bluff, he peered down at the water where stars swam. He saw none but himself in the mirrored universe.

He could not have said precisely when he drowsed off, for it was in that space at the night's heart when time was suspended in the deep wood. It was at some time in that short period when tides were arrested and the galaxies, in their whirl across the valley, stopped to ponder creation before plunging on. Soon the air would shift, tides turn, and Kine, awakening, would recognize the special breeze, the characteristic toss of oak tops which augured dawn and the peal of the thrush again. As he did so, the streak of silver in the eastern sky revealed a slender form on the moist lea, dancing towards the wood.

Then he knew for sure he was off his head. Only madness could explain the tumult within him as Kia returned.

Uncharacteristically her lip curled. So pressing was his greeting, almost bowling her over, that she showed her teeth snappishly. Kine stood back in disappointment and a wren bawled. Above them, in climbing ivy, the sound reflected his ferment, a clamour beyond the seeming scope of the minute bird. Unlike the rook, the wren openly proclaimed his partner's genius: eight pearly eggs in a domed nest. 'I've not slept,' Kia protested, loping tiredly to the pond. 'I need rest. I shan't be sociable till noon at earliest.'

Kine scowled his annoyance. 'Where've you been?'

She slaked her thirst, unresponsive.

The wren crowed. Each of the eight small eggs, little more than a half-inch long, was a masterpiece. Round the yolk and the drop of living matter in it, round the enveloping albumen, round the tissue-thin membrane containing them, the hen had secreted in her oviduct a liquid lime which, under pressure, set quickly to white shell. Finally each pearl had been touched with rosy pigment to celebrate the life in it. The wren's paean from the ivy was jubilant.

Waterfowl on their morning chores criss-crossed the pond with angled washes from their thrusting prows. Kia looked up as she lapped, her chest lowered to the brink, sleek stern raised. There was a dewy gloss to her russet coat, a streamlined perfection of shape about her that drew Kine's eye with compelling force. As she drank, a series of trembling ripples spread outward on the pool from her bright head.

'You should have been with me,' she said at last.

For a while Kine watched her, then sniffed the breeze. There was, he imagined, a scent of weasel on it other than Kia's, but the trace was fleeting, uncertain, and he put it down to maybe a stoat – or no more than his jealousy playing tricks. He was becoming possessive of the female, increasingly heedless of independence. It angered him. 'What kept you so long?' he asked accusingly.

'Wandering.'

On the marsh, he guessed; she was too fond of that place. It was dangerous now and, had it not been, he still would have disapproved, for her interest in the frontier raised a nagging ghoul he could not exorcise. 'By yourself?'

Thirst sated, she lolled by the pond. A frog croaked; another answered. It was laughter, Kine thought, a mocking sound like the gobbling of turkeys, irreverent. Soon the marsh frogs, aroused from hibernation, would swarm the flats, warty and garrulous, their gossip filling the woods from the dykes below. He had known times when it was hard to think for their chatter, and he resented the cackling of the plump frogs.

'No,' said Kia, yawning, 'but if you believe I went near the river, you're quite wrong. I went east, beyond the lane by the ploughman's house. You come to heath terrain.'

'Rubbish land.' Kine damned her wandering. 'You met no one of value beyond the lane.'

'Wrong again.' She lay listening to the frogs, ignoring his impatience, then stretched and resettled where the sun struck between the trees. Poacher's rooster was braying. The breeze was stiffening, jostling lumpy clouds across the far heights. 'You're such a chauvinist,' drawled Kia. 'You don't want to know anything outside your own land. You miss a lot.' She lounged drowsily. 'I met a canny old weasel, a real veteran. You should have been with me.'

'As well I wasn't.'

'He was gallant.'

'I don't doubt.'

'And civil,' she rebuked him, then said forbearingly,

'You'd have got on. He knew the gibbet heroes. He knew lots of things.'

'Maybe. They can all tell tales when they begin to age.'

Enlivened by his annoyance, she chuckled. 'Oh, he was sprightly enough. He'd been in battles. One eye was missing. He'd just one eye . . .'

'A one-eyed weasel?'

'But there was fire in it.'

CHAPTER EIGHT

CRAT crept forward uncertainly. The sound he heard was deceptive. *'Brek-ek-ek,'* it went from the rushes, *'Kroax-kroax'* from the grasses beside the dyke. One moment Scrat thought it came from the plantains; next second from the kingcups. It was loud and persistent, only pausing when the heron flew over, but it shifted: *'Brek-ek'* by sorrel, *'Kroax'* by water mint. The marsh frog's song had a ventriloquial quality.

It worried Scrat. The marsh frog was bigger than himself and could swallow a newt or a small mouse. Bunda, the frog he sought, was a large specimen. His warty olive-green body was four inches in length, his hind legs twice as long. He could spring several feet, and the shrew knew that Bunda was watching him. Inching forward, he strained to spot the ventriloquist.

'Kroax-kroax.' Bunda sang of frog history with exuberance, a declamatory zeal which once had startled Aristophanes. Medieval knights of France had posted serfs to beat the banks of castle moats to keep such frogs quiet. The chant of Bunda throbbed with the nostalgia of the *émigré*.

The frogs belonged to the latest group of immigrants. Valley settlement fell, historically, in three categories. There were natives, such as Scrat himself and the weasels, who had been there since legend started, and earlier. There were naturalized inhabitants – rats and rabbits – once foreigners but established by centuries of valley residence. And there were newcomers, most recently the mink, though the marsh frogs had not long preceded them.

None, Scrat believed, was better placed than the frogs to know the enemy. Introduced from continental Europe at about the time the first mink were brought to England (a few years before the war in which Poacher fought) Bunda's forebears had advanced by the same streams and reedy meres. On the way they had met and learned to revile the mink.

'*Brek-ek-ek*,' the frog croaked, and Scrat, nosing closer, squinted from the shade of a leaf at the waterside. Still the sound rang in empty space. 'I am Bunda the invisible, son of the Founding Twelve.'

Four decades earlier the Founding Twelve had been imported and released in a pond on the great Kentish flats embracing the marshes of Romney, Denge and Walland, soon breeding and spreading from that first pool. Strong swimmers as well as jumpers, they had made their way by a maze of dykes and channels to many points on the broad levels, filling meadows and hamlets with their swelling noise. By Bunda's day, a hundred square miles had been colonized.

'I'm Bunda, everywhere heard but invisible.'

It was not strictly true, for when the sun shone the frogs basked in scores beside the water and, if disturbed, could be seen diving briskly from the green banks. But when they sang they were indeed hard to glimpse, sinking all but their heads when giving voice and throwing their sounds afield. The shrew peered at the dyke and saw only water. Yet the voice was near. 'I can see you. You're close, Scrat.'

Scrat dithered. Ducking under a thistle, he skinned eyes the size of pinheads in a vain search. At least the frog would not risk his skin on the thistle's armament. 'Where are you, Bunda? I need to talk to you.'

'*Brek-ek-ek!*' It was the cackle that had given Bunda his other name: the laughing frog.

'A friendly chat – it might be to your own good.'

'It might be to my good,' the disembodied voice croaked, 'if you came nearer. You're not in pouncing range.'

'I'll stay here.' Picking his words, the shrew added, 'I'm acting for a party opposed to the marauding mink,' and scanned the water for the amphibian. The cut unfolded as far as he could see. It seemed deserted, a

91

silvery road between marching banks. He braced himself. He did not like the stillness, and jumped as Bunda's voice boomed alongside: 'No one defies the mink.'

'Kine will.'

'A weasel? A frog-killer!'

Scrat stood his ground. 'Of course, if you prefer mink . . .'

'I don't trust weasels.'

'A few words only,' the shrew encouraged. 'You're not short of them. I could keep Kine off your neck; he'd be obliged to you.'

There was silence. The reeds stirred and a flight of small birds passed over like drifting leaves. Then, 'I'm here, dwarf, in the shallows by the big stone,' and Scrat saw the head above water, the warty body under the surface, a dim shape. Bunda's legs were marked with dark-green bars, like a rugger jersey, and at each side of his mouth he inflated a grey pea-sized vocal sac. But it was the eyes – the protruberant yellow eyes with their black tracings – which bothered Scrat. 'We might talk on that basis,' the frog allowed.

'Your people' – the shrew hugged the thistle – 'they trekked the mink trails . . .'

'And were butchered.'

'You know the brigands.'

'As well as anyone since the time of the Founding Twelve. If it's evil you wish to hear, midget, I'll sing of it.'

Inflating his cheeks, Bunda recounted the legend of the great frog migration and the deadly raiders who preyed on it. It was a bleak epic, misty with images of meres, windswept willows, swampy hollows, spires of distant parishes beckoning. And as the tribe had advanced, its neighbours the mink had battened on it. In brackish creeks, in dripping culverts, ambush had waited. In ditches, death had stalked. The mink were pitiless. The song of Bunda rang with massacres. Then, at last, part of the tribe had outpaced the mink, reached this valley, found a place of peace.

'There were herons, everyday hazards; a weasel

sometimes,' chanted Bunda, 'but not massacres. Frogs esteemed the memory of the Founding Twelve, but soon forgot the migration and its agonies. Till last autumn. It was almost time to hibernate when a scattering of young frogs came downstream with the bad news. The mink were coming. Already, upriver, they were pillaging and killing with perverted hate. Fish were being dragged from the water and left to stink. It was slaughter not for food but, as we remembered, for its own sake – in celebration of evil. And the priestess of death was Gru the matriarch.'

'The she-mink?'

'The devil's daughter.' The yellow iris of Bunda's eye paled. 'Gru the merciless. Gru of the felspar heart. Gru whose minions redden the streams with blood.' Shaking his head, Bunda reflated the grey sacs and his song became a dirge of grief.

Scrat felt the despondency well inside him. He had held it back, but when Bunda stopped cackling it surged again. When the laughing frog creased to laugh, things were critical. The shrew thought in desperation of Kine's accomplishments. Alone, the weasel inspired hope. It seemed a slender hope to Scrat, but he pulled himself together and found his tongue. 'It's facts I need, Bunda. Kine wants information about the mink.'

'He'll show his gratitude?'

'Wiser to aid a weasel than anger him.'

'Kine would defy the she-mink? He's a lunatic?'

Scrat wondered. He said, suppressing his doubts, 'Make your choice, frog.'

'*Kroax*.' With a swish Bunda vanished, and the shrew was left staring at the faintest of ripples where the head had been. The long dyke shimmered; mosquitoes whined. There was a fine biological scum on the water, iridescent as a rook's wing, and nothing stirred. Scrat's micro-heart thumped. It was uncomfortably quiet, and the lane of deserted water did not embolden him. It was mink country. 'Here,' the frog called abruptly, 'by the reeds, dwarf.'

Suffused with paler green, the olive head reappeared. 'What did you want to know?' Bunda asked.

'Anything you've learned of the invaders – of the matriarch.'

'They call her Gru, spouse of Liverskin, begetter of the twins with the crimson eyes. She's evil, Scrat: she smells evil, breathes evil. The fox won't dispute with her. She's driven the otter from her holt, the chubb from his swim. She's routed the toothy stoat. And she multiplies, sometimes six to a kindle, in the summer months.'

Scrat said nervously, 'Where, Bunda?'

'At the base of the pump-house. She has a concrete bunker in the labyrinth. It's impregnable. Around the stronghold, in rabbit burrows, her marauders have made their barracks, a charnel-house of plucked feathers and stripped bones. By night, when the moon is up and the mists swirl, eerie sounds come from the fastness, and none but the bats will go near the place.'

Bunda shivered. 'The marsh,' he continued, 'is steeped in fear, Scrat. And it will spread, for when victims dwindle on the levels, the mink will turn to the slopes and woods. They'll move by ditches and drains to well-stocked ponds. The name of Gru will strike terror on the high ridge.'

'How best should Kine prepare himself?'

'He should beware, Scrat, tread watchfully, rest wakefully. And tell him this, dwarf – when Gru approaches, he should run like all the cowards who ever lived.'

The Watchman saw Scrat leave the marsh, a shifting speck on the path, and climb to safer ground. For a veteran, the rook had impressive vision. There was little he missed around the wood when he was looking out. From the oak tops he saw an undulating patchwork of fields and lanes, cattle grazing in toy-like droves, the sun-shot windows of doll-sized cottages. But each detail was sharp to the watching bird. He saw the wake of the

94

coot, the sky-blue of dunnock's egg, the doe hare moving her leveret to a safer form.

He saw the magpies working Poacher's hedge, and the man himself at his dustbin, scarcely able to hobble for his blighted joints. The Watchman blinked unsympathetically. He saw the adder in the glade, and the engineer's pick-up parked by the ploughman's garden, where sweet peas and turnips grew. The young man had got out and, as they talked, the girl cuffed his ear with a playful hand.

The rook examined the lea. Kine and Kia were lounging idly in the shade of the thorn at the wood's fringe. With sudden interest the Watchman's eye stabbed down through the trees to a third weasel, unseen by the others and downwind of them. Foliage hindered observation, but the rook had no doubt it was the bellicose stranger from the other land. There was no mistaking his hustling, incautious charge.

Ford took the shortest path through the trees. He had never been in a wood before. There were a few trees on Castle Mound, but no underlayer of herbs and shrubs. Here the wood's carpet engulfed him in its dense pile. Ford charged blindly. The scent of Kia was in his nostrils, and he bulldozed the sappy screen of vegetation with pounding strides. Now the rook perceived him, now he was hidden. On the lea, the two weasels in view remained oblivious.

The wood was a cathedral, its pillared chambers sepulchral in the green light. On every acre grew sixty or more oak trees, great trunks averaging eighty feet in height, their canopy forming a towering roof. It was an awesome vault. In places, thin shafts of sunshine sliced the fluorescence with blades of gold, but Ford's eye was not aesthetic, and his nose ruled. On waves of musky odour he rampaged. Woundwort and wood spurge, bindweed and bryony – Ford took them headlong, exploding through brambles to the clear sward.

With a ruffle of excitement the rook saw the other weasels stiffen, spring backwards, then spin to face the intruder with bristling backs. All three froze, a triangle of weasels in the meadowgrass. Kia collected her wits first. 'Oh, it's *you*. You might have given some warning. What are you doing here?'

'Stand back,' exclaimed Ford. 'I want Kine first.'

He came on and the female, alarmed, intercepted him. 'No you don't. If you're here to make trouble, you can go. No one invited you.'

'Who is he?' Kine looked dangerous.

'Tell him I'm the suitor of Kia,' Ford said boldly. 'I've come to fetch her and crush the snake who runs with her.'

Blackbirds clamoured. Sensing a fracas, they shrilled their outrage from shrub and thorn. Kine sized up his rival. He had imagined Ford a big brute, but no weasel he imagined was so broad of chest. Ford was daunting: his brow was low, his jaw aggressive, flecked with globules of saliva which caught the sun. The grasses he had trampled lay as if a rat had flattened them. Shrugging Kia from his path, he took a wide-spaced fighting stance, neck extended, and glared at Kine. It was a rugged neck. Ford brimmed with battle and the assurance of the muscular. He was, Kine guessed, more muscular than cerebral.

Kine said, 'You're trespassing.'

'I've come for Kia.'

Ford raised his face to the sun and churred a war-cry and love song in the same breath. It was a vulgar sound, fierce as the fever in him, the weasel passion. Then, with a slow stomping rhythm, he began to dance. He did not shift from his ground but rose vertically, fore and aft, rocking and bouncing in savage tempo, the rasping ululation continuing. He had come, he intoned, through storm and thunder for the female, Kia the sinuous, and meant to demolish those who challenged him.

Kia smouldered. Her eyes had narrowed and her tail flicked. 'I'll not be fought for and snatched as loot. I'll make my own choice.'

'There can be only the victor. I've set my heart on you.'

'You'll not win me by aggression, nor will anyone.'

Above them, the rook leered. Kine, biding his time, took in the ground between himself and the bog-weasel. The lea sloped from the wood, and Ford was uphill, a short charge away. Between them the turf was pocked by vole ruts, and Kine, edging sideways, placed the deepest of them in front of himself. He was struggling for self-constraint, to suppress the fury provoked by Ford. He must act defensively in Kia's sight.

'Go peacefully,' he ordered. 'You've heard what Kia says.'

He marvelled at the depths of restraint he found. Instinct signalled attack, yet he contained himself. He played to Kia's rules. It was ludicrous. Not long ago he had shown her a rough paw when she pestered him. Kine remembered her then: the gamine chatterbox. But she had grown on him. Companionship had come of it.

And Kia had aided him. It was Kia who had saved him from Poacher's noose. He recalled her warning. He could have died in the orchard where the hens roamed. And in the owl barn. Kine remembered her healing tongue. She could be tender, a spitfire, a dashing huntress, and he respected her.

But now it was more than respect he felt. To be consumed by possessiveness, tormented in her absence, was something different. The spell had become explicit, an emanation so potent, so urgent sexually, it had drawn Ford to the wood and incited the two males to mutual hate. It was ironical. Kia sought peace; but creation made her, in season, a cause for violence.

'Go,' said Kine, 'or I'll evict you, bog-weasel.'

Ford flexed his shoulders. He pawed the ground. 'I'll leave when Kia leaves.'

'You've no right here.'

'The rights of tooth and claw. What are your rights?'

'Through the wood stands a gibbet; my rights are nailed to it. My ancestors died for my rights here.' Kine paused then said quietly, 'You've much to learn. You are young, hot-headed and beyond your depth. Go while you've time, for I am lord here and Kia is mine.'

There was a bellow, a roar of rage. For a moment Ford quivered, then, still roaring, rushed down on Kine. The charge was bungled, launched in turmoil, unbalanced by the pitted ground. Kine had already pounced on the tough neck, when Kia shrieked.

The sun had vanished. Filled from the west, a low pewter sky, chinked with blue, cast inky shadows amid clumped trees. Clouds scurried nervously. 'Stop it, the two of you. I won't have it! There'll be murder! Kine . . .' She broke off. There was a hush. Blackbirds fled. Next moment the whole wood was quiet, so uncannily silent that the scuffling toil of the combatants was audible. The rooks were rising – oaring grimly, they drew a black banner across the vale. Kia's voice throbbed. The anger was gone from it. 'The Dread! It's the Dread!' she cried.

'Come on,' the girl said, straddling the gate into the wood, 'we can go this way. You'll see the pond.'

'I've a pump to check.'

'You can reach the pump through the wood. It's a short-cut.'

'Through that jungle?'

'Please yourself,' she told him. 'I'm not concerned.' But she snatched his hand when he followed and tugged him after her, exclaiming, 'You can't go everywhere on wheels. Be a countryman.'

The young man eyed the undergrowth. It was thickest at the edge of the harbourage where bush and trees met. Brambles vied with dog-rose in spiky thorn, while the lower boughs of oaks brushed hazel-tops. Farther in, the roof of foliage rose and the passage grew easier. The sounds of birds, conspicuous on the fringes, fell behind until only a whisper stirred the green depths. The girl spoke huskily. 'They say the trees have minds of their own,' she said.

'Like someone I got to know recently.' The man grinned.

'They say trees have feelings in these parts. They reckon a man once cut an elder in this wood and blood flowed from it.'

'You don't believe that?'

She laughed. 'Ask Poacher. You won't get Poacher or my dad to burn elder wood. But the oak's a good tree, a tree of peace.'

'We'll be all right then – provided we can find our way out of here!'

'Don't worry.' Her laughter echoed. 'I used to come here with Poacher when he fished the pond. I know the wood paths.' Shadows splashed over her shirt, dappling strong shoulders, and she raised a directing arm. 'There,' she said, 'see the coot on the water? See the willows? The big one is Poacher's tree.' For a while, unspeaking, she regarded it. 'It's ailing. D'you think it's dying?' she asked. 'All that bare wood . . .'

'I suppose, with Poacher, it's getting old.'

'Can *he* be dying?'

'You're not serious?' He studied her eyes. They were deep, like the pool at the heart of the quiet wood. Leafy skirts overhung the pond's edges, their murky shadows encircling the reflected sky. It had an atmosphere. He could not have defined it as he might the charisma of an engine, but he had read of animism, of sacred groves, and could sense the pagan spirit of such a place. He said, 'Don't tell me you die of superstition here!'

The girl smiled and he reached for her. Avoiding his hand, she slipped away from him. 'Only when a branch sheds, when leaves are speckled, or the annual crop of ash-keys fails. On the other hand' – she dodged him a second time – 'if you dance round an oak you'll marry happily.' She giggled. 'Can you dance?' she said, letting him catch and briefly kiss her. She twisted free. 'Now you've frightened the rooks. They don't like strange men.'

'They'll have to blame you, won't they, for bringing me?'

She watched him thoughtfully. There was a leaf in his

hair where he had ducked through a thicket, and one arm had been scratched by a bramble thorn. But his voice, as his kiss had been, was warm; his grin agreeable. 'Come on,' she said, 'we're almost at the lea. You can see the marsh and the pump from there.' At the far flank of the covert she stopped and gestured him. 'Look! Weasels – they're fighting.'

'I'm damned,' he muttered.

'One's watching. There are three of them.'

'They've seen us,' the man breathed. 'They're breaking up. Looks like the bigger got the worst: he's sloping off.'

'That leaves a pair.' She half-smiled. 'It's no one's business what happens on Poacher's patch.'

CHAPTER NINE

THE first of the Canada geese came up the estuary and into the valley, flew low above the trees then circled the marsh, honking crazily. They were striking birds, more than three feet in length from black heads to black tails, legs tucked in flight beneath pale hulls, but it was the wild trumpeting which gave their return its air of carnival. Deep in resonance, it bounced from ridge and crest, a fanfare of blaring horns.

Kine's spine tingled. The sound was rousing, a proclamation of spring's glory, summer's coming, the time of procreation and plenitude. Kia was close to him. She was nibbling the leaves of the herb rue, a bitter plant said to immunize weasels against adder bites. Kine, listening to the geese, took in her heady scent. He was well pleased. Ford had gone. Kine would have liked to have taught him a sharper lesson, but Kia was happy with the outcome. At that moment Kia's approval was sun and moon to him.

The sky was clear, the land in full bloom. Orchards flowered in benign clouds of blossom, while creamy parsley and golden buttercups lined the lanes. Through a hundred soft fragrances bowled the bumble-bee. Crickets stirred. It was a warm day, rich and sensual – sweet where cow-dung had caked and brown flies gathered; bright where trout fanned; giddy where heifers frolicked; and wild as freedom, mad as passion where the trumpeting geese streamed by.

Kia preened herself. The urge to mate was pressing but she fidgeted. On sudden impulse the female sprang at her companion, bundled him over and with mock ferocity mouthed his neck. For a second she stood back, eyes provoking, then, sure he would follow fled through a hedge to the track beyond. Kine leaped after her.

They burst on to the track separated by a distance of maybe four feet, dust spurting where they kicked down between their nimble bounds. Turning uphill, they flew in unison, legs splayed as they banked, plunging into the hedge again, out the other side, weaving back. Now they were in sunshine, gleaming like red birds; now twisting through shadow where rabbit runs mined the undergrowth. Finches rose helter-skelter. Kia was flying. Kine followed the she-weasel's flashing tail.

He was conscious of little else. Never had he run a rabbit that hard. It was a daft chase. Through green corn Kia led him, through busy labyrinths, by sun-drenched verges, thorny caverns. The rook hailed them. They ignored him. Scrat hailed them. They raced on blindly, the grit from their heels a rude acknowledgement. Marginally, Kine's mind registered mountains that were really trees, and the brilliance of cosmic space. The day was dazzling.

Kia's sinuous form dashed ahead of him. It seemed to glide, barely touching the ground, skimming swallow-like over rut and hump. And as her sleek flanks shimmered, Kine caught glimpses of white bib. He did not wonder Ford had lusted for her. She was pretty as a flower, swift as a falcon, a snake in supple-ness, born to raise kittens of peerless line. She floated. Kine strained for her, leaping past mayweed and bristling gorse.

They raced recklessly. There was a place where a pipe drained water beneath a gate, dry now, and Kia made for it. Plunging in after her, Kine followed the weasel silhouetted against a circle of light. The pipe echoed. It multiplied their scampering exertions, and muffled them, a whispering gallery of cobwebs and spongy moss from which they surged again into dazzling sun.

Then suddenly Kia had sprung like a squirrel up the trunk of a stunted ash where the hedge ended, and was out on a low branch, Kine after her. It was an old bough, underhung with tawny fungus, pitching gently earthward over tall grass. They were nose to tail, hearts pounding, panting breathlessly. Kia jumped, sprawling in the grass, and Kine was on to her. At first she snarled, then received him with throbbing warmth.

Afar, where chestnuts blazed with petalled candles, a cuckoo called. Frogs were croaking. The day bombarded the senses, but in the grass where the weasels coupled, all awareness was expunged in the sublime sensation of sexual union. For an instant, it seemed to Kine, he was lost in oblivion, a consummation as utter as death itself, then perception returned and his head – all Heaven – rang with trumpeting. In streaming waves the geese passed over, their peal a celebration of the sown seed.

Kine rolled drowsily. Fulfilled, he licked his belly and shook himself. The musk of the female adhered to him. For fully a minute they watched each other, no longer mere companions but bound by what had happened – by nature's instinct – and still bemused by it. Then, drugged with satisfaction, they sunned themselves. Midges shimmered. The shadows lengthened. At last Kia murmured, 'Poor Ford.'

And Kine answered her, yawning, 'He'll find another. Ford's a battler,' he granted. 'He'll bounce back again.'

When the sun set, they strolled by the skirt of the big wood. The last rays had filled the glades with liquid colour, making almost transparent the young foliage. Dense herbage had overgrown small flowers. Anemone withered, primrose straggled, taller blooms thrived. Soon moonlight would whiten boughs, endow foaming hawthorn with luminosity. There the weasels dallied. The roar of geese had subsided and the Plough hung inverted in the May sky.

Comment was pointless. The peace was exquisite, inexpressible. It was a long time before Kia said simply, 'It's a good place.'

'The best,' Kine said. 'It's our place: to hunt together, stroll together.'

'A place for our offspring . . .'

'And their offspring.'

They ambled dreamily. It was one of those moments when all the essences of earth meet in the warm night. Somewhere, from some tangled thicket, a shy brown-grey bird rose to a dark perch and flooded the afterglow with melody. Only the nightingale possessed such music, could have crowned fulfilment with so apt a sound. 'Listen,' Kia said, and the weasels paused in the scented bower. No bird she had heard sang so movingly. By day his notes were part of the general medley of woodland song, but by night his pulsating bursts touched the soul, and the weasel sighed. She was content.

Yet contentment, she knew, was transient. For a week or two the nightingale would sing, intense and tireless; by midsummer his transport would be spent, his voice forgotten. Contentment frightened her – like the mink. 'I don't want to lose it,' she said quietly, 'this land of the valley, this weasel wood.'

He weighed her words absently.

'Never mind,' she said, 'we'll be together.'

'Right here – it's your home now, our place to share.'

'Yes . . .'

'Kine country.'

'Yes,' she said with a tremor. 'I love it, Kine.'

The voice from the dark brakes soared thrillingly. Throbbing, rippling, the notes of the nightingale rose and fell. So varied and contrasting were the passages, the deep succeeding to high so remarkably, it seemed incredible they came from the same throat. The pauses tantalized. A dozen times, in piercing crescendo, a single note would issue, followed by a trilling refrain of different quality. To cap the song, a second nightingale answered in harmony.

The sound was flawless – as flawless, Kine mused, as his new mate. The stars shone for her. Kia was a comet, a jewel of evening. How his mother, the old she-weasel, would have applauded his day's work! Who would not admire his partner's qualities? Kia had everything: speed and grace, intelligence, courage, tenderness. She was a spitfire of tested doughtiness, a diplomat, a little lost kitten, wry and mischievous. To walk with Kia was to tread clouds.

Woodmice fled from them: their eyes bulged, cordy tails flipped, and they vanished through serried stalks. Kia pounced playfully, dancing back to her companion in skittish form. From time to time she nosed him, exploring curiously as might a stranger, then, nostrils alert, lolloped on again. Kine paced ardently. He felt an overwhelming attachment, a fierce protectiveness such as no other creature had roused in him. All her daughters would be perfect, he claimed; the sons in Kine's mould.

Kia said, 'Don't tempt the gods. They hold hostages.'

'It's in the stars. Our line shall prosper. We'll grow old and respected in this best of lands.'

'I hope so,' she breathed, the tremor returning, 'I hope so, Kine.'

'It's our place.'

'And we're together,' she said. 'That's what matters.' They reached the Moon Pond. 'We must live day by day. The night is beautiful.' The pool indeed looked enchanted in the pale gloom. Pointed shadows of reeds striped islands of duckweed and lily-pads; floating willow leaves curled like gondolas. Great trees whispered where rooks slept, and the voice of nightingales soothed the wood. Kine called Kia to the bluff and they looked over it. Kia said, 'Us in the water, and the ripe moon.'

'As it was meant to be,' Kine said, 'the two of us.'

Kia herself ripened in the next few weeks, though the swelling in her did not bloat her slender form. A casual eye would have overlooked her pregnancy. Indeed, the ploughman, dressing barley in the long

105

field, was not only ignorant of her condition when he glimpsed her from his tractor, but could not have told the sex of the small beast. The first change Kine noticed in her was her appetite. A small eater before, now she foraged greedily.

The sharp-fanged adder kept away from her. Kia killed snakes and became addicted, as the days passed, to the flesh of moles. Their runs attracted her. Kine knew he would find her at mole workings. As he waited there, a mound of loose brown tilth would stir and Kia would emerge, bright-eyed and bustling, from the earth's depths.

He found her, once, at the great untidy mole fortress at the wood's end. The earthen pile, pushed up clumsily round a tree and joined to a network of rambling tunnels, had become overgrown with fern and coarse grass. Kia popped out beside a protruding tree root and shook her head. 'It's uninhabited,' she said, 'almost derelict. Not a mole about.' Her air of gloom tickled him.

'Why moles, Kia?'

'I've a yen for them.' She cleaned her muzzle. 'A sudden longing. It's odd,' she said, 'but I recall being fed on mole when I was young. I must be reverting to infant tastes.'

'No harm,' allowed Kine, 'if you like the things.' He did not, nor did the bore of the tight holes appeal to him. 'But the fortress of the mole is a winter haunt. It's deserted in the summer months.'

'So it seems. I ought to conquer the craving, but it's hard,' she said.

As it proved to be. Kia became an expert on mole activity. She knew the runs in Poacher's orchard, every mound in the barley and on the lea. When she was missing, Kine knew she would return flecked with tunnel soil, mole on her warm breath. It amused him – not least Kia's smugness when she had gorged. Others, including the Watchman, found it less droll. The rook was hard-pressed. The rearing period, never easy for rooks, had drained the old male.

At first he had slaved alone to feed the young and his brooding spouse. Shuttling between rookery and feeding grounds had been exhausting; hacking food from the drying ground was tortuous. By the time the female joined him, he had become a plumed wreck. Several of the male rooks had starved themselves close to death to feed their families. Even when the young flew, at about a month, the fledgelings depended on adult care, and now, into June, the Watchman's problems intensified. The moult had started. On the one hand, rooks needed extra food to regain condition; on the other, worms and grubs became fewer in the surface soil. Summer was mean in the rook calendar.

'Fads!' The Watchman glowered at the weasels. 'Some would like the luxury of feeding fads!'

Then the adder complained of Kia's fickleness. Kine had never disturbed the snake's tranquillity, but Kia's pre-natal eccentricities riled the reptile. Where the sun shone, and grass grew warm, the painted adder liked to rest or move in languid rhythms from glade to glade. Now, instead of his usual sinuous flow, an angry jerking marked his movement and he reared his head dangerously. 'Can't you handle her, Kine?' The breath came in hisses as his lung compressed. 'She's hunting everywhere.'

'As she's a right to do,' Kine rapped, dancing warily. 'Kia is mistress in Kine's land.' He was watching the shifting coils, for the eye of the snake was uncommunicative, rigid under the transparent skin. The adder was in good fettle. He had not bitten for a while and his poison waxed. Kine challenged him. 'Don't bite me, adder. The bile in your bladder is an antidote. Bite me – I'll kill you and swallow it.'

'I've no fight with you.' The glinting eyes stared. 'Just warn your mate, Kine.'

'I'm warning *you*, snake!'

Kine was a zealous champion of Kia's rights. But the mole-hunting missions began to irk. Some days he scarcely saw her; when he did, her abstraction began to aggravate. She was secretive. She mooned about privately, slinking off again. There was more, instinct told him, to her obsession than simple foraging. At last, intent on discovery, he crept after her.

She made, that morning, for a dried old mole mound at the wood's edge. Kine, hidden in the herbage, saw her glance round cautiously, sniff the excavated entrance and dive below. Approaching the tunnel, he examined it. Her footprints were thick in the crumbling soil. She had used the mole tunnel many times. He paused distastefully. Rabbit burrows he enjoyed, but not mole tunnels. The narrow tubes constricted movement, oppressed the mind.

He remembered following one mole lane to a grisly larder where mutilated worms squirmed. Half a dozen had been stored alive, sufficiently bitten by the mole to prevent escape. Kine had stumbled straight into the squalid hoard. Now he entered the mine without enthusiasm.

Kia's scent led east, where the working ran under hazel and woodland herbs. There was room for the weasel, but only just, and he bored forward blindly, body flattened. The walls were smooth, uniformly curved to take the barrel-shaped mole who had dug the passage with powerful hands. It was not a new run. In places root fibres had grown through the roof. They combed the fur on his neck and he held his head low in the black void. It was quite dry, and the air had a warm, somewhat stale taste more redolent of ant-life than moist worms.

He sympathized, in passing, with the old rook. Until it rained, worms would lie beneath the depth of the Watchman's beak, and the bird would be tested to find many grubs. The earth was hard. Kine felt dusty particles crumble as he advanced, whiskers guiding him. He found the flat, uncustomary gait arduous.

Then, in the gloom, the tunnel rose and he was labouring up a steep, brief incline to reach a dead end. Kia had gone. An undisturbed earthface confronted him.

Kine felt a stab of alarm, then bewilderment. Not only had Kia disappeared into solid walls, a tunnel just below the soil's surface had terminated with an abrupt uphill gradient. It took a moment to begin to make sense of it. The passage must have climbed into a hillock, a mole's nesting mound, containing a false by-lane in the dome. He had passed the true entrance, which led to the chamber under it. Backtracking, he explored the walls until he found the space. It was minimal, but, squeezing through, he entered a roomy nest of dry grasses which comfortably accommodated himself and Kia.

She said, 'Do you like it? Once I found it I remembered those earthy smells. It took me right back. My mother nursed us in a mole's nest. It's perfect for size, and it's ready-made.'

Kine was horrified.

'You don't like it,' she answered for him. 'What's wrong with it?'

'You can't rear weasels in the soil. Not our kittens.'

'It did *me* no harm.'

'You were lucky.' He sniffed disgustedly. 'What protection is a mound of earth? It can be dug out or scraped away. Tunnels can be flooded by heavy rain. You can't give birth to our kittens in the realm of the worm, where life decomposes and the blind grope. They need the sky, the flow of sap around them. They need stout protective walls, a leafy canopy. I was born in a tree of life.'

'I know,' Kia said.

Kine said, 'In the Life Tree at the wood's heart. That's a nest fit for weasels.' His tone was puzzled. 'Why come here, Kia?'

'I know the tree has been good, but I'm afraid of it.'

'Afraid?'

'Some of its branches have withered. It may be cursed, Kine.'

He laughed, relieved by her quaintness. 'Is that all – a few boughs? Is that why you've been seeking another nest? Just think of the scores of trees with bare limbs. There are oaks in the vale with half their boughs barren, and sturdy poplars with bald flanks. They still throw leaves in abundance; the sap still rises. They don't fall down, Kia. The willow's a rock of strength.'

'It just seemed ominous . . .'

'Come on,' he urged fondly, 'you love the glade. The Life Tree's stout and airy, and the pool gleams. This is no place.' He led her back and she thought, as they went, that he was right, that her condition had deluded her. 'I think I'm going off moles, Kine; coming to my senses.' It was the old Kia. 'Poor Kine,' she said, chuckling, 'did I frighten you? What a trial we are, me and these heirs of yours!'

'You gave the adder a turn,' he said pithily.

They spent the next days hunting and preparing the tree nest with moss and leaves. It began to rain as they finished, the wood sighing, drops of water infiltrating its great hood. Kia's time was close and Kine left her in the hollow and prowled the pool. Rain whispered on its surface. It was fine rain, mild and steady, such as the rooks, faces upturned, had wished would fall. Kine ignored it. Cascades spattered from leaves, damped his coat. He paced about absently, oblivious of puddles.

With the rain came new colours: deeper greens as vegetation was freshened and washed of dust. Slowly, drips became trickles, trickles ran to rills. Soon culverts were gurgling, ditches moist again. Droplets brightened thorns and tawdry nettle flowers. Alone on the bank, Kine marched and counter-marched until, drenched and impatient, he called out to Kia. The low whimper from the willow was triumphant. He raced to her.

110

She looked up proudly from the kindle she was cleaning, pleasure profound in her husky purr. There were five kittens. Pink and helpless, their unopened eyes bulged and they jerked aimlessly. They were not, viewed objectively, beautiful, but to Kine they were matchless, entrancing gifts, and his vision misted as he gazed at them. He was overwhelmed. The mystery awed him. 'You're wet,' said Kia. He could scarcely believe his part in this miracle.

CHAPTER TEN

THE engineer pulled up by Poacher's cottage and walked round the big Humber at the shabby gate. There was a jotting pad above the fascia with a list of addresses on it, and on the back seat a copy of Blackwell's medical catalogue. He stroked the machine with a respectful hand. It was too good for a dirt lane. Had he owned such a vehicle, he would not have risked the sump on that rutted track. It was not a pick-up, a working bus.

She was engrossed at the cottage door with a visitor. He was middle-aged, pallid beside her tan, and wore a lounge suit. There was a tension, a gravity in their manner that made the younger man hold back. 'You know,' the doctor's voice came clearly, 'that he ought to be in hospital?'

The girl rubbed her forearm, as she did when anxious, from wrist to elbow, mechanically. 'It's hard enough to keep him in bed,' she said.

A mower thrummed, drowning conversation as it neared the lane. Spinning on the headland, the machine tossed up pollen and dust in a drifting cloud that had the visitor reaching for his handkerchief. When it had passed, he said, 'Aren't there relatives?'

'Not as I know.' Her fingers soothed the brown arm. 'I drop by when I can. We're the nearest folk.'

The doctor snuffled. Looking back through the door at the parlour, he slid a watery gaze to the garden, its rampant weeds. The hedge had burgeoned: it was wild with brambles in bud and flower. No one spoke. The drone of bees replaced the snarl of the tractor. Their drone was sultry and constant in a twisted old syringa beside the path.

'I see.' At last the doctor added, 'It's very difficult.'

'He's difficult, all right. Near impossible.'

'We'll have to do something. Since he refuses to be moved . . . I'll look into it.'

The girl stroked her strong, downy arm and said, eyeing him frankly, 'I wish you would. I'm worried. Being neighbours, we're concerned for him.'

She had, the young man at the gate thought, a simplicity of manner and emotion which somehow matched the place, its neglected charm. With a roar the tractor returned, another swath cut. It stopped, engine throbbing, and from the cab her father bawled, 'D'you need me there?'

To which she answered 'No, pa!' and waved him on. 'Poacher'll do more for me than for him,' she told the doctor. 'If anyone can manage, reckon I can.'

'He's not' – the doctor paused and amended the phrase – 'he's got his mental faculties, the patient?'

'Poacher? More chance of catching a weasel napping than catching Poacher out!'

'I wondered.' The drone of bees was steady and he moved up the path towards the waiting car. Placing his bag inside, he gazed back at the small window behind which his patient lay. 'I just wondered,' he muttered, shrugging. 'You get all sorts. He mentioned something about a tree. He seems to think his misfortune . . .'

'The old willow by the pond – Poacher's Life Tree. You don't want to take no notice. He's a heathen devil, full of fantasies.'

'I see.'

The girl forced out the question: 'How bad is he?'

She knew already; she had known when Poacher took to his bed, for it was unprecedented in her experience. He was feeble now. When she thought of his hardiness, the tough all-weather Poacher of her schooldays, she glimpsed the brevity of vigour in life. Her mother had been the same. Not once had she ailed – until the day she complained. The next week she had died. But somehow Poacher had seemed different, indestructible. Poacher had never changed. He had made no concessions to time or age. Her

113

throat filled, and she dug her nails into her arm to reprove herself.

The older man considered her. She was a bit of a country girl in knock-about jeans, yet who else was there in this deserted vale? He said, 'The hay smells nice but gets up the nose. There's a lot of seed about at present. It *is* quite serious,' he confessed in the same breath. 'I'll do my best to arrange something. Meanwhile, someone has to manage. He mustn't get up. He must be kept still ...'

'You'll give him something?'

'Can you collect it?'

'Yes,' the younger man put in quickly. 'I'll drive her in. Don't worry, I'll bring her to town and drive her back again.' He placed a hand on her shoulder as the Humber, lurching deeply into potholes, departed up the lane. 'He'll fix it,' he told her. 'We'll get Poacher well doped. He'll pull out of it.'

'The rotten beggar,' the girl exclaimed, 'him and his tree! He's gone and frightened me.'

'Last night, when the sky was black and unimaginable spirits gripped the marsh, they say not even the bats would fly by the square pile where the dyke meets the river near Castle Mound. Last night, they say, the evil of the place was seized by restlessness; that Gru was sleepless with moaning appetite. Then, where shadows floated like corpses at the pump's end, the dark dungeons of the stronghold stirred and eyes in cold close-set pairs caught the fitful moon.

'For an hour, they say, in bunker and earthen barracks, the band of Gru twitched and snapped in hungry readiness, the vapours of the night thick with mink stench. The marsh shuddered. Streaming clouds drew fear in clawing waves across the levels. Creatures trembled. Then the she-mink spoke and her minions received the word. It passed from Liverskin, her spouse, to the crimson-eyed twins, and down through the dark ranks. Each, receiving it, slipped swiftly from their fastness and set course.

'This, they say – and more is conjecture – will be a day of grief and plundering far afield.' Bunda told it, and Scrat, shaking, reported as the sun rose.

But since the birth of Kia's kittens Kine's interest had been limited. Kine was euphoric and summer glossed the marsh with deceptive innocence. Beside river and dyke, where the grey brood of the swans was strong and well-drilled, growth had increased with tranquil density. Mauve-seeded reeds spired. Shady docks, with rush and iris, formed gardens where birds sang.

When the sun shone, evil seemed far removed. Reed-buntings chirped and dipped in flight between osiers. Sedge-warblers babbled, their silky nests strung to clusters of cane-like stems. Wagtails flitted. In some cases, denizens of the ridge had been attracted there. Woodpigeons and blackbirds watered where steers had wallowed, and the perfume of meadow-sweet drenched the flats.

In sunlight even the pump-house looked innocuous. Ragged nests of sparrows made frills round the flat roof. Scrat was not fooled by appearances. True, many small birds escaped the tyranny. But ask the hare or the lapwing what was happening. The hare no longer dropped her leverets on the levels, but sought the greater safety of sloping land. The lapwing had gone elsewhere to rear her second ground-nested brood. Ask the heron: he knew why the number of fish had dwindled. Ask the frog why he feared for his croaking clan. Terror ruled the marsh – and its name was mink.

Scrat was waiting at the marsh gate when Kine appeared. 'It's bad, Kine. In Bunda's view things have worsened. The news is grim.'

But Kine had good news. The infants ruled. They had ventured at last outside the tree. Kia had ambled by the pond and they had romped with her. The picture delighted Kine, who had watched their development with mounting pride: their weaning, the bloom of fur, their shaping character. One little female, very small, had all the fire and cheek of her mother in her, leading the mischief with sparkling eyes. 'They'll be hunting soon, then watch out for your skin, Scrat. You're just the size for them!'

'Bunda says . . .'

'You know,' the weasel dreamed, 'my own nursery outings seem like yesterday.' He eyed the field where the hay lay in ridged swaths. In uncut corners moondaisies mingled with flowering clover in reprieved clumps. He remembered first discovering clover and yellow trefoil; recalled the crackle of gorse pods in the noon sun. With Kia he would take their small tribe on such nursery jaunts.

Scrat implored, 'The mink are breaking new ground. They moved last night. They may be raiding the ridge. I can't be sure, but if they went by the ditch . . .'

'You've come from Bunda?'

'Yes.'

'A frog fable.' Kine was sceptical. The ditch was empty. He followed it by eye to the wood's edge. Orchis flowered there, bright and small, beside campion and foxgloves in tall racemes. He said, 'The frog's an alarmist. He'd like to think I was scared, to settle scores with me. Mink move by water. If they were coming, they'd have come when the ditch was wet.'

'No one knows them better than the marsh frog. If once they reach the culvert, the pond is theirs.'

'Across dry land?'

'Who's to stop them? Who, Kine? Poacher might have, with his gun, but Poacher's out of it. You asked for news,' despaired the shrew. 'Yet you throw it back at me!'

His wail touched home and Kine conceded, 'You're right. Don't give up, Scrat. Keep the information coming – you never know. But I can't see it this time, not a catastrophe. If Bunda had it right, it would be that. Besides, the rooks – they'd have flown the Dread. When the mink leave water they're conspicuous.'

His gaze returned to the wood. It seemed, somehow in his mind, to have darkened. He was beginning to labour the point, and when Scrat spoke again the dwarfish voice echoed the weasel's doubts. 'The rooks have given up a look-out. They're on the feeding grounds.'

'All the same . . .'

'Yes, Kine?' The midget waited, but Kine was silent, his mind distant, so that Scrat knew contact was impossible. Somewhere far from the valley a summer storm growled. When a weasel stood thus, still as stone, head held high, eyes immobile, his mind had shifted beyond the normal to another plane. Scrat had known them stand trance-like for several minutes. At last the weasel said, 'Well, the kittens need food. Today I hunt. Tomorrow we teach them the first lessons of self-sufficiency.'

The far storm rumbled. That was not the call that had come to him – the sudden pulse of anguish, the silent scream on some frequency unidentified. But the sun was shining; bird-song tinkled. And the mental image he had just received of the Moon Pond, with monsters rising, had surely been, like the scream, inspired by Scrat's yarn. 'You might try,' he said, 'a word with the heron. He's dependable. Bunda gossips. Unless Bunda's croaking, he's not content.'

He worked slowly up the hedge, sniffing in crannies and dim retreats, the smell of newly cut hay a distracting force. The nostalgic scent took him back, like so many summer things, to nursery times, careless hours revived in the new pleasures and cares of parenthood. They were a joy, Kia's kittens, the smallest a special treat. She had a wicked little snarl and, when ignored, an attention-demanding nip. She was so like Kia – so self-willed yet so gifted at

117

pleasing, a sly mite. He had watched her stalking a beetle, all quiver and pounce, then, catching sight of him, grabbing his tail and tugging impishly. Next moment she had slumped in a heap and was fast asleep.

A phrase returned to him: hostages to the gods. It was appropriate. Piled in slumber, the tiny tribe evoked such depths of protectiveness in Kine's breast that their vulnerability was scarcely bearable. Kia had known it before their birth. The phrase had come from her. Now their need was for meat, and he quickened pace.

The rook saw him in the hayfield, among the thick swaths. The cutters sometimes left carrion in their wake and, though Kine preferred to kill his own food, the demands of young mouths overcame pride. Porpoise-fashion he threaded the waves of mown grass. The rook drilled wearily. He was accompanied by a gawky son who still sported nasal bristles and face feathers where the adult was bare-faced. 'Join the workers, Kine. Parenthood's a hard punishment.'

'A high reward.' Kine bobbed up from the hay. 'A five-fold blessing, Watchman. A high reward.'

'*Huh!*' the rook said, stabbing the soil. 'Five more weasels in the land – we should celebrate!'

The great bowl of the vale darkened as a cloud passed, then shone again. Kine looked down on the marsh, its raking waterways narrowed by summer growth. Mink in the Moon Pond! The levels were their habitat, their haunts the wild banks of stream and dyke. Where the stem of reed met oozy silt they slid to water, dragging under the struggling duckling and swimming vole. The marsh fowl fell to the killers, so did Bunda's kin. But the nightmares of the frog community could not be foisted on the slopes! The horrors were marsh problems. And until Kia's kittens had grown, Kine could not attend to that troubled realm.

Bunda croaked. From the hayfield his clack was just

audible. There was little rest from his turgid themes.

'Last night, when the sky was black and shadows floated like corpses at the pump's end, the dark dungeons stirred . . .'

Kine was not listening. Nostrils flared, he paused a moment in the close stubble of the grass, spine humped, and sifted the air with his keen nose. The prevailing scent was hay, but there were nuances of many herbs and creature life. The scents of prey were cold. He disregarded them. One trace put his back up. Bouncing forward, he stopped and sniffed again. In a series of quickening spurts, fur bristling, he reached the overgrown ditch at the field's end. Its crop was tall. Thistles towered above him like ships' masts. Giant grasses bent under seeds as large as oats. He stretched his neck. The smell was as plain as it was sickening.

He followed the effluvium of mink to the culvert, ran the pipe to the stunted ash where Kia's brood had been conceived, took the ditch by the lea, then pierced the wood's depths. His head was a maelstrom, all thought in it deluged by the vile stink. His mind seethed, and at the core of the vortex was dread: a blind dread such as Kine had never known before.

The air was tainted, green and still where the oaks made avenues of vaulted space. The big boles were lime-shaded; broad-leafed grasses smooth as lilies thronged at the feet of them. Kine did not notice. Nor did he notice the still ranks of nettle stems or sombre burdock at full growth. Even at summer's height, the rotting leaves of last autumn mulched the herbs there, and the fallen twigs he leaped were putrified.

All he noticed was the deadly odour and a distant *churr*, like a swiftly pulsing ratchet, which grew louder as he ran, disturbing the silence in angry bursts. That it came from so small a throat as the wren's might have surprised a stranger, but Kine knew that *churr* of outrage and was chilled by it. 'Prepare yourself,' exclaimed the wren. 'Be prepared, Kine.'

The coot's feathers were on the bank of the pond in a small heap, a grey-black heap, and there were specks of blood in the vicinity. The heap stank of mink, as did the trail to the water from that grim pile. Kine's back tingled. Scarcely daring to do so, he moved forward. There was a roach laid high on the bluff with its head removed. He knew what was coming and, before it came, was benumbed by expectation, an icy prescience.

Kia's flayed body, snarl fixed in defiance, was not far away. For a time he could only stare. Inching nearer, he put his nose down to it. It was another Kia. The scent was Kia's. The flesh was Kia's. But it was a cold Kia, torn and defiled by atrocious jaws.

He nudged the carcass, stood bemusedly guarding the crumpled form. He was stunned. Slowly, he circled it, his emptiness filling with disbelief. It was impossible. The shape was twisted, intestines uncovered, beset by ants, but Kine could not believe it would not move again, that the staring eye had no sight in it. Nor that the nest was deserted, obscenely vandalized.

'There was no time,' the wren churred. 'She tried to shift them to safety, but there was no time. They gave no warning, simply towered from the water and fell on her. She stood ground. She was a sprite against giants, but she stood ground. She defended her small ones to the last breath.' The bird hopped agitatedly from perch to perch. 'She was heroic, Kine, a fireball of despair, a spitting fury. She fought them bleeding and drove them back. She repulsed them in her agony. Barely able to crawl, she went at them. It was terrible. She lay paralyzed, still snarling at the end, as her life ebbed.'

'The kittens?'

'Then the mink fell on the kittens. They are no more, Kine.'

'They must be.' He cast round him. Somewhere, there must be kittens. The playfulness and mischief, the *future* could not have perished since the sun rose that morning. The urge of parenthood churned in him. Five mouths to feed! There had to be mouths to feed. Obsession tore against reason, and distractedly the weasel began to search. He searched the pond's bank. He searched the ivy-clad stump, and beneath fallen ash poles. He looked in the niche by the rotten post. All it held were wood beetles, funereal crustaceans which formed lifeless balls. Hope failing, he explored the remotest depths of holly thicket and secret pit. He found old food stores, moist seed-leafs, centipedes – that was all.

He searched a dozen bowers – summery now, but witches' caverns on winter nights. It was neither summer nor winter in Kine's consciousness. It was *no* time. When time returned, he told himself, they would come with it. But would it *ever*? Would the howling emptiness fill again?

At length he went to his dead mate and hung his head. For a moment he saw her, bright and supple, against stars of blackthorn as hail fell cleanly from an April sky. *'I'm fond of you, Kine. I don't know why,'* she said laughing, *'but I really am.'* The scene changed. She ambled dreamily at sunset, and a nightingale was singing as she turned to him. *'I don't want to lose it, this land of the valley, this weasel wood ... I love it, Kine ... The night is beautiful.'*

It was fleeting, and when the moment passed she was gone with it. He knew the shape before him was inanimate. The wren churred and, in the space above the pool, a pale ghost of the moon lingered into morning, cold as Kia herself. Kine did a strange thing. Stooping slowly, he rolled against the small corpse. It was a purely instinctive act, a last symbolic contact before the crows, or some other scavengers, picked the bones.

Then, decked in the scent of the tortured body, he began to dance, to undulate in a measured, head-swinging dance of hate. He faced the marsh, the distant stronghold of Kia's killers, the den of Gru. And as he danced, the Blood Fury rose in him.

CHAPTER ELEVEN

IT might have been any midsummer evening on the wooded slope. In the gloaming, rabbits of all sizes dotted the lea, from 'starters' not much bigger than blackbirds to raw-boned adults. They could have passed, until they moved, for mole hummocks. Observation showed the small ones the twitchiest. Startled, they streaked like shrimps out of view, while their elders, shrewder judges of danger, paused to take stock.

The burrows at that spot lay in a bank of bare hard soil overgrown with brambles and deeply cracked. In these cracks wasps built the cellular combs of the nests, or bikes, which the badger sought on his nightly rounds. The badger dug out the larvae while the wasps slept, and, crumbling the delicacy, ignored the barn-owl prowling the gloom where wood and field met. Doves and pigeons were settling in the smaller trees, their crude nesting platforms resembling black rafts.

The doves flew low, white tails fanning as they pitched to the covert in swift arcs. They made the slowly gliding owl, with his extemporary escort of smaller birds, look ponderous. So did the swallows, shooting back and forth amid the insects they supped on. Before the swallows gave up and retired to roost, bats were winging above the wood.

It was an odd light. Peering into the gathering dusk, a stranger might have perceived that objects rising from a level – clumps of herbage in a grazed field – acquired a shadowy prominence they lacked by day. This was true of hares, who often browsed in groups on the mead at twilight, reaching high on their haunches for tasty food. They stood out more clearly in the greyness than in the brightest sun. Around them, beetles, rising in the coolness from rings of cattle dung, toiled to new places on droning wings. Where the dung dried, rank grass spurned by grazing steers formed dark keeps in which insects and the spores of fungi dwelled.

Later, when days turned humid, fungi would burgeon in many places, often as toadstools of seductive form. Some, with delicate stems and domed caps, were as pale and translucent as porcelain; some were gaudy in colour, like paper parasols. Others turned black as they grew, then festered mushily. Bracket fungi, jutting from trees, were sometimes present for many years. There was an alder near the pond which played host to great brackets with brown-flecked tops like well-turned omelettes. They had barely changed in the last decade.

The owl flew beyond the alder to a lonely oak which marked his turning point. He seldom varied his circuit, and knew each tree in it. There were several isolated oaks between ridge and marsh, smaller than the oaks of the covert, and in their senile years. Evidently they died from the top down, for such foliage as remained was near the bottom, their lifeless limbs reaching up like drowning swimmers in the fading light. Wheeling, the owl turned back towards the wood again.

The badger was down a hedge now, digging where bumble bees had their nests. Like the bear, which he resembled in shape, the thick-set growler of the shadows had a sweet tooth. The bee nests tended to cluster in buried groups, several occurring in a single bank. By morning, the only trace of them would be the badger's scrapes. Small birds in the hedge flapped apprehensively. Always jittery as darkness settled, they erupted in flocks which a sparrowhawk might have plundered, but which were too quick for the gliding owl.

After a while the hares began to move, loping in Indian file down the slope, one doe veering off towards the lea and the woodland path. She came casually, with the somewhat ungainly gait of hares when strolling. At speed their straining bodies were flat and graceful, but at leisure the long hind-legs had a disproportionate, stilt-like look. She came languidly, though the great amber-mauve eyes were wary, the sinews in the lean frame prepared for flight. Suddenly, at the wood's edge, she froze. With a bound she hied back across the meadow and was lost to view.

From the trees came a piercing call. It was not quite the cry of a stuck pig, nor quite the whiffling squeal of an angry horse, but had something of both, and was wholly startling. The vixen who had uttered did not repeat it. For a moment she paused, her triangular black-backed ears cocked, then, unanswered, walked quietly on – as her kind had walked the forests since primeval times.

Now the moon made a halo on dewy grass. Deep in the moist sward it gleamed on velvet and, as a tiny figure scuttled, the owl swooped. Disgruntled, he soared again. It was the shrew, a creature shunned by discerning predators, for on each flank of the dwarf a series of minute glands produced, when activated, an offensive taste. The owl rose steeply, passing with dispassion the darkened gibbet, himself unsaddened by the latest news.

The death of weasels did not dismay the barn-owl. They culled his prey, and his leg remained stiff from Kine's assault on it. He spared no sorrow for Kia, for her progeny or weasels crucified. Dipping, he seized a vole, found a suitable anvil and smashed the life from the struggling beast. In the darkness, he preened himself. A window was glowing in Poacher's cottage. Faraway headlights blinked and vanished. The owl screeched savagely.

Kia – the mate of Kine – and their brood were dead.

The girl went outside, the light from the door she opened illuminating fuchsias and a cottage lawn smooth as a billiard table. There was washing still on the line and, while her father smoked indoors, she filled a bucket with clothes and dropped the pegs on top. Beyond the line, where the hedge was trimmed low, she could dimly see the road and the darkened vale. After sunset she preferred the neat garden to the fields beyond.

On a midsummer's night, when the owl screeched and the fox howled, it was easy to imagine strange happenings on the wooded slopes. The girl's forebears, with flickering lanterns to stem the gloom, had believed the shadows held eerie threats: supernatural padfoots, black dogs which strode backwards, gnomes with donkeys' heads. There was much that mystified, not all imagined, and the ploughman's daughter, despite – perhaps because of – her valley roots, did not like the dark.

Her eye was drawn to the lane by the slightest of movements on the far verge. As she watched, a snake-like head parted the growth, and in five or six bounds the small dark shape of a weasel crossed the macadam to her own side, disappearing in the direction of the wood. Hardly had it gone before a second weasel crossed, and a third appeared. 'Heck,' the girl called, 'the night's stiff with weasels running Poacher's way!'

'Weather, maybe.' Her father stood in the doorway. 'It's been a dry spell. Creatures shift with the weather.' He puffed smoke. 'Another night without rain, we'll make some sweet hay.'

The girl folded the washing and he considered her. The brisk, competent gestures were familiar: she had her mother's manner in so many things. She would make someone, perhaps the young engineer, a lively wife. The widower grinned, eyes crinkling behind curling smoke. He was not possessive, but as genial a father as the ruddy quick-smiling face implied, and she would, he knew, command her own affairs. 'It's a mood,' he harked back. 'Creatures are moody. I reckon it's a mood got into them.'

'Gipsies say weasels hunt by night as families.'

'Maybe. Books do say they go alone; that's my view of them. I've watched them from the tractor – mostly lone hands.'

'Poacher says he once saw a weasel tribe.'

'Aye, Poacher says . . .' The man compressed the fuel in his pipe with a stubby forefinger. Rekindling the ash, he breathed the night air. He could smell the last of the hay he had turned that evening; and would bale tomorrow if the weather held. There was a mouse on the step, killed and left by the cat, which was overfed. The clouds were teasing, and the bowl of the vale exhaled warm draughts.

Beyond the garden, through strings of runner-beans and trees black as oblivion, a light gleamed feebly under Poacher's eaves. The man turned back to the parlour – to the straw dolly in the corner, the crocheted table-mat made by the girl's mother in her dying days. She and Poacher, he used to reckon, were the strong ones. Life was curious – life and death. The mouse on the step. An untold history ended by a cat's paw.

'Mind,' the man said, 'when Poacher and me were lads, there were a lot more creatures around than nowadays. Rats moved in swarms; weasels preyed on them. You could meet a swarm of rats, scores of the beggars, on a dark night. By night a lane would seem alive for the rats a-marching it, that's a fact. When me and Poacher were lads, rats were everywhere.'

'Poor old Poacher,' said the girl. 'Will they be shifting him?'

'To a hospital, to do as he be told? Not a hope of it.' The man rubbed his chin with a calloused hand. 'Poacher put on by nursing women?' He smiled reflectively. If Poacher had ever succumbed to the will of a woman, Poacher and not himself would be the widower; the girl would not, like her mother, be telling him where he might and might not knock his pipe. It was the ploughman who had succumbed. Poacher had gone to France and won medals killing men, as at home he had killed most things which ran or flew. 'He'd rather die in a ditch,' the girl's father said.

'The damn fool.' She stood on the step, looking into the garden, where shadows rustled, things passed in the night. She slammed the door. 'The damn fool,' she said, 'him and his weasel tribes!'

Kia was dead, screeched the owl, and in the wood the restless sleep into which her mate had fallen ended with a jolting sense of loss and loneliness. Kine was in the Life Tree. He heard the owl. He heard the frogs on the marsh and a lapwing mewling beyond the trees. There were many noises in the darkened wood. Branches creaked. There were snores, grunts, whimpers. It was not what he heard that chilled the weasel but what he missed in the tragically empty nest.

Once, in his nursery days, he had wakened and been alone there. His infant peers had crawled outside where, heart thumping madly, he rediscovered them. Now he knew Kia and her kittens were unrecoverable. Their warm bodies, their moist breath, would not greet him in the hole again. He no longer cared much for the willow, remembering Kia's fear that the tree was cursed. He had slept there from habit but, stirring, had no wish to hang around.

Rage returned to him. Outside, the patter of what might have been a rabbit lingered a few seconds then drifted off. He heard the squeak of a woodmouse, shrill almost as the bat's cry, but was unmoved. He had no taste for the hunt. The only blood Kine lusted was mink's blood. He bared his fangs. He wished to close them on the neck of a monster and set them in a death lock, a lock even his own death would not break. He owed Kia a mink's life.

There was another sound and the weasel listened. In the depths of the hole, he gave a low hiss. This time it was not a rabbit, but a step more deliberate, more dangerous. Kine bristled. The lapwing was still wailing, its cry distant, unrelated to the prowling in the dark wood where, apart from the *blip* of bats, hush had fallen. Again the sound came, a scuffling hint of intrusion, then the night was still.

Kine looked up at the hole, the worn lip of his exit to the glade and pool. Whatever had moved was light of foot. Stretching his neck, he peered sharply from the willow den. In such a manner had he first glimpsed the outside world as an inverted image in the Moon Pond, and now the water brimmed with images: moon and trees, stabbing reeds, and the weasel – the unfamiliar and unexpected weasel there. It shimmered in the water beneath the bluff. As Kine watched, another joined it, then more, until the pool quite suddenly filled with weasel shades. For a moment, compelled by the reflections, Kine was mesmerized. At last he switched his gaze to the bluff above.

The land sloped smoothly to the little escarpment, clear of growth save for some thin mossy grass and a straggling briar. Toxic berries of belladonna hung nearby and, where the coot had perished, plantains clustered. The weasels stood on the incline, groups of two and three merging in larger clusters. Others joined them from the shadows, slipping from the herbage to the pond's brink. They came by lea and woodland gate, marsh and ridge, instinctively drawn to the dusky glade.

Astonished, Kine looked out at them. The bank was silvery. Thin fingers of willow foliage admitted the moonlight in lacy beams which bleached insects, plated the crusty bark of ancient boughs. The tribe grew. Kine saw bog-weasels, heath-weasels, weasels from woods and pastures, some aggressive, eyes beady with suspicion, all curious. The glade seemed choked with them. Above, where the massed constellations swung in orbit, a shooting star blazed, and a gust of midnight wind gave the covert a nervous twitch. It made the pigeon's roost sway, and the pheasant's perch. Tendons tightening, the swaying birds gawped at the weasel pack.

The adder streaked away from it. The wren churred: 'Where Kia fell, the tribe gathers. News spreads; Kia was popular. Where Kia fought, the clans assemble in tribute and for revenge. Watch and marvel – watch the dance of the weasel tribe!'

It was a dance of sorts. For perhaps thirty minutes – as their numbers rose to a score, and still increased – the scampering, sniffing weasels galumphed aimlessly. The glade seethed, but only slowly did a pattern of dance evolve. When it did, it was a war dance, a leaping dance of red warriors, a dance of rage. They danced like leaping fish, like jumping crickets, vying with each other in height and energy, whirling grim-faced.

Sucked into the frenzy, Kine felt giddy. There were stamping, undulating weasels on every side, and he recognized none of them. Yet their dance was his dance; their rage his. It seemed appropriate on his territory, a justifiable intrusion, this hypnotic rampage beneath the great trees. The Blood Fury was running; he saw it in the eyes of small high-raised heads and the set of jaws, as he felt it in his own veins. Swaying, bobbing, he pranced and bounded, and suddenly Ford was along-side, wildly pacing him. 'She was joy, Kine. They'll suffer for what they did to her.'

'They'll rue the day, Ford.' He would have killed Ford once; now he whirled and chanted, 'They'll rue their wickedness.'

'We'll destroy them,' Ford grated. 'We'll rip out their throats, drain the blood from them.'

Faster the weasel tribe stomped in the glassy light. Mobbing the willow, it swirled away across the glade and round the deep pond. Kine went with it. It was, he knew, an anachronism, a denial of independence, this red mob, yet he needed the release, the abandonment. He needed to share his fury, to join the outcry. 'Death to the monsters!'

'To the mink dens!'

'To Mullen's dyke!'

They were pouring through the gate to the track at the wood's skirt. There, in rayless shadow, they pounded silently, vengeful sprites whose onrush awed spectators of hedge and verge, small beasts who goggled and dived to earth. The shrew scurried; voles blinked anxiously. At last, where the gibbet stood, the tribe halted and Kine drew breath. They stood in homage, the rotting cross-bar of relics above their heads. A breeze

130

puffed, stirring spectral blooms of elder, then died again. For a second, bones in withered skins rattled – dead weasels whispering.

Framed by clouds and dark foliage, the martyrs hung in crucified ranks against the galaxies. Thin and shrivelled, no greater in length than a man's boot, each decomposing husk had once housed the huge defiance of the weasel breed. Awed, the living bunched closer beneath the mummy-cloths. 'They stood alone and unafraid, daring the owl and diving hawk, the man and the man's dog, against giants – and in our own trials we'll not forget. In battle, we'll remember them.' Kine recalled his mother's praise. Stars twinkled. He heard another voice. *'I'd feel less frightened,'* Kia had said, *'if there were more of us.'*

Ford shoved through the concourse. 'Enough time wasted. To the marsh,' he snarled, 'to avenge Kia and her kindle. Follow the bog clan. Death to weasel-killers!'

'Lead on,' spat a young heath-weasel. 'Let's be rid of them.'

'Death to Gru, the she-devil, and Gru's brood!'

The pack heaved, hissing and stomping as rain threatened, driving currents of air across the wood's face. There was a fury in the tribe, a raging passion, as tangible to Kine as his pounding blood. The clans jostled. Weasels bickered. Every now and then one would jump high above his fellows, bib flashing, or dart from the mob in a lone dance near its periphery.

'To the marsh,' raged Ford.

'Death to mink!' came the chorus.

'Advance the bog brigade!'

But as they moved a warning broke, and they turned to the gibbet with searching brows. The moon had fled, obscured by cloud, and in the hay-scented gloom the newcomer was a tortured shade, a sable wraith whose yell of caution halted the tribe. 'Wait! You've the minds of chickens, not weasels. Where's your strategy?'

'To the dyke,' screamed Ford. 'To the devil's stronghold!'

'Death to mink,' came the chorus. 'To Mullen's dyke!'

Ford turned to the stranger. 'That's the way of the weasel, to engage and kill.'

'To think first is the way of the weasel; to scout and plan.' For an instant the cloud parted and the old one-eyed weasel stood full in moonlight, the sage of Kia's travels, of Moon Pond memories. Kine struggled to place him, then the gleam was gone and shadow returned. It said huskily, 'Mink are deadly; the deadliest foes you've ever met. Are you taking them on without a plan? On the marsh, their own ground? Has any of you yet faced the monsters?'

'Kia did,' Ford thundered. 'She fought heroically – as we'll fight to avenge her death. This is a weasel war.'

'A righteous war,' cried the young heath-weasel. 'We're unafraid.'

'War,' the veteran told them, 'must be planned, especially a war against great odds.' He glanced upwards to where a front of massive cloud-heads blocked the heavens. 'The weather must be considered, and the strength and disposition of the enemy. You can't fight the first battle where he's strongest, on his own terms. You must plan and wait, use surprise, exploit his weaknesses.' The single eye flashed. The matted coat, Kine could see, was striped with battle scars. The old oracle added, 'You need a strategy. Who's leading you?'

'Ford,' a shout came.

The flashing orb picked out Kine, and with its lingering gaze came responsibility. 'I am,' Kine said. 'I lead the tribe, for Kia was mine, as were her kittens – and is this land. I am lord of this domain and know its byways. I know its denizens. I am Kine, rat-killer, owl-fighter, weasel champion ...' Ford was glaring, remembering their tussle. 'If you dispute with me,' Kine invited, 'fight for leadership. But I am Kine the unbeaten, and will vanquish you.'

He saw Ford grit his jaws, struggling against impulse. Then a sudden draught whipped up dust, presaging rain, ruffling weasel fur as the tribe watched the bog-weasel shrug. 'He was Kia's mate,' Ford conceded. 'I'll take his leadership.'

'And be my deputy?'

'Accepted.' Ford beamed ruggedly. 'Forward to the dyke with Kine!'

'No!' Kine barked the rebuttal as the rain fell. 'We've heard wise advice from an old weasel warrior, and we'll act on it. First, a council of war. First, the plan, then the fury. We'll not hold back, but we want value for sacrifice, the best revenge . . .' The initial raindrops were mighty, printing stains on the gibbet, pitting soft dust. Gradually, in the darkness, they came faster, like hoofbeats on the hood of the sleeping wood. *Rat-tat*, they sped on over barn, over Poacher's roof. Kine stood under the elder and, as the tribe split for cover, contemplated the old weasel with sharpening memory. 'It's been a long time,' he said at last.

'Yes.' Leaves shuddered, spilling water in blobs which became so frequent they formed small cataracts. 'I'm sorry about Kia,' the old animal muttered. 'You know I met her. She was a fine creature; your mother would have welcomed her.' One-Eye sighed. 'She died, too, your mother. Perhaps you heard . . .'

'No.'

'Last winter. She had started to weaken. The frosts were cruel to her.'

'I hadn't heard.' The rain was a torrent now, flung about in the night by a wind which snatched at boughs, tossed fledglings from nests, flattened fronds and ferns. Kine flinched. He had not seen her since his youth but the loss hurt. Water swirled in ditches; the pond fizzed. It seemed impossible so much water could come so quickly on a summer's night; that clouds could have carried so vast a weight. He thought numbly of Kia and the kittens – and now the old she-weasel had been torn from life. Kine said, 'I never saw her once I'd grown and she moved on with you. Were you still her mate?'

'Until the end, Kine.' The torn face had done with suffering. It wore a kind of scarred serenity, as if its single orb had seen the final peace.

'You grow up and grow apart, that's the weasel way.'

'Territorially, but not in spirit.'

The squall was now passing. The wind dropped and the rain, free of tension, fell vertically in thinning rods, easing to a drizzle which barely dimpled the puddles so swiftly filled. Culverts gurgled; in the washy gloom drips plopped and splattered from countless leaves.

'Not in spirit,' Kine said. 'You're quite right.'

His father nodded. 'And you've a war to plan.'

CHAPTER TWELVE

GRU swayed to the thunder, to the roaring of the pump. The power and violence of the churning screw attracted her. She enjoyed the lash of water in the steel coil, the frothing cauldron where it clawed the dyke, the slamming pressure on the outlet valve. The field of suction fascinated her. Lumps of wood, of floating weed, were drawn to the catch-grid with swirling force. It pleased her to imagine the consequences to a creature caught in the tow, pulled through the grim bars. Each pummelling turn of the screw excited her. She thrilled to the fury, the mincing thrum.

The rain-filled dyke gradually drained. Gulls, scavenging, hailed the matriarch with sycophantic squeals. The hard-eyed gulls owed easy pickings to the mink. They saluted her. Gru's lip curled. The grin, if such it was, exposed saw-edged teeth in daunting ranks, chill as the gulls' affection, and as cynical. 'Salute me,' it said, 'but beware. I grant no privilege.'

The dyke swilled. Gru swayed to the foaming violence. At last the level dropped below the pump's electrode and the power died. It had the abruptness of a heart attack. There was a final churning, vibrating heave and the screw shed its load with a sighing jolt. For a while the tow in the dyke continued, cheated now, thrown back in a low wave which soon expired. The she-mink stirred. Purposefully she gained the shoulder of the emplacement and surveyed the pool.

Beneath her, a fall of possibly five feet, the dyke was black as Gru herself and, dropping plumb as a stone, she vanished into it. There was scarcely a splash, then her skull reappeared and she stroked for the metal grid. A scummy raft of drifting rubbish clogged the bars. Mounting it, the matriarch stood where the pump had threshed, glared into its maw and made obeisance there. The gape awed her, the sense of power, devouring appetite. In the jaws of the giant she felt affinity.

Her voice echoed in the chamber; Liverskin was listening, and her bunker guards. 'The power of the grinding jaw is implacable. Only Gru understands its churning poetry, its mangling music, its capacity to crush as simply as Gru crushed the spitfire of the Moon Pond for her insolence . . .'

Kine climbed the stunted ash to the fork near its crown, and looked down giddily. Though an agile climber, he lacked the squirrel's head for heights as well as the long balancing tail of the tree-lover. At the base of the ash, One-Eye and Ford seemed far off, and Kine clamped his claws in the blemished bark. The platform gave a clear view of the sultry vale.

The day had dawned sweatily. Already the sun, burning mist from marsh and river, was teasing steam from the rain-washed slopes. Only the distant crest looked cool, in a blue haze. The stream rolled muddily. Where globules from the night's downpour underhung barbed-wire fences, cobwebs glistened. Dykes shimmered. Hay, soaked where it lay, no longer held the promise of the day before. Kine descended the tree and joined the other two.

'Every ditch,' he said, 'is running. They've got the conditions they like for foraging.'

'They'll come,' One-Eye said gruffly. 'They've only scouted. They'll want the pond. They mean to colonize.'

Ford scowled. 'I can smell them out there. Let's pitch into them.'

'In good time,' cautioned One-Eye. 'You can descend on the pump-house and be massacred, but I doubt Kia would thank you. You need to learn how to fight them first. I've fought most things in my day, from rats to terriers, and the secret is to know how their minds work; how they come at you. The rat is devious; a dog comes straight for you; a stoat hesitates. But the monsters –

how do mink fight? You can learn by skirmishing, iso-lating individuals and setting ambushes. Discover how many weasels a mink can match. Find out where it is vulnerable. *Then* march on Gru, my friends, prepared for her.'

'When half the tribe has gone,' Ford said.

'Perhaps – but not the best half.'

'They've got their own lands,' Kine pondered. 'They can't neglect them indefinitely.' He looked round edgily. The stunted ash at the foot of the wood, where the trees tapered to scrubby hedge, was their watch-post. Nearby ran the ditch the mink had used on their grim ascent. Other ditches climbed from marsh to ridge at field-spaced intervals, now patrolled by scuttling weasel groups.

'Ford's right,' he confessed. 'It's hard to just sit here. It sets your fur on edge. The mink are down there. You know they'll come. But when and where? How many?'

And would he keep his nerve, Kine wondered, faced by the malign giants. He recalled the black monster on the river strand, the wedge-head, the trap-like jaws, the great back of the brute, and the broomy tail. He remembered the torpedo speed of the mink when the beasts submerged.

'It's getting hot,' he said fretfully.

Ford snapped at an insect. 'Sitting here waiting isn't weasel work.'

'We must keep our heads.'

'*Bah!*' The rook lazed in the ash tree, his glare sceptical. 'If you had *heads* you'd migrate and forget the mink.'

'Would *you*?' asked Kine. 'After all the seasons you've been here, would you run from them?'

The Watchman temporized. 'I'm too old for changes. Be lucky to last the winter, anyway.'

One-Eye grunted. 'You and me, rook – be joining our ancestors before much longer. But, you know, this place was theirs from the beginning. Rooks and weasels were here before rabbits, rats, pheasants were heard of; when Poacher's kind lived with bears in caves. We can't abandon the valley like that, rook. Besides' – the hoary jowls tightened – 'it's not a lost cause. Kia fought them. She didn't run. If she could face them, one little she-weasel, what may the tribe achieve?'

'Ah, Kia . . .' The bird's voice softened. 'She was a bright flower. I'm no lover of weasels, but Kia was special. I thought a lot of her.'

Kine said, 'Then you'll help us, Watchman? For Kia's sake you'll join with us?'

'The mink-fighters,' prompted One-Eye, 'need us old hands.'

Ford groaned inwardly. They would be fighting, if he had his way, not wooing aged birds. Bog-weasels, battlers of the frontier breed, did not wait for the enemy to come to them. It was not Ford's style to kill time, to sit on a ditch while danger drew closer, and each movement of the grass brought a tingle to the spine and made the pulse jump. The heat ruffled him. The prickly humidity made him irritable. There was menace in it, threatening sounds in the hedges. With a start he rose on his haunches and scanned the grass-heads.

'Get down!' cried Kine, and as their bellies hit the soil the nearby herbage parted and a breathless animal fell on them.

They recognized the young heath-weasel. His lungs heaved. 'The ditch by the gorse,' he said, 'where the land-drain empties . . .' He was straining for coherence. 'They've ambushed a mink, a brown monster.'

'Stay here.' Already, Kine was running. 'Wait with One-Eye. Come on, Ford!'

They burst full-tilt through the hedge to the track and headed uphill, scattering dusty sparrows and sunning doves. Shafting barley was on their right, the tangled growth of the woodside – fading nettles, snaking brambles – on the left, as they flew abreast. Seeds of dock, crisp, brick-coloured, peppered them. The weasels rocketed on. Side by side they drove, pebbles spinning, droplets splashing from puddles as they hammered down.

Kine thought of Gru's spouse, the only brown mink he knew, the loathsome Liverskin. A half-grown rabbit fled their path; a jay scolded in the covert. Above a jungle of flowering thistle, Kine saw the barn and, sheering off through dog-daisies, the two weasels shot the hayfield gate like red arrows in low trajectory. A cattle-trough loomed, fell behind, its valve hissing, leaky as always.

A brown mink! If not Liverskin, another monster. Any mink, thought Kine, would do him – any evil brute.

Swaths of hay stretched ahead. The sun blazed. A band of gold indicated the gorse hedge, a bold line beyond the field, the sight of it urging the weasels to greater speed. Ford, marginally the less nimble, dropped a length behind Kine. Hay steamed. Somewhere a tractor growled and pigeons, rising from mown grass, watched the runners pass below before sinking back. Then, with brisk finality, Kine was plunging to the ditch where water tumbled from a land-drain, Ford after him.

A weasel climbed from the chasm and shook his head. He shook it frantically, as if an insect had stung him, and when the shaking stopped the wound was evident, a gaping tear from eye to ear, oyster-raw where bone appeared. The creature kept shaking, trying to slough the pain. 'In the water,' he muttered. 'There's no life in him.'

'Where?' Kine said.

'Beneath the drain.' He turned back and the others followed to the frothy sump. A limp shape wallowed there, lifelessly twisting in the effluent. Kine saw it was a dead weasel. The heat was fierce. A fly buzzed round the head of the wounded animal. 'He got a neck-hold,' he reported, 'but the monster took him under. We did our best. When the brute was in water we stood no chance. It wasn't even a big mink – three-quarters grown – but it made mice of us.'

'Got away?' Ford said miserably.

'Couldn't stop it, not in water.'

'No.' Kine fought his disappointment, stepping back from the drowned body. Linnets were chattering as if nothing had happened. 'You tried,' he told the injured weasel. 'You made a brave attempt.'

Ford shrugged wearily. Kine, catching his eye, said, 'We'll take more losses, I fear, before . . .' He paused. His faith in success deserted him. '. . . before it's over,' he concluded. He left it that way, gaze fixed on the mink-infested waterways. Could a band of weasels, he wondered, really save the valley? Could anything? Was vengeance at the price of self-destruction anything more than weasel madness, a foolish curse? Kia and the kittens were irretrievable. Perhaps the rook had the answer – migrate and start again.

'We'll beat them, Kine, as you vanquished the rat. We'll fight beside you and Ford until we've done for them.' The wounded weasel stroked his eye, rubbing blood away. Flicking his head, he snarled defiantly. 'Next time I'll have one of the brutes. I'll leave my mark on it.'

'Right,' Kine said, 'we'll teach them!' He felt his eyes smart with shame and looked back to where the wood stood tall in the sun, full-canopied; the wood Kia loved, where the tiny female kitten had played with her. He had betrayed them. For a minute he had wavered. He despised himself.

The drowned weasel began to drift away from them. Kine took one more look then turned and moved off with Ford. The heat was intense. Skeins of cirro-cumulus streaked an otherwise cloudless sky. In a good season Kia could have graced the land with four broods, each five weeks in gestation, Kine thought bitterly. A weasel summer – it could have been a sweet summer. It was a brutal reflection, self-torturing.

Ford said darkly, 'First chance bungled.'

'They gave their best.'

'And it got away. Bog-weasels would have stopped it. We should have bog-weasels posted on every ditch.'

Kine let that pass. There was no gain in squabbling, and Ford could have laboured a sharper point. Had Kia gone back to the bog, as Ford had hoped, she might be alive now, even flourishing. The idea nagged him, and Kine, struggling to banish it, asked, 'How far?' and when the other looked blank, 'It got away. We haven't asked ourselves how far it would have gone.'

Ford stopped. 'You're right,' he said.

Kine said, 'Maybe to the marsh, but not inevitably. It might be resting a short distance down the ditch. On the bank, perhaps. It had the best of the affray, so why should it run far?'

'You're right,' Ford repeated, brightening. 'What are we waiting for?'

'It's worth a look.'

The sun blazed on the gorse but did not penetrate it. Dark with fox alleys and twisted stems, the heart of the hedge was a hidden world. In tangled privacy, the pheasant froze unblinking on her nest there. The squatting partridge was invisible. Rabbits hid in black hollows, betrayed only by the round dry pellets they left like gunshot in scraped earth. Rabbits and hares redevoured their droppings after feeding, so each meal of herbage went through them twice. The final crotiles had little substance left in them. Kine sniffed forward. Stepping lightly on the ledge of the shaded ditch, the weasels followed the flow which murmured downhill.

The marsh was hazy below and frogs sang woefully. On the edge of the hayfield, ants were scavenging; they manned an ancient molehill, streaming out from it. They reminded Kine of Kia's corpse, and Ford's voice, through the nightmare, almost startled him. 'That's the scent,' Ford exclaimed. 'Fresh. We're on to him!'

'Softly, Ford . . .'

Kine began to urge caution but Ford was gone, already ahead, bounding recklessly. Cursing, Kine followed. Keeping low, he watched the bog-weasel bounce through streaming sun, bristling, blundering. Ridged hay broke the view, every swath a potential ambush, but Ford was hell-bent. At last, panting, he halted and Kine caught up with him. The ground shelved downwards to their front. Unimpeded, their vision extended to where the brown mink sat.

It had hauled itself from the chasm and was several yards from the gorse and into the meadow. Kine stared fixedly. His belly had contracted and his skin prickled. This brute might have been among those who killed Kia. It had certainly killed the weasel in the ditch, and seemed less than ruffled by the experience. Lean and muscular, it sat drying in the sun, streaks of black in the jacket and flaunting tail. There might be larger mink, thought Kine, but it was bigger than any rat he had seen, and dwarfed a weasel. And it stank – it stank of its kind, and of the Moon Pond massacre.

Ford said, 'He won't escape this time. He's ours, Kine.'

'We'll have to flank him, cut his line to the ditch.'

'Never mind all that. Let's get into him.' Ford charged on again.

Kine dived for the gorge and the deep ravine. Ford was mad. It was vital to attack from the water flank, divide the monster from its element. Plunging to the rill, he left the bog-weasel batting on open ground. On either side of Kine the banks were vertical, land-drains disgorging muddy cataracts. Dark shapes wallowed there. Something swirled towards him and he drew back. It was the drowned weasel. A stone delayed its macabre passage, and Kine, slithering and splashing, dashed ahead of it. Springing back to the brink, he surveyed the field.

Ford galloped with a heart Kine admired despite its foolishness. The charge was ludicrously long and conspicuous. It seemed interminable. Almost at once the mink was up on its haunches, watching scornfully. Lip curling, it met the smaller beast with a stunning swipe and, as Ford was bowled backwards, Kine saw only disdain on the monster's face. Diving back to the ditch, the shrewder of the weasels pursued his course.

He was searching the bank now with urgent darts of his sharp head, nosing anxiously. Above the shadowy corridor, oblivious of violence, linnets chattered. He heard the rap of a woodpecker. Water tumbled. It filled a dark frothing sump, and beside it in the wall of the ditch was what Kine sought, a small landslide worn smooth by the feet of thirsty creatures, an inviting ramp. It had invited the brown mink; the brute's spoor was warm on it.

War-chant throbbing, Kine leaped to the field athwart the mink's path. It was well judged, for the monster was barely a skip away, Ford molesting still with stubborn pluck. As Kine appeared, it raked the bog-weasel casually with razor claws, then turned chillingly. Kine thought of Kia. She had faced the chiselled heads of its monstrous kind. He danced savagely, so close he could see blebs of moisture on the mink's nose. 'Watch your throat, mink! You must pass me to the water – watch your brown throat!'

Steam swirled, and through the vapour the mink's teeth were pointed ice. Kine heard them snap as he swayed and saw Ford reeling wildly, a battered wreck. 'Revenge, Kine!' The croak was demented. 'Revenge or death!' He bored in and Kine watched as, almost lazily, the mink turned, smashed down the weasel and poised with gaping jaws. Kine lunged. Striking coarse oily fur, he closed his own teeth.

Now battle was joined, he felt curiously fatalistic, as if the outcome were already judged in some vault of the heavens unknown to him. He felt his destiny hinged to the mean brown monster whose flesh he mouthed. He had found a shoulder, barely penetrating the thick coat, but the mink reared and, as Ford limped clear, Kine released his hold and dodged the brute's wrath. The sun was dazzling. He pranced awkwardly. Grassy stubble, standing high against the weasels, foiled their finer steps. Like snakes they froze, then moved suddenly, hissing, chivvying the powerful foe.

'Next time,' Kine chanted grimly, 'I'll take a neck-hold. Show your neck, worm of Gru. Pay your debt to me.'

'Your debt to Kia,' hurled Ford. 'Die for Kia's brood!' He sallied and, as the mink swung to fend him, Kine went in again.

He missed the neck, striking hard unyielding ribs beneath stifling hair, then was under the giant as it rolled on him. Its weight emptied his lungs. He could not breath. He was smothered by the monster, lost in darkness, gagged by foul-tasting fur which filled mouth and throat. Dazed, he rolled free while Ford drew off the mink's threshing claws with a reckless cast.

The field was spinning. Something swung like a flail and Kine was down again. He rose groggily, avoiding the monster's tail as it lashed back across the stubble, large as Kine himself. Seeping mist filled his mind, the sun hammered. Through clouded eyes he saw Ford on the ground, the mink rampant, and knew the struggle was at crisis point. Ford was weakening, his defence was feeble – and, for a paralyzing moment, Kine's own sinews were flaccid when he strove to help. The long back of the monster flexed as the blow was aimed. Galvanized, Kine hurled himself at it. He shouted, 'Move, Ford!'

There was, for a fraction of a second, a break of action. Then the mink bucked, jerking and twisting to throw the weasel straddling it. Kine's teeth sought the spine and his claws gripped. He hung on, but the neck was like timber, brown-matted and powerful. It seemed impervious and he read the brute's mind. It was heading for water. It had drowned one weasel. Either Kine could dismount or ride to suicide.

Clawing fur, he tore with his jaws as the giant ran. It went in scuffling bounds, accelerating, bulldozing hay swaths so that soggy grass enwrapped the weasel, almost toppling him. Askance, he saw Ford find his feet,

144

shake an agonized head and stagger after them. Incredibly, the bog-weasel was charging, once more bellowing. 'Hold him back from the water! We'll have him yet, Kine!'

'Take the throat, Ford!'

They were flank to flank, Ford straining tiredly to pace the monster, Kine grimly attached to the plunging back. He saw the flat head stab sideways, frothing jaws seeking Ford – saw Ford stumble, run out and veer back again. It was an extraordinary stampede of snapping predators, the mink increasingly crazed as Kine's teeth pierced, Ford doggedly straining for the brute's throat. They passed from sun to shadow. The gorse was close. Again Ford pounded in; again the mink stabbed. Flecks of brown fur were scudding as Kine toiled. The monster shuddered. The bog-weasel had taken hold. In union the three shot beneath the gorse to the chasm's edge. Like leeches the weasels cleaved, then were tumbling, hurtling to the black sump.

Kine came up blowing water, swearing bitterly. He had meant at all costs to maintain his grip. Submersion had thwarted him, and only Ford's reappearance, soaked but living, was consolation. 'Are you all right, Ford?'

'I had the devil.'

'We couldn't hold him.'

'I had the throat, Kine.'

There was a stir, a muddy movement in the water, and bubbles rose. Slowly the brown mink surfaced, belly uppermost, blood diffusing from its torn neck. Ford beamed suddenly. His punished head was grotesque, but he was jubilant.

CHAPTER THIRTEEN

THE kestrel hovered above the slope, almost motionless. It was the best part of two hundred feet up, from which height its eye held some small and unsuspecting creature perhaps a couple of inches long in the field below. Tipping air from a wing, the hawk slipped smoothly to one side as its quarry moved, passing behind a tree, so Poacher no longer saw it through the window in the cottage eaves. Watching made his head swim and he lay back beneath the low-pitched timbers of the old roof.

Beside the rude metal bed the black-eyed dog scratched. Poacher felt for the liquor bottle and drank from it. It burned but strengthened, enabling the man to reach the gun he kept near him and cradle it. Alert, the terrier viewed the weapon hopefully. The man coughed. 'Them days are gone,' he advised. 'It's truce to rabbits. Just insurance.' He tapped the gunstock. 'Against them who know best, in case they come for us.'

With an effort he focused on the wood outside, where the willow stood. His people had been born here; he had been delivered here where he lay of a mother who had died beneath the same roof – who had named his Life Tree, treated his youthful ailments with herbs and berry cures. He put the gun aside. He intended to die in the valley among the same woods.

The dog turned his attention to a foreign sound. It came from the garden, a plaintive mewling which sent the terrier bounding downstairs to the door, where he sniffed and scraped. Poacher drowsed, ignoring the commotion until the dog began to whimper, then he sat up shakily. Listening, he heard again the feeble mewling, the dog's quickening response as the bed moved. The man wheezed his displeasure. But he was curious and, slipping into shoes, advanced unsteadily.

Standing increased his dizziness. Drab walls seemed to sway as he leaned on them. Reaching the stairs in the corner of the attic, he paused. Once, a ladder had joined the floors; now the narrow steps were steep and hazardous. Halfway down he sat and rested while his head swam. When it had cleared he continued, mumbling fretfully.

There was a strange neatness about the parlour, as if already it had a new occupant. The smell was summery, of wax polish, cut roses, wood-tar from a chimney unused since winter's end. It was like returning to an old haunt possessed by spirits of another world. The dog jerked his stump, whining eagerly. 'Get back,' Poacher muttered, 'you're going nowhere. I'll take a look myself.'

The room was shadowy. Beyond the windows, untended growth blocked out daylight. Dusty shrubs tapped on panes when the breeze rose. Poacher gritted his teeth with effort, lurched to the table, and spread his palms on it. Bent across his arms, he eyed the scene through the casement and screening leaves. He had never been a gardener, but the chaos offended even his own standards and he pined for the strength to swing a levelling blade. The thin call came again. Now the dog yapped.

'Gi' me time, you patch-eyed beggar. I'll take a stick to it.' Poacher braced himself. The door seemed far off, as did the briar stick. Hobbling, he reached the stick and, leaning heavily, slipped the latch.

The brightness surprised him. Sunshine, striking through the surrounding trees, flicked and dazzled as the leaves moved. He had to fight a resurgence of giddiness. It passed and, with hooded eyes, he took a couple of short steps. It was quiet outside. Flies thronged aimlessly. In the glare he heard only insects and a distant aeroplane. Then the cry – not quite the cry of a fledgling – but hungry, desolate.

Turning, he quizzed the thicket of broom beside the door, and, where the wall behind it met parched earth, the tiny starved creature huddled there. Poacher had

147

seen young weasels with their parents on hunting trips. Once, by the barn, he had heard chattering and watched a she-weasel leave the woodpile followed by four young in single file. A moment later, returning to the pile, the scolding adult had reappeared with a fifth kitten to join the others.

But never had the man seen so slight a kitten on its own. It was a pitiable miniature in a white bib. Across the neck an ugly gash spoke of escape from violence, though not from danger, for, too young to fend properly, Kia's smallest daughter lay exhausted and mewled for food. Poacher raised his stick. His vision blurred. He put the stick to the ground, resting on it. Then, sight sharpening, found the kitten glaring up at him. They were, he thought, two of a kind, both in dire straits.

Tentatively he pushed the stick towards the weasel and watched her teeth flash. Barely strong enough to move, she was not giving in while there was breath in her. That was dandy hounds for you, he told himself. 'Damned vermin,' he muttered. Then, almost tenderly, 'Never known a weasel forsake her young. Let's have a look at you. What you need is a meal. You stay there a while.'

It was ten minutes later when the girl arrived. She found him, pale and exhausted, in the parlour chair. He should not have been up. His appearance shocked her and she went for him. 'My God, what have you been doing? What a state you're in!'

'None of your business.'

'That it is. Doctor's orders, you stay abed.'

'Last orders I took were in the war, girl. Be damned to orders in my dying hours.'

'Poppycock!' The girl tapped an impatient foot and spat the word, cursing her concern for the wretched man. He was impossible. Twice a day she had been in to cook and care for him, take the dog out, and this was how he repaid her. 'Dying!' she snarled. 'Being a nuisance is more the size of it.'

'I've seen the tree, girl.'

'Pagan idiot!'

'That I'm not,' Poacher rasped.

'Seen the *tree*!'

'For no pagan saw God,' the man protested, 'and I've seen Him, many times.' He licked his lips. 'Aye, many times, girl. In the eyes of a pheasant, in the shimmer of a fish, in a bobbing scut. I'll die with that much.'

'You poached His rabbits!'

'Enough for the pot and a bob or two.'

'And blasphemed Him,' she sighed with compassion. 'That's the sum of it.'

'The poaching's done. The woods are done with me.'

'You're softening, Poacher.' The girl went to the kitchen and ran the tap. 'Best pull your socks up, for mink are murdering. They got into Mullen's fowls; killed thirty of them. Just left them lying there. I'm making some tea, then it's bed for you.'

She came with mugs and cake, saying, 'If you went into hospital they'd get you fit.'

'You're scheming with them.'

'Nobody's scheming,' she snorted, 'I'm telling you. You should be in hospital, that's the place for you.'

'Let them come,' Poacher told her, 'I've got the gun.'

'What a fool you are!'

His eyes narrowed. 'You don't really think that. We've had some good times. Remember, I took you fishing and berrying, catching elvers on the marsh when you were so high. Showed you the fisher bird, filled you with wild pears. That old plank broke, remember, down Long dyke. I hooked you out of it. Damned if your mam didn't fry me. Remember them times?'

'I remember.' She watched suspiciously. 'Why d'you think I'm here now, taking care of you?'

'Your mam trained you right,' Poacher wheezed. 'You've not grown up bad.'

'Oh, haven't I?'

'Not as handsome as your mother, but a good girl. Can

bake a reasonable cake. We had some good times.' He paused cannily. 'Reckon you'd warn me,' he wheedled, 'if they were scheming . . .'

'That's it, Poacher, bed!' She was on her feet. 'Upstairs, I've had enough of you!' When she had helped him, she went back to the kitchen to put his supper on. He lay, sapped by his effort, listening carefully. The kestrel had gone and it was quiet outside. For several minutes he heard the girl shifting about before she called to him, 'You've had a leg off that rabbit, you rotten beggar, and I was cooking it!'

'Dog was hungry,' he lied.

'I fed the blamed dog.'

He heard her cussing and grinned, despite the pain he felt. Clumsily he eased towards the window and looked down from it. The little weasel had not moved. She was still tucked by the wall, behind the shrub. But there was life in her. She was tackling the leg of rabbit like a trencherman.

Where barley ripened, the weasels danced. Another mink had been killed and they stomped with gusto. It was a red-eyed mink, one of the dun-coloured sons of Gru. As they danced they sang of victory and extolled themselves: 'Hear the song of the tribe, daughter of darkness. We shall visit you.'

The sandy sons of the she-mink had been ambushed at the wood's fringe. Suddenly, weasels had been everywhere. They had burst from rabbit tunnels and hollow stumps, leaped from low branches, swept from tangled groves. Hate had hurled them at the monsters, and tribal vengefulness. A heath-weasel had sprung from a trench beneath the enemy. A bog-weasel had charged from a brake of thorn. Startled, the invaders had retreated, but one had died.

'To the bunker!' sang the weasels. 'Enough of waiting. Ask the red-eyed corpse – we are formidable!'

'It's true,' Ford told Kine, 'the time has come to attack, to strike at Gru herself.'

'I have a strategy.'

'To take the stronghold?'

'Yes,' barked Kine as they danced, 'but not as Gru would expect: not by frontal assault, to be mauled by her guards. I've another plan.'

'Tell me.' Ford halted expectantly. 'What way is there?'

Kine drew him aside. 'Think like the enemy. If you were Gru, where would you least expect trouble? From the river, am I right? From across the water, the mink's element. From your land, Ford – cross the stream to their rear. A surprise raid.'

'By the back way!'

'From Castle Mound, on the far bank. Can you take us there?'

Ford's eyes shone. 'Can I take you? It's a brilliant ruse, Kine! I can take you there.'

'Good. Listen. We leave One-Eye and the young heath-weasel to guard the wood. The rest of us cross below the reach to the scrub at the bogside. That's your domain.'

'I was born there. Depend on me.' Ford projected his gaze to the riverbank. 'The frontier's rough,' he declared with sombre relish, 'but we'll cope with it. Between the scrub and Castle Mound lies the great swamp. We must travel by sheep trails. The cover is sparse and there'll be harriers, other dangers. But we'll handle them. Once we reach Castle Mound, only the river lies between Gru and us.'

Kine nodded. 'Surprise is vital,' he said. 'They won't be watching the rear. We swim the river again, get into the bunker by a back way.'

'To the labyrinth.' Ford showed his teeth. 'Then for Gru! We'll take her, take the lot of them! They'll be cold as the twin when we've done with them!'

Kine was serious. 'It's not infallible; no plan's infallible. But with courage and luck . . .'

'It's a masterplan.'

'One-Eye approves. I've consulted the veteran. But

the swamp will be risky. It's up to you in the other land.'

'I know every trail. I know where to feed and where to rest. Leave the bog to me, Kine, there's no better guide.'

'Then tell the rest of them, Ford. I've got to slip off; there's a last job.' He looked back as he left and they were jubilant. It was a small pack, for some had departed, but the best remained eager, perhaps a score of fighting weasels, and the dance whirled. It was a war dance. They bounded and churred, revolving round Ford like a spinning firework, elated by the news he brought. Their chant followed Kine on the warm air. 'Hear the song of the tribe, Gru. We shall be calling! Sleep uneasily!'

'Listen hard in the night, for our steps are delicate!'

'We shall come like the breeze, like the soundless snake!'

'And the kiss of the weasel is oblivion!'

Kine heard the voice of the stripling and felt sad for him. 'We'll be heroes; we'll feast on glory, awe and reverence!' The heath-weasel had yet to learn Kine was not taking him. The raid was for neither the callow nor the long-in-tooth. It was a gamble. There were perils in plenty, but it had to succeed. Weasels were neglecting their own lands, their patience fraying. It had to be done before the pack dispersed.

He went down beside the corn, excitement and misgiving in each step he took. Frogs were croaking, rooks chattering. A mink had been killed; the news was passing. Kine stepped briskly. They would have something to clack about soon, he thought.

Scrat was early at the marsh gate, waiting anxiously. 'You've stirred it up, Kine. One mink killed and one bloodied – the devil's sons. You've got them gossiping!'

'So I hear.' Kine listened for a moment. 'What does Bunda think?'

'Bunda sings of Gru's rage. But Bunda chuckles again. The marsh frog laughs again. Hearts are lighter on the marsh. Of course, there'll be retribution, but a mink is dead. That's good news here.'

'There'll be more very shortly; news to celebrate.'

Scrat eyed him hopefully, sick of his task on the hostile and stiff-grassed flats. Slopes of yellowing grain brought wistful yearning. Perhaps corn fields had once been more beautiful – in the days of poppies, corn charlock and marigolds – but the ripening ridge, with its hedges and woodsides, looked good to Scrat. Bells of foxglove still nodded on stems whose lower blossoms had seen haytime; spiring loosestrife was flowering, and lilac water-mint. It was, in the days after Lammas, a purple period. Heather burst, echoed by thyme and banks of massed thistles with purple coronets.

'I've done my best, Kine.'

'Your mission won't be forgotten. It means a lot to us.'

'A bit of danger,' Scrat said, flattered, 'that's a spy's job.'

He stuck his tail up and strutted, but his gaze held the slopes where succulent insects abounded in flocks which made him drool: crane-flies struggling in tasty thousands from pupa-cases, caterpillars on willow-herb. His belly rumbled. 'Don't suppose there's much more *I* can do,' the dwarf said hopefully.

'Not much,' Kine responded. 'Just one more task, Scrat. In strictest secrecy, we're launching an assault on the enemy stronghold from over the river, through the other land. Cross downstream, pass deep behind the frontier, re-cross from Castle Mound. Failing disaster, we'll astonish them. We've a job for you.' He described the role without fuss, making little of the hazards. 'That's all there is to it,' he drawled matter-of-factly. 'We'll do the rest.'

'*All!*' Scrat shrieked. He was quivering.

'It's not a lot, Scrat.'

The midget gawped. 'Just wait on Gru's doorstep . . .'

'At night, by the river. It'll be dark.'

'Show the way?'

'Up the bank,' Kine agreed.

'The mink bank!'

'No one will see you.'

'To the labyrinth?'

'You know the holes. We need an entrance at the rear, Scrat.'

'The devil's bunker!' Scrat was wailing. 'You've lost your senses again, Kine. You're mad . . . mad . . .'

Kine scuffed impatiently. Dark crescents of swifts streamed above them, hawking crane-flies, grey-bodied daddy-long-legs which flew clumsily. The swifts skimmed the weasel, swooping with characteristic delight past the land-bound, so that the buzz of their wings was like the hum of bullets. Kine said, curling his lip, 'Yes, I'm mad, Scrat, mad and dangerous. I've sworn revenge . . .'

Soon the swifts would depart. How quickly, he thought, the corn had ripened; it seemed only yesterday grass swayed in hayfields, and Kia was dancing in the soft and seeding waves. How soon the opal of June became Lammas gold. 'Don't provoke me. If you'd lost what I lost, Scrat, you'd understand. I ask this now of you . . .'

'I understand.' The dwarf was trembling, but his voice held. He shook his snout. Kine thought he would weep. Instead, the velvet mite gulped. 'She was good to me,' he said almost with firmness. 'She was good to me.'

'A bit of danger,' Kine prompted.

'That's a s-spy's job.'

'We depend on you.'

'I don't envy you your march, Kine, through the great swamp. How will I know when you're ready at Castle Mound?'

'I'll send the rook, Scrat.'

'Take a tip, Kine. I'm not valiant like a weasel but I know the marsh. Make for the reeds as you swim, by the outlet valve, then at least you'll be hidden while you regroup. It's open from there to the bunker – you'll have to sprint for it. I'll show you how to get in. The pump-house skirting has crumbled, and you can reach the foundations. Not me, mind. I'll be staying outside. Mayhem's a weasel trade.'

'Leave it to us.'

'That I shall.'

'And Scrat . . .' Kine broke off, saying quietly at last, 'Never mind, Scrat. You understand. They didn't spare a single kitten; not a single one . . .'

Part Three

THE DANDY HOUNDS

CHAPTER FOURTEEN

KINE led the raiders briskly from the wood, made sou'east to the farthest point of the territory and halted them. Scouting forward, he watched the flow of the river from the home shore. It moved smoothly, flat and glassy in the light of early morning, black beneath still banks. Across the stream lay the otter's holt.

A distant relation to Kine, of ancient lineage, the otter was seldom home. He used his shelter on this reach only sparingly, an effacing, solitary creature flitting by night between lodgings several miles apart. His kind moved restlessly. Now he paused in the vale, now passed to the sea, haunting cliff-caves; now, by estuary and channel, returned again.

Weasels since the Ice Age had shared the vale with the big waterman. Kine knew his habits. And knew then, by spraints and marks, he was in residence, at watch in his muddy holt. Suddenly, the broad face appeared, eyes like lamps, and with a flip of rudder the otter vanished to guddle for trout on some other reach.

Kine called the tribe. As one by one they breasted water, he looked back at the wooded ridge. On the eve of departure he had gone to the Moon Pond and stood alone there. It had been a last vigil before the raid, a brooding pilgrimage. The place had a lonely, neglected air. Duckweed, fading as if bleached, cloaked the pool, while brambles infested its crinkled edge. In the Life Tree the hollow gaped. It was ill-starred. Only insects frequented the morbid opening.

Kine had shuddered. Going slowly to the bluff, he had peered over it. Stagnant weed had met his gaze, and thin yellowish scum. Then, with sad memory, he had seen the lilies – wild white water-lilies with crimson hearts. An uncanny sense of presence had come over him. 'Kine,' a voice had stirred the silence, 'Can I talk to you?' Its owner had moved forward. 'You must hear me,' said the youthful heath-weasel. 'I've got to come on the raid. I must come with you.'

Kine had watched the lilies.

'Please, Kine. It's a chance that won't come again. Let me march with you. This will be a great campaign, weasel history. Let me be there – be able, if I survive, to spread word of it. I don't mind danger. I don't think I mind death if it comes to that.'

He had looked terribly young, a stripling, his coat yellow-brown, the unlined face fresh – little older than Kia's kittens, had they lived. The thought had irked Kine. 'I can fight; I'll carry my weight. I'm eager for the fray, Kine. We live in stirring times. Historic times.'

'Do we?'

'I mean, they'll look back on our fight, on our stand for the vale against the aliens. You're leading a crusade, Kine, a mission. If I missed being with you I'd die of shame. It's all I think about, the raid. Let me go with you.'

Kine had pondered the lilies, lost in memory. How long he had stood on the bluff he could not tell, but when he had turned to leave, the youngster had still been there. It might have been his own son. And if it *had* been? How then would he have answered? He had stomped away in fractious temper, pausing fleetingly. 'We leave early,' he had growled. 'Be there punctually.'

Now the river was before him, the V-shaped wakes in straggling convoy making for the other bank. From above, where the Watchman circled, it was as if a rippling ribbon were very slowly being threaded on the tide, and the rook flipped in salute, despite himself, to the surging animals. They would come to no good, in the bird's opinion, but courage was courage. Swooping low across the weasel flotilla, he lumbered up on fingered black wings and flipped a second time.

Kine waited. One weasel was still on land. It was the

juvenile. 'There's no water on the heath, Kine, I can't swim. I never learned.'

Red heads were bobbing in the flood. Some were nearing the distant shore. Kine was praying the stretch would be free of mink. He said with menace, 'Can't swim? You begged to come on this mission and you can't swim?'

'I'd never been to a river.' The youngster's eyes were bulging. 'I didn't realize.'

Kine snarled. 'Realize? What? That water would be wet, like your ears? That it's broad and deep; that death lurks in its coils? You didn't realize?' Kine regarded him grimly. 'Well, hear me, weasel, and listen carefully. We can *all* swim. We just walk into the stream and we keep on walking. That's not difficult. Walk in. Keep on walking. Understand? Have you got it? Then, by the god of thunder, get on with it!'

As the other obeyed, Kine snapped his teeth at him. 'Walk, by thunder! Kick into the current.' The tone relented a fraction. 'You're swimming now.'

They went side by side, the stripling gulping and blowing anxiously. The haul was slow. Their destination, low and green, seemed far ahead and Kine, recalling his last venture in the river, urged greater speed. He had escaped the flashing topedoes by the breadth of a hair, and plumbed the drowning depths. 'Faster!' he called, 'Put your back in the effort. Mind that weed. Watch the eddy by those boulders. Breathe steadily.' Lines of sedges were looming. Shadow beckoned, swamping dog-day brilliance with heavy gloom. 'Keep it up.' Cool leaves towered. His claws raked into silt and in a moment he was growling, 'You made it – not so bad for a weasel who can't swim.'

Damply, they scrambled the incline through the river growth. Great banners of water-dock unfurled there, almost tropically rank, and roots of bushes were naked where wavelets lapped. It was a place of dark shafting blades and funereal tassels on bare masts. It had a sombreness unbroken by the lighter plumes

161

of the shore they had left behind. Here was neither valerian nor meadowsweet. Little blossomed. Stalwart rue cheered with its yellow petals, but was sparse. So was the hemp agrimony near the otter's holt. Miry hollows spawned mean whippy scrub beyond which, it seemed to Kine, lay an endless level of grassy tufts whose nature betrayed an oozy, forbidding base.

Mist still hung there. It was not often the great swamp was free of mist.

It dipped and drifted across the trail from the flanking mire in white skeins so dense in parts that Ford seemed insubstantial, a weasel wraith. Here and there, where the mist was thinner, could be seen the distant scarp of the hinterland and, far west – depressingly distant, Kine considered – the hump of Castle Mound. The weasel column stretched behind them. Its rear members were invisible, and Kine complained of the vapour for the umpteenth time.

Ford said, 'There's nothing wrong with mist. It conceals us. As long as we stick to the sheep trail . . .' On either side of it lay the grey-shrouded alternative: a squelching morass which periodically opened beside them in yawning pools of liquid, black as Gru herself. Tufts of grass made spiky islets. 'What we *don't* want is rain. Much rain and these paths very soon flood.'

Kine could imagine it. The route was primitive: a causeway through interminable slough, thrusting deeper and deeper in swirling murk. Wolves had trod there. Sheep had left their white bones in the black bog. All it needed was rain to ruin everything. He said, 'We'll have to eat soon. We can't afford to lose strength; there's a long way to go. The real test doesn't start until the assault.'

Ford agreed. 'There's a mole cantonment ahead. We'll refresh ourselves.'

'Hold on.' Kine had stopped. 'Someone's calling down the line,' he said, straining his hearing. 'Hold on, Ford.'

The call was taken up nearer. It came plainly and

Kine repeated it. 'Harriers!' He looked back through the vapour. 'Cover! Take cover where you can. Don't move, anyone.'

He saw the dim shapes of weasels merge with tufty bog growth, but, lifting his sight, he was prevented by mist from seeing more, or spotting the danger. He swore an oath. Then, scrambling from tuft to tuft, he reached the weasel who had raised the cry. It was the animal scarred in the first fight with the brown mink. 'How many?' Kine asked.

'A pair, making ground in this direction; but the murk closed and I lost sight of them. They were keen, though, quartering low, unhurriedly. Watch your back, for they know their job. They're old hands, Kine.'

'Curse this bog mist.' Kine squinted uselessly into the rolling cloud. It was fickle, too restive to be dependable. Any moment it could vanish, exposing them. He watched it wafting and writhing where bog grass shafted, a pale ghost thickening and diluting unpredictably. Dense as cream, it would diffuse suddenly until the sun's rays all but cleared it, then condense again. 'There!' breathed the other weasel. A chink of blue had torn open the gloom to frame the two birds.

They were turning slowly above the trail, great brown-flecked hunters on broad wings which canted upwards as they glided from the vapour. They were owl-like predators. They had the same lazy move-ments, the same thickly ruffed necks as the barn-dweller. They were just as dangerous, and the weasel tribe froze as they slid overhead.

Kine watched the female, slightly larger than her mate, swoop low across the path, alert for movement. He saw the bright acerbic eye and thought she must have glimpsed them; but she climbed away, the male following. They circled clumsily then, veering from the sheep trail, and abruptly disappeared. Kine churred his relief. on his haunches he said, 'Right, let's move. Let's get on again.'

Through clearer breezes they advanced apprehensively. The mire stirred as it warmed, emitting surging rumbles and stagnant fumes. Bog-snakes slithered and frogs submerged. Kine's skin tingled. He felt uneasy, and when the path began to tremble he stopped a second time. The sun was hazy. It greased the swamp with the cheerless gleam of a raven's wing. 'Feel that?' he asked Ford. 'Vibrations. The earth's shuddering.'

'You know what that is . . .'

'You're the guide.' Kine's coat was bristling.

Ford glared to their front. 'The mob,' he growled. 'The benighted mob.'

'Getting nearer.'

'Coming fast. A plague on our luck – the whole mob.' It was visible. At first it looked like a mist rolling back down the causeway, a massive worm growing moment by moment until the ground quaked. Then the leading components were conspicuous: marsh sheep. It was a ewe mob. Kine could see their fat, close-sheared bellies and thrusting necks. Their hooves were pounding. They filled the trail. They packed the path in a stampeding column a hundred strong. There was no evading them save in the swamp on either side.

'We can't outrun them,' Kine bawled.

'Run?' Ford roared above the thunder. 'Run from fool sheep!' He squared his shoulders.

Kine's gaze was riveted. The leading ewes, tough bog veterans huge compared to the weasels, were looming fearsomely, a wall of sinew on limbs shod with punishment. Kine had walked with indifference by grazing sheep, placid creatures. But he knew the stamping challenge of a roused ewe – and that a mob at speed was a charge of cloven hammers that could smash a dog. Old trail-marks witnessed the weight behind those hooves. Yet Ford faced them like a buffer, braced and swearing; and Kine, drawing back, wailed, 'Jump, Ford! Jump, you idiot!'

Then Ford was under the leaders, his form dwarfed. Kine saw him spin in the dust of the mob like a dead leaf, before his own senses reeled and he was on his back amid a forest of threshing legs. Stunned, he watched soil-clogged hooves crash around him, and tried to move. It was a lottery, pure chance delaying the lethal stroke. Half-rising, he was hit again, bowled nearer the bog. Again he floundered as hooves skimmed him.

Now he rolled in a ball like a hedgehog, inhaled dust then jerked suddenly sideways to the path's edge. A horny hammer scorched his flesh; he scarcely noticed the pain. The mire was inches away. A final twist and he was looping, somersaulting from the scrum to flop breathless from the causeway into black yielding sludge, out of the mob's path. For a moment the oily liquid supported him.

Ford had gone. Kine searched the tumult of streaming legs without a glimpse of him. Ewes were bucking and kicking as they galloped nose to tail along the narrow track. There was no break in their onrush, just the din of thudding hooves and the glare of obsessive eyes. Already the leaders were out of sight, and Kine could see no end to the pounding tide. Lean tough-knuckled limbs toiled with piston force. No life could survive beneath those massed hooves.

A sense of sinking returned him to his own plight. Insidiously, the bog was embracing him. The goo was treacherous. Too thick to swim in, it was sufficiently fluid to suck him into it. It sapped the energy. It seemed to treble his weight, make stone of legs which, once embroiled, resisted the urge to fight for him. Nearby, a tufty islet of grass promised sanctuary but, striking for it, he doubted his power to cross even that short gulf. The more he struggled the more he sank. The hooves, he thought, would have brought a quicker and cleaner end.

Chest and abdomen engulfed, Kine fought to keep his neck free. The racing sheep were oblivious of him, mindless of the speck of desperately striving fur. He was getting no nearer the clump. His neck weakened.

The mire crept higher. Lunging, he strained to grasp the tuft, but was short, and his mouth filled with sludge. His jaws gaped wretchedly. Forced to rest, he felt the bog reaching up for its final grip.

This time despair and weasel obduracy joined strength. He spurred himself. 'Kia fought to the end. Gru shall not escape me this easily.' The heave he gave wrenched every nodule in his spine. He felt his neck crack. But his teeth closed on swamp grass, and he clung to it. He did not move. With a life-saving hold he could afford to pause, and recover energy. Then, very slowly, he heaved his mud-covered body to the grassy island.

The big beasts of the mob were still passing. He cranked his vision round to the soggy margin of the trail they hammered. The mire glistened. At intervals beside the track the black morass was dotted with clumps of growth such as the one he had reached, and atop them, like frogs on so many lily-pads, he perceived the scattered tribe. He gave a grim smile. Raising his head, he sang harshly, 'We're coming, Gru. You can't escape the Blood Fury! Mire and mob – a thousand obstacles – cannot stop us. The tribe's still travelling!'

In ones and twos, as the mob drew away, they regained the path. Kine joined the tribe with a single leap. He found it gathered where a trampled form lay lifeless on the trail, and his voice shook. 'He wouldn't budge. He faced them all. Ford was that kind of chump. He had no fear in him.'

One of the weasels turned. 'It's not Ford, Kine.'

'Who? Not the stripling?'

'No, the youngster's all right. It's the weasel who was scarred by the brown mink.'

Kine dropped his head. 'He raised the harrier warning. He alerted us . . .' They stood in silence a minute before Kine asked slowly, 'Then what happened to . . .' He got no further. The earth quaked and suddenly two late-arriving ewes came up the trail abreast, necks

craning, eyes demented, racing madly to catch up with
the mob ahead. The tattoo of their hooves rose like
a drum roll, reached a crescendo as weasels were
skittled, falling away again. The smaller creatures
remustered angrily. Dust hung over them. It made a
plume far up the track, and, as gradually it dispersed,
a bedraggled figure limped out of it. Ford was muttering.

Kine said, eyes pricking, 'Fine help *you* were, bog-
weasel!'

'Sheep!' Ford grumbled, spitting dust. 'Gormless
imbeciles.'

The mud on Kine was caking in the moist heat. The
sun was fierce. Divested now of haze, it swam in a blue
roof above the frontier, penetrating an almost too
perfect atmosphere. Only far west was a trace of cloud
visible, like a fin on the skyline, dark but remote. The
tribe advanced. The fin grew. Soon the fin was a tower
of cumulonimbus, then a craggy massif of black vapour
and bizarre effects of light. The swamp turned amber,
mauve, orange. The sky was sulphur-yellow. A great
stillness fell, and from way across the marsh a green
woodpecker yaffled the cloudburst's imminence.

CHAPTER FIFTEEN

'KINE ... are you there, Kine?' The small voice came closer. 'Kine,' it called, and again, 'Kine.' One-Eye lay hidden, too wise to move until the caller was revealed to him. The voice came shrilly through the wood, part plaintive yet sharp with frustration. 'Kine,' it pined. There was reproof in its insistence. One-Eye yawned. Only the rash proclaimed themselves to all in earshot. But he was curious.

Thistledown tumbled on the draught between the timbers, and, light as thistledown, the she-weasel skipped in sight. 'Kine,' she bleated. With a sigh of annoyance she paused to scratch. A peacock butterfly, sun-drenched wings brilliant, floated over her. It was a picture, thought One-Eye. She was wholly unself-conscious, sleek with budding maturity but scarcely more than a kitten. The dainty stranger quickened his tough old heart.

He said, surprising her, 'What do you want with Kine?'

She spun round, eyes flashing, and he thought her indignation at being caught unawares suited her. She had a brave little temper, snapping hotly, 'Who are you?' and, receiving no answer, 'It's no business of yours.' But when he made as if to leave, her need for company was touching. 'Well, it *might* be,' she pleaded. 'Kine's my father. He's the only kin I have. The rest were murdered by the mink. I can't find him. In fact, you seem to be the only weasel in the wood.'

She did not flinch at his scars or the empty eye-socket, and he warmed to her. 'You're Kia's daughter? I thought the whole brood was slaughtered, but I can see – I should have known right away.'

168

'You knew my mother?'

The veteran nodded. He should certainly have known. It was remarkable. He took in the small-boned elegance, the supple form. She was younger, but Kia to a whisker. He said, more moved than he showed, 'Kine's my son. That's why I'm here. I'm minding the wood while he leads the tribe to avenge its own.'

'You're my *grandsire*,' she exclaimed with what he thought was undue emphasis. It had the ring of antiquity. It consigned another season to the past, and seasons were short for One-Eye. A generation had grown while his back was turned. The chicks of spring had taken wing beside scudding troops of woodpigeons and lapwings. Young starlings foreshadowed winter's armies in roving companies. August! Swifts were leaving. Willow-wrens, still yellow with youth, faced the daunting world. And the little she-weasel said, 'You must be very old. I can see why Kine left you behind, but I shall go to him.'

One-Eye grimaced. Dunlins climbed from the marsh in a speeding phalanx, switching tack with a flash that changed their colour from grey to white. Feathered tribes passed restlessly. Curlews and redshanks, sweeping low, skimmed over herons spaced like posts on the frontier, and were lost in mists beyond. The old-timer shook his head. 'No one can reach the tribe now. It's on the great swamp.'

'Then I'll wait for him here. I can help defend the wood until he comes back.' She eyed the male with pert defiance. 'I can kill, you know. I'm not an infant. I've killed mice and voles. At first I was helpless. Poacher kept me going – put meat beneath the broom bush. He still does, but it's not the same as freshly killed. Well, *is* it?' she insisted when One-Eye spluttered. 'Poacher's meat is cold.'

'Poacher!' The old weasel was appalled. 'You mustn't go near Poacher. He's anathema.'

'Nonsense. I wouldn't be here without him – without the food he throws.'

'It's a trap.'

The female giggled. Her chattering chuckle disturbed a grey squirrel, who left a cob-nut unburied and shot aloft. 'Poor Poacher. Poor sick Poacher! His days are ending. If he likes to watch my dancing movements, admire my sheen from his window,' she said with mischievous conceit, 'where's the harm? Come, I'll show you.'

One-Eye scowled. She was leading him on, the teasing witch, flexing her charms on his hoary susceptibilities. Dancing movements! She had the cheek of her mother. She deserved to be trounced, but you could not trounce an elf, a beguiling imp; you could not belabour a bubbling spring. 'Go on,' he challenged reluctantly, 'prove your fantasy.'

They went towards the barn along the woodside, Kia's daughter skipping ahead of the old warrior. It was warm, and butterflies – tortoiseshells and commas – sunned on brambles, though the mass of wild bloom had gone and already the nights breathed autumnal airs. A few white yarrow-heads, a spray of sow-thistle blossomed. One-Eye missed them. His single orb saw only one flower: her chestnut head and snowdrop bib were delectable.

She stopped in Poacher's hedge. Scarlet berries of arum thrust from spotted sheaths. 'You can come,' she invited shortly, flouncing forward. 'There's nothing to fear.'

One-Eye's growl was earnest. 'Enough's enough. This is perilous.'

Her voice rippled. 'You'll just have to watch me then.'

Scorning concealment, she had bounced on to the path, where she brazenly turned and made a bob to him. Then, with a sniff of importance, she moved on again. The sun lit her as she danced; her paws twinkled. Approaching the cottage door, the glossy sprite paused and, poised on her haunches, began to preen. It was pure bravado, and continued until she glimpsed her human audience. Conspiratorially, the face in the upstairs window cracked with amusement, the pane misted and was wiped. The wan features of Poacher beamed a second time. Suddenly, the small creature flicked her tail, executed a prancing circle and disappeared. She reappeared from the broom shrub with laden jaws.

Back in the hedge she placed the joint of rabbit at One-Eye's feet. He was dumbfounded. In all his seasons he had seen no trick to match it. She had yet to see a winter, but Kia's daughter had Poacher mesmerized. To hold a rabbit spellbound was not impossible. To mesmerize a man – even witnessed, the feat was scarcely credible. 'It's always like that?' he asked bemusedly.

'Always has been.'

'Have you a name?'

'No,' she smiled, 'I never had one.'

'It's "Wonder",' he growled, 'I've just christened you.'

'Because you like me, One-Eye?'

One-Eye snorted. 'Because it's a wonder you lived,' he told her. 'Because it's a wonder you behave as you do; and because, Wonder of wonders, you get away with it!'

The drone of the combine-harvester accompanied the girl from Poacher's den along the ridge. She was reminded of her mother by the harvest; of a doe-eyed, tough-willed woman, full of mystery, who spoke darkly of the marsh and gipsy *chis* who could turn into hares and back to girls again. But best of all were the tales of the Corn Spirit which, at harvest time, would take refuge in the last clump of standing barley or wheat, among the rabbits there.

No reaper was anxious to cut that clump. So the men, in those distant days, would share the task and, even then, be chary of going too close. Standing back, they would hurl sickles at the clump until the stalks fell. Then the sheaf would be clad like a woman and left out in the open to avert storms. The girl smiled to herself, swinging her hips as she made for home. It was a slow smile. She strode with the loose gait of the country, used to rough tracks, and humped Poacher's washing with casual ease.

Her mother had talked of the Last Carrying – how, on the final day of harvest, the last wagon would be drawn by bell-decked horses, and how the people would carouse and holler harvest rhymes. The girl remembered her mother chanting lines her own parents, and their parents, once clamoured as the lumbering wains concluded the labour of August's gathering.

> We've ploughed, we've sowed,
> We've reaped, we've mowed,
> We've carr'd our last load,
> And aren't o'erthrowed.
> Hip, hip, hip . . .

Today, when it was over, her father would step alone from the combiner, bale the discarded straw by tractor, and burn the stubble. The Corn Spirit was forgotten. But not everything changed. She hitched her burden. He would still be filthy at the end, his clothes fit only to join Poacher's in her washday chore. Lord, I'm late, she thought, spotting the pick-up, and the young man by the gate. She dumped the bundle in the garden. 'Have you waited long?'

He greeted her moodily. 'I'm used to it.'

'I had to stay. The poor beggar's alone too often.'

The young man huffed. 'Can you wonder?'

She frowned, a hand to her hair, which had blown awry. He had been patient on the whole, helping when he could with errands for Poacher, uncomplaining of the time taken up by her extra work. She liked him for it. She expected it and met his tone with a warning glance. 'I get on with old Poacher. He'll put up with me.'

'So would I, in his position.' For once he overrode caution. The wilful glance roused him, as did the

172

uptilted arm and dishevelled locks. 'A fussing girl in and out. I'd like the chance.'

'What does that mean?'

'You tell *me*.'

She did not answer, and the thrum of the combiner stole into the vacuum. The young man eyed the vale with hostility. They ganged up on him: its wildness, her own untamedness, Poacher, the marsh, everything. He was, he brooded, an outside diversion, nothing more, in her life; and he cared too much for the girl to be content with that.

She said, 'I believe you're jealous,' then with coldly mirthful scorn, 'of *him*, old Poacher! I never thought you were daft, but . . .' She watched him, lips pursed. 'For heaven's sake!' she mocked.

'It's you who's daft. I'm concerned for you.'

'For heaven's sake,' she persisted, 'old Poacher! He thinks more of that young weasel he's been feeding than of me. He's like a child with it.'

'What weasel?'

'Is it important?' she said, intrigued by his jealousy. 'There was this orphan weasel, and Poacher nourished it. It comes for meat, bold as a robin. He can watch from his window. It makes the day for him.'

'Once he used to shoot them.' The man threw his hands up. 'Now it's people he threatens. He shouldn't be left there.'

'No one comes for him.'

'They'd have to if you insisted. It's no kindness, hanging on to the old devil, you know that.'

'Maybe.' She shrugged, watching the growling matchbox that was the harvester on the slope. Perhaps Poacher was just a relic, a Corn Spirit, better tidied away than left rotting in the valley when winter howled. Yet there was spark in him. '*We've carr'd our last load, And aren't o'erthrowed.*' Poacher had carried his last load but had not surrendered. She said, 'Maybe you're right. God knows, I keep telling the beggar he should go away. For his health's sake.'

'Best chance of lasting.'

'Aye,' she concurred, 'like taking a wild thing into captivity. Tend it carefully, it'll likely last longer than in its wild place.'

'More than likely.'

The girl plucked a grass. As she bent, she saw a hare truckling quietly in the verge, almost invisible. Its soft eye fixed her, nose barely quivering. Then, aware she had seen it, the creature sprang up the lane towards Poacher's place, paused, and looked back at them. Relaxing, it loped on, the whole spread of the valley ahead of it. Musingly, the girl sucked the grass. 'Reckon there's lasting' – she spat the stem – 'and *living*. I could last somewhere else, could be richer, comfortable, have things done for me. But only place I can live's where I belong, in the valley. I'm free here.'

'And if you marry?'

Her gaze swept him with amusement. 'What's that to do with Poacher?'

Half turning, he said, exasperated, 'To hell with arguing. There's not much time. I'm due on shift in another hour.'

'You'd best be going, then.'

'I can spare a bit longer.'

'I shouldn't bother.' She closed the garden gate on him. 'I've got the washing. I don't need you to spare me anything,' she purred, hefting the bundle and departing, her hair swirling.

He watched her go then kicked a tyre on the pick-up with sudden viciousness. 'Damn!' he said.

There was a scuffle in the orchard, and birds scattered protesting with metallic cries. The small weasel bounced in the sunlight, whirled twice in pursuit of her tail, chattered gleefully. 'Wonder! It's a good name, I like it. Furthermore, One-Eye, I no longer like being alone. I like finding another weasel. Not *just* another weasel, but my grandsire. Kine's father,' she exulted, 'that *is* wonderful!'

Churring, she danced away through tall brittle gicks and the gnarled boles of fruit trees, whirling tilth from dry mole works, bursting through gossamer so the dew on the webs sprayed. She made One-Eye feel young at heart, though decrepit physically. He lost sight of her. Dizzily, she pranced into view from a grassy tunnel, to spin round him in a circle and shimmy off again. She was the spirit of youth in that age-old place.

Poacher's orchard overhung them with lichened limbs, a mossy mausoleum of human labour long run wild, yet still gaudy in patches with ripening fruit. Each winter its archaic occupants all but perished. It became a graveyard of grey-fingered ghosts, a grisly no-man's-land of scarred trunks and snapped branches. Fungi battened to the carnage like clotted blood. But in spring an obstinate resurrection stirred ancient boughs to adorn themselves almost bizarrely in leaf and flower.

Suddenly, from wizened tree-tops, the missel-thrush flung out his song; while, in an ancient fork of branches, the silver cup of the chaffinch's nest appeared. Soon, fruits of nostalgic obsolescence began to swell. Old trees dangled little red apples like Christmas baubles. Others produced varieties, green and bitter, whose use – perhaps for some type of cider – was forgotten. Purple damsons, little bigger than sloes, hung in clusters near small ochre pears with abrasive skins. There were mulberries, too. They grew on a tree so desiccated, so age-ravaged, that their inky red moistness seemed a miracle.

Withal came deeply varied scents: in sun-mottled arbours, the mellow perfume of sweet apples joined the heavier fumes of bruised and fermenting pears. There were fruits of aromatic fragrance and subtle headiness. Strongest was the smell exuded by the fallen globes, their flesh bored by wasps who worked incessantly from nests in the fissured earth.

The place was quiet now. Only the resonant buzz of

wasps in the caverns they had fashioned broke the stillness, until the thud of a falling apple stopped Wonder's onrush. She sniffed the contused fruit. Its smell was pungent, but not so powerful it banished the trace of mink. The repellant reek of the monsters soured her spittle, and suddenly her ebullience drained. 'They've been here, round the hen house,' she blurted.

One-Eye, snuffling forward, agreed with her. 'But the scent's cold. They probably came some time last night.' He saw the small creature's tenseness and sympathized. 'Don't worry, they'll have gone. Most likely scouting, and couldn't find a way in.'

'The same stench as the nightmare . . .'

'Don't worry. We'll be ready if they return, but they've a bigger surprise than us awaiting them,' he cheered her. 'Kine on their doorstep with the weasel tribe!'

'Yes.' She brightened. 'I'm not frightened of them, One-Eye. My mother wasn't.'

'Kia was valiant.' He glanced sideways at her. Too little time had passed to heal her memories. In her mind the trauma of the Moon Pond was an open wound. But the young were resilient. He said, 'I don't like the stillness – it's going to rain.'

She laughed, high spirits regained. 'Rain? From a blue sky! Why, the sun's shining, ripening the apples. Don't be so gloomy, One-Eye. I'm going to dance again.'

She skittered off beneath scarlet-streaked fruit and lanky suckers of damson, the mink forgotten; and the old weasel caught glimpses here and there of her bright bib. It flashed amid nettles, bobbed from grasses, shone in flying arcs round weathered boles. Now she penetrated shadowed bowers, now pursued wasps. It was at once a game and a test of fleetness for sterner times.

One-Eye raised his neck to view the far sky. An ugly cloud covered the bog beyond the river. Black and mountainous, it already spat dark shafts of rain on to the great swamp. It was the worst of all his fears that the tribe would be caught on a flooded mire.

Wonder stopped her race, and panting she came up to him. 'How right you were, One-Eye. It *will* rain. Shrewd grandsire!' Then, perceiving his disquiet, 'You're worried. It's Kine – you're worried about him. I can see you are.'

CHAPTER SIXTEEN

THE tribe crouched with backs to the weather, tails tucked low, longing for the shelter it did not have. The wind which came with the cloudburst drove the rain in stinging torrents, penetrating fur and drenching chilled skin. There was no escape from it. Kine watched sheets of gushing water turn silver, darken a moment, then flash again. The sky pealed. He looked at Ford. Ford's coat was slick, droplets fringing his chest. Periodically the bog-weasel shed them with a fierce flick.

Kine said, 'We'd be better on the move if this is going to last.'

'It won't last.'

'If it does, we're in trouble. It's pushing the level up.'

Ruffled lakes had grown in the downpour and, where clumps had once formed islands, no more than the tops of grasses stood up from the deluged swamp. The trail had narrowed. Soggy patches intruded from either flank, trickling into the shallow dips. Indentations left by hooves had already filled with water. All it needed, thought Kine, was a dip in the path, and the way to Castle Mound might be impassable. 'It can't last like this,' Ford asserted. 'It's a freak squall. It will end before we know what's happening, and the sun will shine.'

'Possibly.' Kine was dubious. The optimism of a weasel who had sought to halt the ewe mob single-handed did not reassure him. 'All the same, I intend to press on. Get them travelling, Ford.'

The weasels stirred again. There were grumbles as they leaned into the downpour, marching wretchedly until a series of muddy hillocks loomed ahead. Then their shout was eager – 'The mole cantonment!' – and the tribe broke into a sloshy, spontaneous charge. The young heath-weasel passed Kine, grinning avidly. 'Food!' he shrilled through the rain. 'I'm going to gorge myself, Kine. I'm ravenous. Let's get underground!'

He plunged into a tunnel and Kine, scratching the tilth, found another hole. Dropping through, he was gasping suddenly for breath in the mole chamber. The black tube was awash with rain. Nosing the roof, where air was trapped above the water, Kine filled his lungs, struggled back to the earth's surface and shook dismally. Other weasels were surfacing, too. Mud dripped from their flanks, and they were spluttering. 'It's flooded,' moaned the heathland stripling. 'They've abandoned it.'

'We'll feed later.' Kine eyed the cheated tribe: it looked a sad group. The rain was still pelting. 'Let's march again,' he churred harshly.

'You see,' Ford insisted, plodding stolidly, 'it's easing. The storm's letting up. We've seen the worst of it.'

'*Tchk!*' A grey lagoon now lapped the causeway, and a snake swam in it. A pair of gulls skimmed the water, barking gutturally. 'Save your breath, Ford! Perhaps the worst of the rain is over, but the level will rise as the heights drain. This lake's going to spread. What's the trail like ahead when the flood mounts?'

'Wet. You're in a bog,' Ford growled, 'not a garden of roses. There'll be paddling to do.' The stalwart shrugged. 'We're wet already. Once you're wet, you're wet.'

'Once you're hungry, you're hungry.'

'We'll eat on Castle Mound.'

'If we get there.'

'Bah!'

'It's no good, Ford. We've youngsters with us who weren't reared like you to bog conditions. There's a limit to what they can take of this. It's serious.'

'I never said it wasn't dangerous.'

'Just how dangerous?'

Ford shrugged again. 'Perhaps rather worse than paddling. We may have to swim in the tricky parts.'

'Bad as that . . .'

It proved worse. Ten minutes later they passed a line of dripping osiers and were forced to halt. A small rill was in spate, a gushing, unnavigable barrier. The weasels watched helplessly. All summer seemed to drown in the murky tide. It bore the litter of hills and copses, of field and heath. Flotsam raced in it. Besides rafts of torn reed and swirling seed-heads, the broad waters carried berries, fragments of petal from distant eminences. Bedraggled bracken, quitch, brashings drifted with leaves and heather bloom. When the spate subsided, buntings and other birds would hunt the high-water mark for stranded seeds. Now the flood rose.

Kine seethed with frustration. 'Not a hope of swimming,' he snarled. 'What next? We're running out of time, Ford. Scrat will be waiting. What's the next move?'

'Can't sit here,' Ford said gruffly. 'Have to turn back.'

'Turn back!'

'Find another path. It may be possible.' The bog-weasel glowered. 'I'll not be balked by a stream. We'll take another trail.'

'I didn't notice one.' Kine turned on Ford grimly. 'There isn't one, is there? Admit the truth, Ford.'

'Whose land is it!'

Kine retraced his steps slowly. 'It's your land, but it's not your weather. You can no more stop a flood than a flock of sheep.' He went back past the osiers, his gait bereft of its normal bounce. Only part of his emptiness was hunger, and he barely saw the bleak pollards or noticed how much narrower the path was, suddenly. At the end of the stunted scrub he seemed to stand now at the heart of a boundless lake, its surface no longer broken by tufty grasses, but smooth and grey as a heron as far as eye could see.

Sprouting from dumpy boles, the thin osiers waved

feebly, marooned spirits reflected where water lapped. A sense of isolation overwhelmed the straggling, dejected tribe, and Kine, watching, felt as remote from home as he thought possible. The touch of dry ground on paws, the scent of woodlands, a nourished belly, were sensations recalled from another world. He conjured up images of sloping meadows and woodland ridge. How much he had taken for granted in a land which now shone starlike in his yearning for it – and he reproved himself. Sourly, he shook his feet. When he put them down they filled with mud again.

'Kine!' A weasel ahead of him turned urgently. 'It's closed across the way we came – we're cut off,' the creature gulped with distress. 'The trail's gone. There's water everywhere.'

Kine ran forward. In a moment he was stopped by the scummy rim of the lapping flood. It was true. The path from the river was now beneath the lake. They were standing on the last strip exposed; and that was shrinking perceptibly as they watched. The weasels shivered. Splashing to one end of the soggy island they sniffed the tide fearfully, then scampered to the far end. Denied escape, they clustered together and viewed the flood's breadth.

Ford examined the pollards. 'Sorry, Kine, it's a curse of Gru. There's a spell on us.'

'Just bad luck. The trees?' And when the bog-weasel nodded, 'Into the osiers! Everyone move! It's rising fast. We'll have to sit it out until the level drops.'

They climbed wearily. The rain had stopped. Instead, the wind had risen; and dusk, cheerless as the flood, blurred their damp shapes. The wind snarled. It was biting, whipping waves against their perches, portending a raw night.

'Will we survive, Kine?' The youngest weasel sought reassurance, his voice desolate.

'At least,' Kine jollied him, 'we won't die of thirst. Let's see in the morning. Get some rest now.' It was hardly possible. The wind stabbed continuously.

Another time it would have driven a weasel to a warm niche, a cosy hollow. Now they crouched like mice on corn stalks, alone in the darkening flood. They heard no insects; they saw no birds. Only later, when the tide ran black, did a frog break the silence, its woeful monologue abrasive on Kine's nerves.

'For pity's sake,' he called sharply. 'A frog in water! – you've nothing to moan about.'

'You've not heard?'

'Heard what?'

'There's been a massacre. Gru has fallen on the clan of the Founding Twelve. She's demented, crazed by the killing of the twin she spawned. First, she set the monsters against the marsh frogs. The dykes were gruesome with slaughter. Not since the days of the great treks has such death occurred. Frogs were massacred. Among them, Bunda, sage and oracle . . .'

'Bunda!'

The frog was moaning. 'It's just the start of the killing. The mink are blood-crazed.'

'What of Scrat?'

'Who?'

Kine was silent. Water sloshed. The eye of the night held little hope for him.

Morning dawned with a mirage: a flood fantasy. The lake gleamed, and on its surface had gathered great flocks of birds. It was extraordinary, as if every aquatic fowl in creation surrounded the half-drowned stems where the weasels perched. Fragile terns rode sun-flecked wavelets with big scowling gulls and fleets of wild duck. Coots swam; teal dunked. A herd of swans preened, twisting lissom necks, and standing up from the flood to stretch vast wings. There were drab birds and flamboyant ones. Shellduck sparkled, their white and chestnut liveries seeming scarcely real. Wings whistled and a skein of mallard, necks outstretched, slanted down on to the water with scudding grace.

Kine blinked. It was dazzling, but the spectacle did

not alleviate the stiffness of a cramped, hunger-ridden night. Nor did it offer escape from a worsening plight. Enfeebled by exposure and lack of food, the weasels clung vulnerably to the marooned stumps. They were conspicuous: harriers or sparrowhawks would spot them from far off. Kine said, braced uncomfortably between osiers, 'There's got to be some way out. We can't perish here.'

'The way out,' Ford said, gaze spanning the water, 'is over there.'

Kine focused on the distant crest of the hinterland. Strange woods stood up from fields of stubble which sloped, wreathed in blue haze, to the flood's edge. The shapes of copses, the tilt of meadows were unfamiliar, and he suspected dangers were plentiful; but at least it was dry ground, a source of food. By following the rim of the flood they could still reach Castle Mound. 'All we need,' he said wrily, 'is the strength to swim twenty times as far as possible.'

A flight of swans took off powerfully. Wings thumping, they lumbered across the water cutting wakes with their feet until speed provided lift, then, with a throbbing roar, were airborne in tight formation, yelping twice as they droned north. Within seconds they were over land. It looked so easy, Kine was sickened. Turning round, he took in the blue above his far home. A tiny fleck blotched the sky. He nudged Ford. There was no need to voice fear, for Ford was bristling already. 'A hawk,' he growled.

'No.' The dot had grown larger. 'Too clumsy,' Kine breathed with relief. 'Could be a crow.'

'It's a rook.'

'You're right, Ford!'

'The Watchman?'

'No mistaking him!'

For a moment the bird was lost, as more mallard cut in front, landing noisily. Widgeon followed. In the commotion the mire resounded with raucous cries, then the rook was overhead, his black wings oddly misplaced in that watery haunt. Slowly, watched by craning weasels, he circled, then tumbled down towards them. His grating '*Caw*' was sarcastic. 'More guts than sense,' he rasped, his glance withering. 'A fine predicament!'

Ford scowled. 'We don't need taunts . . .'

'Or squabbling,' Kine interposed. 'You're a welcome sight, Watchman. You've come from One-Eye?'

'From the marsh. I saw the massacre.' The rook examined their perches with a cocked head. Bark peeled where water had buffeted the grey stems. It peeled in shards like the rotting scales of dead fish. Beneath the surface, bunches of slender shoots waved in the shifting flood. He thought of the torn limbs of frogs, disembodied legs which had jerked after the slaughter with nervous energy. 'I saw Bunda die, Kine. He dived deep but they pursued him.' The hard beak tightened. 'There was no escape. You're well out of the destruction. At least you're alive on these blighted stumps.'

'More than Gru will be,' Ford howled, 'when we get to her.'

'Scrat? Did you see him, Watchman? Is the shrew alive?'

The rook ruffled, surveying the lake. 'What do *you* think? You know Scrat – who's going to find him when there's danger? And if they find him, who wants to choke on his miserable mini-skin? The shrew lives.'

'That's something.' Perhaps an omen, Kine reflected; a sign to raise weasel spirits, inspire escape. 'Tell us, Watchman – you've looked down on it – is there any way we can cross this fowl-infested flood?'

'How far can you swim?'

'Not as far as the mire's rim.'

'You surprise me,' the rook jeered. 'The boundless prowess of the weasel has met its match.'

'Well?' Kine bit on his temper.

'Well, there's a way, but you'll need to swim the first leg. Beyond the swan herd there's a ridge, a barely-covered bar protruding from the shore.' The rook paused and the tribe waited. 'You could wade it,' he said. 'Swim to the extremity – you could wade the rest. But it's a good swim. If you're game, I'll guide you – fly ahead of you.'

Kine looked out to the swans. It was a good swim, all right; a distance to tax the strongest weasel, and the tribe was low. The prospect daunted him. But so, he mused, did starvation.

'Are we game?' he demanded.

Assent was vehement.

They took to the water with the strength of revived hope, Kine setting the pace. Ford swam close to him. The rook flapped over them. He swooped wave-high and they felt the draught of his wings before, batting ahead, he emulated the kestrel, hovering adroitly. He was a shrewd old bird, irascible maybe, but Kine trusted him. Kia had liked him, so did One-Eye. His tongue was sharp but his heart was true, and he spurred them on now with gruff encouragement.

It was an odd sight. Led by the aged rook, the straggling convoy of small mammals surprised the birds on the flood, who veered suspiciously. Bustling and splashing, a moorhen took fright, alarming some teal, which sprang away like rockets, sun darting on their black and green specula. Kine swam doggedly. The breeze was moderate: it chucked a slight swell in his face, and each time he hit a trough the rook seemed to drown in the crest ahead.

They swam interminably, it seemed. Muscles agonized, strength was ebbing so that each breasting thrust demanded greater effort than the last stroke. 'How much farther?' Kine's query sank unanswered. The rook had drawn ahead, and the leader of the tribe toiled with growing doubts. There seemed no end to it. Leaves floated by in shoals, and Kine cursed when they wrapped around him soggily. Never had he swum so far before. He was struggling. 'How much farther?' his mind was begging, 'how much more of it?'

He glimpsed Ford and could tell the bog-weasel shared his own thoughts. There was no returning, no regaining the osiers. The bar was their only hope. All depended on the rook now. 'If he's misjudged it,' Kine thought bleakly, 'it's the end of us.' They would die very shortly on the flood's breast. There would be a few bubbles, a last anguished thresh, a sodden corpse or two when the lake drained.

Ford was spluttering, attracting his attention. 'We're coming up to the swan herd. Keep going, Kine.'

'Do we skirt them? If they've a mind, they'll attack us – drown the lot of us.'

'Straight on, friend. Too late for caution. We'll never make it if we don't take the shortest course.'

He was right. This time, Kine thought ironically, the incautious Ford was all too right. They had to risk upsetting the massive fowl, and hope the temper of the white giants was equable. The swans sunned drowsily. Kine drew abreast a towering cob, and saw the great bill above him, fiery orange flaring from the ominous basal knob. One stab and that weapon would consign him to the flood's depths. Painfully, he paddled the long flank, limbs enfeebled by hunger and the endless haul.

There was a snort of aggravation from the swan and the herd stirred. Inquisitively the big birds stretched trunk-like necks to investigate. The small fleet of sorry weasels stroked frantically. Kine's head was throbbing and his lungs heaved. Another cob had pushed forward, hissing angrily. Kine caught the half-lift of wings, the peevish eye, and dived beneath black-webbed swans' feet, striking desperately through a liquid curtain of murky flood.

How far he swam underwater he could not tell, before the pain of suffocation forced him up again. Then he saw that the white herd had dropped behind. His head was splitting. He was spent, floating helplessly in a twilight world of dizzy lethargy. Dazed by lack of oxygen, he heard the calls of weasels from what seemed a vast distance, another plane. But they came nearer as his head cleared, and Ford was spluttering. 'The rook, Kine!' Others were bobbing, gulping breathlessly. 'See, the rook, Kine . . .'

The Watchman walked on water with strutting gravity.

Kine stared bemusedly. Comprehension and elation came simultaneously. The bar! The rook was standing on a lightly-washed causeway fingering landwards to fields of stubble and green slopes. They had done it: they had reached the bar. Threshing forward until his own paws touched bottom, Kine lay limply in the shallows, recovering.

He could see trees. He could see willows by the water. There was a creek enclosed by vegetation, a bed of green matted reeds, a knoll with cattle grazing on it. He saw oaks and limes, here and there a leaf prematurely yellowing. There were thickets of bramble with crimson tints. It was a dry land, cropped butts of corn crisp in rising fields. Rabbits sloppeted there. Grey and plump, they browsed with a leisurely creeping motion which signified tranquillity. It was a land of food.

Chapter Seventeen

THE Fordson driver jacked the plough and drove the tractor off the stubble to view his handiwork. He had turned a dozen furrows round the field, excluding the lower side, which was by the mire. That was one place a firebreak was superfluous. 'An hour to fill, a month to drain,' it was said of the bottom levels. But, in fact, they never did drain properly – had not done so since Creation, he would bet a pint.

Dismounting, the driver knocked earth from the ploughshares, took a blow-torch from his cab, and pumped up the pressure before lighting it. Systematically he fired the stubble along the topside of the field, so the breeze would carry the line of flame down the slope. When the stubs of straw had burned he would complete the ploughing. Meanwhile, dousing the torch, he climbed back into the blue cab and ate his sandwiches.

For a while the man watched formations of duck racing above the flood. Climbing and diving, they circled with seemingly pointless fury, like wall-of-death riders he had seen once at a local fair. The sheer splendour of the morning, the gleam of water, filled them with crazy energy. Lower, lapwings scudded in loose flight across ploughland. Gulls fought for crusts the driver tossed to them.

The fire had taken hold, begun to crackle downhill, leaving a spreading trail of black ash, above which images crinkled in the rising heat. The man unscrewed a thermos flask. For a second he thought he saw something jump in the stubble, then steam from scalding tea blurred the window and he wiped the panel. Smoke from the line of fire intervened, but again something moved, and he kept his eyes trained.

The creature was small, mostly obscured by the residue of straw, bouncing spasmodically into view, like a stoat or weasel. There was, he thought as he watched, more than one of them. Indeed, were it less than improbable, he would have sworn there was a band of small animals advancing up the field from the flood level. If so, they had yet to perceive the fire approaching them.

The tribe stopped in a bare patch amid the stubble where the corn had failed and the ubiquitous mayweed had made its nest – a soft, earthy place full of sun and wild flowers. 'This'll do,' Kine observed. 'It's time we rested. One more push, then the assault. Make the most of the break, for we shall need strength.' He felt suddenly, deeply drowsy, overwhelmed by the escape, belly stuffed with rabbit after hunger. They had come off the causeway on to spongy grass and a sprinkling of willow poles, some with old nests of pigeons in their sketchy limbs. There had been rabbits galore. Rather fewer now remained. The tribe had fed at last.

The young weasel from the heath stretched with fresh courage. His nervousness had gone and he affected a mature tone, rich in confidence. 'We're doing all right, Kine. We're making history in this land. Victory summons us.'

'We're surviving,' Kine told him. 'I said we'd survive the flood. Now I say it's not over; the job's ahead.'

'With Kine we conquer! The tribe's strong. Danger yields – ewe mob, swan herd, ordeal by storm, they yield to us.'

Kine yawned. 'Just leave me alone,' he growled. 'The tribe's tired.' He lounged reflectively. The stripling would find his feet. If he came through, there would be no holding him. He would have a fine conceit. The phrase lingered: 'A fine conceit!' It rang with Kia's chuckling humour and Kine was struck by his own transformation since the time she first reproved him, not so long back – in another epoch of experience. He had been as vaunting as a bantam cock. He crowed no more. It consoled him that as time passed he felt more like One-Eye's son.

Ford slumped beside him. 'It's not always *that* bad. We were unfortunate . . .'

'You can keep your bog, Ford.' The stubby straw was dry as tinder. Kine spread himself. This was more like his own land: wooded slopes, sheltered combes and dingles, the scent of good soil. He had glimpsed hazy crowns of plantations as they climbed, a distant farmstead. Tops of pylons had ribbed a far crest. 'You should move to these slopes,' Kine suggested. 'You could stake a domain worth hunting. It's foreign terrain but it beats the swamp.'

'Soft country,' Ford teased, 'fit for seekers of easy-living. I was brought up a harder way. It's not so easy to change habits.' He raised his nose and said, 'Burning . . .'

'There'll be plenty of burning now harvest's over.' It was the season of smoke. For a while the valley would fill with the thick fumes of bonfire and field-burning, scented mists drifting for mile on mile.

'Besides' – Ford dismissed the smell of fire – 'if the mink prevail, no domain, bog or wood, will be worth a rat's paw. We're near the reckoning. By the bones of the ages, I can't wait for the brutes!'

'How much longer to Castle Mound?'

'Be there by evening.'

Kine forgot his tiredness, a mental picture of the bunker, its monstrous garrison, stimulating him. To gain its rear, peer down from the mound at the loathsome citadel, had been the plan, but had long seemed remote. Now the prospect was suddenly imminent and his lethargy vanished.

'From here,' Ford said, 'we march on firm ground. We've put the swamp trail behind us. We'll canter it.'

'The river?'

'The flood's below the pump-house. The stream should be safe where we cross.' Ford grinned. 'What's a river?' he said happily. 'After what we've just swum it will seem a ditch.'

'*Then* they'll pay!' Kine paused and said it with quiet

violence. '*Then* they'll pay, Ford. They'll pay, I promise. Even if I die in the belly of the labyrinth, Gru shall die with me.' It was not simply revenge, though revenge was a factor. To rid the vale of the monsters was imperative. No weasel would submit to the rule of mink. Death was preferable.

'We'll destroy them, Kine. It can be over by morning if we cross tonight.'

It seemed to Kine that the smoke was thickening, beginning to catch his throat, but Ford's suggestion worried him and he countered, 'Not by night, it's too risky. We can't predict the current, and the tribe could flounder in the dark – be swept off course. We'll cross at first light. Scrat must be in position. The rook will carry the word: we attack at dawn.'

Ford nodded, wrinkling his nose. The reek of burning had strengthened. 'It's too close,' he muttered abruptly. 'I'm going to look, Kine.'

Kine listened. The fire was audible, a sound like cartwheels on gravel, then fiercer: a crackling, a mounting roar. Charred straw was floating past them now in smutty clouds. A hare stood tall in the stubble, black-tipped ears cocked. She had stopped in downhill career to glance back. She was gone in a moment, and a flock of starlings passed over like a dark shadow, succeeded by darker smoke. The smoke thickened. Suddenly, above the bristling corn stubs, the tribe saw red tongues of flame and heard Ford's piercing, 'Run for your lives! Run as you've never run!'

Smoke billowed. It surrounded Kine, stinging his eyes, fouling nose and throat, a choking black cloud which bore no resemblance to the sweet-scented blue-grey halo of a woodman's fire, or the aromatic plumes of a garden bonfire, but gushed in a reeking blanket, as smoke from burning rubber or waste-oil. Straw burned filthily. Kine, breathing the noxious fumes, felt overwhelmed by them. His frame shuddered. Gagged and blinded, he retched to expel the poison, and was saved abruptly by a kink in the draught. It brought a rift of fresh air. He was no longer with the others but could breathe, and looked around him for signs of life.

A few small creatures were moving in confused flight. Voles dithered between running and tunnelling. Harvest mice climbed the short stems in panic, or scurried in circles, uncertainly sniffing their own kind. The scale and speed of the threat bemused them, and Kine, a stranger to such fire, was stunned by its fury and seeming boundlessness. Like scarlet hounds the flames approached with leaping vigour and roasting breath. There was a crash of stubble and the young heath-weasel was beside him, urging frantically, 'This way, Kine. We must return to the flood. It's the only way.'

Kine wavered. The note of authority surprised him, and the other, noting his hesitation, explained hastily, 'Heath fires, Kine – there are many on the heath. We know we must get out of the heather, away from the growth to water or a barren patch. There's no safety in this stubble. We must race the flames to the flood's edge.'

'Then we follow the drills . . .'

'Like the wind,' advised the stripling, 'or else incinerate!'

Kine was moving already. 'Sound thinking,' he bawled above the commotion. 'Good for you, my young friend! Like the wind it is!'

They fled down the drills. Smoke was swirling, flames roaring behind them, the heat intense. With each straining, scudding bound, Kine gained height to see over the flanking stubble to where belching fire scorched the field's breadth. On the right the furnace had overtaken them, racing ahead in a blaze of black and orange which appalled the weasel with its savagery. An isolated tree stood in the fire's path. Momentarily, flame engulfed the bole then charged on, leaving the trunk as dusky as the charred straw. Avidly the fire stretched for new ground. Tongues leaped from the inferno, hurled sparks in smoking cascades, were sucked back into the wave of heat.

On the left, too, the red wall had outpaced the weasels. They were speeding, Kine perceived, between the horns of a blazing crescent whose centre licked at their retreating heels. A slight swing of the wind and either horn could veer inwards, cut their flight, make cinders of their slight, tormented frames. He missed his footing. 'Faster!' Stumbling, he bounded forward. 'The breeze is strengthening.'

A rabbit crossed their path feebly, blinded by myxomatosis, the rabbit plague. Panic-stricken, it lurched blearily towards the smoke-cloud and disappeared. Then the weasels themselves were running blindly, caught in the choking tide, steering by the fence of upright corn stubs either side of them. For a second the smoke was banished by a more fearful canopy of flame, and in that second Kine felt a heat on his back so excruciating that his flagging sinews found renewed life. He shot forward in desperation, the stripling pacing him.

'See the others?'

'Too much smoke.'

'Let's hope they're in front ...' It was scarcely uttered when a gap in the streaming soot revealed a weasel to their flank, undulating through the stubble where smoke was pouring. The smoke swirled and the animal vanished, to reappear to Kine in a glimpse, as brief as it was horrific, of burning fur, engulfing fire, before the vision was blotted out. Heat was bearing down on him in scorching gusts. It was dark beneath the gas cloud, like dusk when the last reflection of the sun ignited the gloom in a crimson blaze.

In the ominous glow another weasel ran ahead, and Kine could see it was Ford as he closed the gap – and that Ford was starting to labour, to lose propulsion. Kine drew abreast, eyes streaming. Fumes choked him, broke his churring exhortations into heaving gasps, 'Keep going . . . not much farther . . . keep running, Ford . . .'

Flames were towering. The roar of fire, exploding, crackling in their wake, was deafening and the shriek of the stripling, still close to Kine's shoulder, barely audible, 'The wind's veering – it's swinging. We must alter course.'

Kine took in the right flank with swimming vision. The horn was turning across them, licking inward to trap the fugitives. Hope dwindled. The weasels would have to run obliquely now, forcing through the bristling stubble, to beat not only the flames behind but those threatening their escape route to the flood ahead. Wheeling half-left, he smashed diagonally through the stumpy drills like a weary race-horse on a hurdle course, leaving a trail of gaps in the obstacles. The slower bog-weasel followed, making use of the path. The stripling sped with them.

Fire was everywhere. They seemed barely a jump ahead of it with each leap through the scratching stubs. The field was a furnace, an inferno raging with such fury about the diminutive predators that Kine believed the world would burn with them, the entire universe. The very air boiled. It baked his lungs. Searing flames numbed the senses, singed the hair, seemed to shrivel him. Red tongues stabbed. A line of straw turned black with heat as he barged through it, and charged another drill. Ahead, the horn raced to thwart them with fiery violence.

Streaming from the flank, a wall of vaulting fire was closing their escape like a sliding door. The corridor to safety was growing narrower as they ran its blazing gauntlet and breathed its black fumes. It was thick with gases; with sudden frenzy they exploded, hurling flame across the path. Stunned, the weasels recoiled, broiled and desperate. Kine whirled on the barrier. 'Straight through, don't falter,' he barked. 'It's our only chance!'

Together, confounding every instinct, they charged

the fire. Kine shut his eyes and was hurtling in burning space, nerves screwed against pain, against searing heat. He seemed to roast midair, to dehydrate, to fill with fumes which stifled consciousness. Then, with a jolting, deluging splash, he was sprawling in water, the others beside him, and the flood lapped them gently as they soaked in it. Weasels dotted the swamp's brink, dunking, wallowing. They watched the flames. For a time no one spoke, then Ford challenged, 'Say what you like about the bog, they can't set fire to it.'

They stood amid the ashes of the fire as tractor and plough ranged the far headland, and Kine paid tribute to the fallen: those whose lives had been lost since the raid began. The cold black work of the flames made sombre viewing. Here and there in the charred acres a streak of buff indicated where the holocaust had spared a few drills for a yard or so, but the blaze had been thorough and the field mourned. It was difficult to imagine growth springing within days from that deathly slope, yet the plough was already turning up rich soil and robust worms.

It would bury, however, the scorched bones of several members of the tribe who had failed to escape, and Kine ranked them with the gibbet martyrs. 'We'll not forget. None who died on the trek will be forgotten, whether crushed, drowned or burned. We'll remember them.' Flecks of soot blew on the breeze, and a flight of swans added the wild harmony of their bugle-cry to the requiem. 'They came,' he said, 'to do what remains to be done. As we face the last step, their spirit inspires us. Let's get on again.'

The air was dry, invigorating, and the unfamiliar hedgerows by which Ford led them were thick with fruit. Blackberries dripped from brambles in great clusters like grapes; thorn was dotted with glossy-skinned sloes. Everywhere, vermilion hips of wild rose vied with cherry-red haws to catch the sun's rays. It was a welcome aftermath to fire and flood, that last leg of the march, and the weasels attacked it with renewed bounce. Culverts gurgled. Skirts of spinneys grew warm. In moist corners stood pink-gilled toadstools and lichened relics of fencing which seemed as rooted as the hedge itself. The raiders progressed with mounting confidence.

Those who saw them – and human eye was not a witness – remembered the uniqueness of the sleek band, rarest of country sights, advancing on Castle Mound with a panache scarcely hinting at the ordeals endured, the task ahead. Bright bobbing coats gave the dandy hounds an air of carnival, of deceptively dainty mischief, cloaking the grimness of their enterprise. Mobs of young sparrows, exploring the valley, bustled round the weasels with sporting interest. A siege of herons on a stream stretched with tetchy curiosity, while, in a meadow, an old goose-rumped pony blinked at the only weasel pack he would ever see.

Occasionally hedgehogs, ancient virtuosi of the survival art, whispered caution from thickets as the tribe passed. The drowsy hedgepig was well equipped. Not only were his spines a sharp defence, but his rugged constitution was invaluable. It was impervious to the poison of the adder, his old enemy. He could 'sleep' away winter at low temperatures. Probably, though, the main factor in his widespread survival throughout the vale was that he hid by daylight and worked at night. Then his voice, oddly noisy, pronounced the merits of nocturnal life.

'Strike by dark,' he said. 'Whatever your strategy, strike by dark.'

Kine was not persuaded by second thoughts. He had weighed the gains of a night assault, and they were surpassed by the risks of swimming blind on a fast stream. He still favoured a dawn attack. It would be dark enough, he reflected, in the labyrinth. He envisaged it: the terrors of the bunker, its hated occupants. He had no doubt the decisive conflict would be underground.

But now the sun warmed their path, and when at last the mound came in sight, it looked surprisingly tranquil, more a crown of peace than a battle post. They had come by a sketchy copse to a lay of rough pasture, a crumbling stile, its wooden step rotting, and suddenly the hillock rose ahead in the beams of evening, a dumpy island, serenely wooded and undisturbed. Its slopes were smooth and grassy. Where the sun pitched on great trees the foliage was golden, turning purple in places where shade prevailed. Hidden birds sang.

'There you are,' Ford growled with satisfaction. 'Keep close from this point. We must go carefully.'

'Are there mink prowling?'

'Everywhere. We'll be on top of their stronghold when we climb the mound.'

Kine eyed the eminence. 'Of course,' he muttered. It looked inviting – so inviting it was hard to believe they would peer down from the top at the den of the priestess of death herself.

CHAPTER EIGHTEEN

THE speckled hen opened an eye but it was dark outside, and a shutter of skin closed the round lens. For several minutes she ignored the crunching of wood near the slatted floor. The night was full of noises and the fowls huddled close on their perch in the chicken house. The hut was aged, doubly neglected since Poacher's illness, yet the hens felt safe, shut in by the girl who came up at night.

They were a mixed lot – crossbred Leghorns, Rhode Islands, Sussex – about a score, their pecking order led by the speckled bird. She had scratched Poacher's orchard for several years and was the boldest of the group, but now she fretted as the gnawing grew louder and the others stirred. Fangs were tearing at rotten wood, boring powerfully. They worked quickly, pausing only to eject fragments of splintered plank.

In four or five minutes the noises stopped, a tremor ruffling the perched birds. An unfamiliar draught was blowing, bringing something from outside which slithered eerily. The speckled hen screeched. In her mind she could see every inch of the enclosing hut: the nest-boxes behind the perch, the soiled slats, the red mites where the wood needed creosote. But she could not envisage the thing on the floor, the intrusive form – or the shape which joined it through the crude hole.

The hen house resounded with throaty nervousness. Squawking birds shifted anxiously, necks craned, wings fluttering. For a while the strangers did not move. Unseen yet tangible, they constituted an evil force in the air which dismayed the fowls. The hut had ceased to protect. It was no longer an asylum; it was a trap, and the speckled hen knew her kind had little chance in it.

They would panic. Their best resort was the perch

but, with the sureness of self-knowledge, the speckled bird knew they would panic, erupt blindly to the hut's constraining corners. The urge to fly thumped in her own breast. First one would take off, then the rest would go.

It was predictable. A scuffling on the slats and she could sense the hysteria, the tensed wings as the evil shifted and prowled invisibly. The birds would doom themselves. Already, their nervy clucking was tumultuous. They seesawed, feathers tossing. Tail plumes quivered. At last, a whirlwind in the gloom, a Rhode Island flew with a shriek. She crashed headlong into the planks, a sister following. In the ensuing chaos the intruders crouched patiently as wings pounded, plumes drifted, hens batted in terror from wall to wall. Only when the hens slid gasping to the slats did the mink move.

There was massacre. One by one, the necks of the birds were ravaged, feathers clotting on bloody laths like daub and wattle. The speckled hen, clawing vainly for a foothold atop a nest-box, slipped and fluttered to the floor in numbing fright. Dead fowls were everywhere. She landed on a limply-sprawled Leghorn whose gored gullet was warm and damp. Shrieking, the hen crashed to the far corner, sensed the lurking jaws, and flapped to where another victim floundered. Breathless with fear, she hit the wall beyond. Her neck throbbed. It was the last in the charnel house to be defiled.

The sky was brightening when the mink emerged. Gru, eyeing the eastern glimmer, licked bloody chops. 'Let the dwellers of the ridge count the corpses. Let them ponder the mark of the new regime.'

'The mark of Gru.' Her mate looked back at the hut.

'Before we head for the bunker we've another job.'

'The she-weasel's daughter?'

'The little fugitive. She skulks by the pond with the one-eyed ancient, full of impudence. Like her mother' – the cold gaze flicked to the oakwood – 'a trifling job.'

They were still in the orchard when Poacher stirred. He thought something had roused him, but it was quiet. The air was still and the birdsong, when it tentatively rose, bore a wistful note, an awareness of autumn beckoning. He turned painfully. Dawn streaked the window. There would be windfalls in the garden; Spanish chestnuts in the dew at the wood's skirt. It was a dawn to stride in, not sniff from his bed like a dying dog.

Time was cheating him. It seemed only yesterday syringa had bloomed, bees dwelt in the white cups. It seemed yesterday lime had poured scent from tall boughs now casting leaves on the cottage path. Now floodwater gleamed. Far off, the myriad dots of migrating wildfowl wheeled in great flocks. It was a morning to be ferreting. He viewed the wicket gate through a smeary pane. Incarceration was not living, for man or beast.

Spotting what he took for a black cat, he looked more carefully. It was not a cat but a mink – a gigantic mink. Another followed, brown, almost as monstrous, and the cause of his awakening came back to Poacher: the rumpus of frightened hens. He had no doubt, in that instant, what the mink had done. A massive anger welled in him, a weasel fury. It galvanized the spent frame to heaving effort. Somehow the man reached the threshold, despite his agony. His head was whirling, his body racked. He drove his legs forward. Rage alone was his strength – and the gun he held.

He saw no sign of the killers. They had gone towards the wood, he thought, the pond their first stop. Then by culvert and ditch to their marsh retreat. He squinted savagely. They were gorged, and would move with indolence. If he could stay on his feet he could still overtake them. His lips jerked. 'I'll have you.' Poacher's eyes searched the track. 'If it's the last thing I do,' he pledged, reeling insecurely, 'I'll have the pair of you.'

The bent and brute-like silhouette surprised the

barn-owl. Daylight fractured a grey sky with silver clefts. The owl watched thoughtfully. The shuffling scarecrow was a strange sight. Poacher had not attempted to dress himself. He had dragged on a jacket, pulled on boots; for the rest, he wore pyjamas and a cartridge belt. He was staggering, lurching like a sick ewe. Zig-zagging, he almost collided with the woodpile, veered wildly to the gibbet, clung a moment to its post, advanced again.

A flock of titmice, twitching briskly up the woodside, seemed to mimic his progress in jerky flight. When they vanished, the place was still, even thistledown undisturbed. There was silence, one of those hesitant moments in dawn's birth, a moist intertia which would lengthen now each morning as autumn neared. Summer's vigour was draining. In parts, meadowsweet still flowered, but pallidly, its odour much reduced. The tang of smouldering field-fires was everywhere.

The calm of nature was not echoed in Poacher's head. He breathed the smoke and, in his anger and pain, recalled another wood, another enemy. He squeezed the gunstock. Webs shimmered. Boughs shed the night's vapours in twinkling drips. He could still hear the bullets, the scream of shells. Yet this wood was sepulchral; it was briar, not barbed wire, that ripped his clothes. He caught no glimpse of mink and, vision misting, hugged a tree bole to stay afoot.

'I'm beat,' he thought. Then, despising the thought, he fumbled forward, torn by thorn and bramble hooks. Fallen poles, their rind stripped by rabbits, conspired to obstruct; burrs stuck to him. 'Chicken killers!' In the silt of a drying puddle he saw their prints and was charged with fresh fury. 'Poultry murderers!'

To the wren, he seemed to move almost blindly through the deep growth. Tangled thickets reared, black arbours where creatures would limp when winter crippled them. The blackness swallowed him and, when his senses returned, the man realized he had fainted, though not for long, since the damp of the ground had not worked into him. One hand was painful. Moving it, Poacher disturbed a spiked shell, the chestnut opening to release its polished fruit.

That did not change – the pleasure of childhood, rich and brown, like the stock of the gun which lay beside him. He eyed the chased silver buttplate and cursed himself. Time was racing again. The sun was rising. It ducked into the vault beneath a hem of foliage, gilding the soft mould. The wood stirred. Prowling pheasants sought its rays; small birds preened in them. Pigeons rustled. From the marsh, a curlew cried, another shade of Poacher's childhood. He tried to rise. He got as far as crouching, could do no more, and went down again.

Painfully, the man stretched an arm and pulled the gun to him. The scent of loam – inhaled close to the ground, as a weasel breathed it – inspired a ripple of strength, and Poacher started to crawl, to drag himself, the weapon braced in his elbow's crook.

Above, a few rooks flapped and cawed in the wood's roof. Since their young had flown, they slept away from the vale in their winter roosts. But each morning some returned, as if drawn by nostalgia, to the empty nests in the high crowns. There, in swaying, bedraggled nurseries, spiders lurked; and scraps of shell, yet to be ejected by autumn winds, bore witness to the passing of seasons and life itself.

Wonder said, 'D'you think the tribe's at Castle Mound? D'you think Kine's safe?' She had skipped brightly into the wood, pranced for One-Eye with elfin vanity and, fickle as a cloud, asked, 'Will he ever come back? What if something awful's happened? I daren't think of it!'

'Don't,' One-Eye said gruffly. 'He'll be all right.'

'How do you know?'

'He's had a lot of experience.'

'Not of the other land.' Of that hazy frontier of uncertainty, she thought with sudden anguish. She peered from the wood at the distant flats. Who knew what perils had faced him beyond the stream? It was not, like the home marsh, drained by dykes there. The great swamp was inundated, its trails drowned, its far slopes concealed in smoke. What did they know of the dangers, the mysteries of those slopes and their blue woods? 'Suppose,' she wailed, 'they never *do* get to Castle Mound?'

'It's Ford's country,' the other said brusquely. 'He'll see to it.'

'And if they do, they've still got the mink to fight!'

'That's what they went for.'

'Oh dear, One-Eye . . .'

'They're battling weasels. They've proved themselves.' His voice was irritable as he considered her. In a moment she would be unconcerned once more, full of tireless bounce. Unlike himself, she only worried in spasms, but either way her intensity wearied him. He was too old, too abidingly anxious since the tribe left. He said, 'There's nothing we can do, and chatter won't help.'

'No, of course.' She skipped away, unabashed. 'Just you rest. I'll keep an eye out. You can doze a while.'

She watched the sun glance the Moon Pond, picking out the mosquitoes and smaller gnats. Weed floated patchily and, where the rays touched, small night-closing lilies opened their petals; those under the bank still in sleeping balls. There was a thin layer of scum round their leaves. It clung, also, to dipping stems of bittersweet from a brambled promontory. The air of loneliness was undiminished by a solitary moorhen among the reeds. It was an immature specimen, brown and gawky, with a nervous twitch. Spotting Wonder, it raced a few yards then vanished beneath the water, leaving emptiness.

The place had evil memories for Kia's daughter. She preferred Poacher's garden. 'Has Kine always lived here?' she asked broodingly.

'You ask me questions in my sleep?'

'It's just that it's spooky, a dismal spot.' She shivered,

glimpsing the hole where her kin were butchered. Half one side of the willow had ossified. Lifeless limbs jutted ghoulishly, haunting the foliage of neighbours with brittle fingers. One branch had fallen. It lay, grey and rotting, on the bank beside a graveyard of lesser twigs. How much longer, she thought, before the rest fell? 'A tree of doom,' Wonder muttered, 'I don't know about a Life Tree. A thing of pestilence.'

'Like a chattering juvenile.' One-Eye stirred with a rumble. 'In death is life, and all life changes,' he rasped, 'except the endless chat of the uninformed.'

'I dare say you preferred it to silence when you were my age.'

'When you are *my* age, a wink of sleep's worth a month of words.'

'Then we're in the right spot, for it's quiet as a tomb.' She titivated her whiskers, musing audibly, 'I suppose I'll come here sometimes to think of my mother, but not to live here. It's morbid. I'd sooner settle near Poacher. He's been good to me.'

'Bah!' It was a paradox – weasel saved by weasel-killer – beyond the veteran's comprehension and he snoozed uneasily, thick with doubts. Once, rousing with a start, he imagined Wonder was still chatting, but she was gone, the wood peaceful, and curling up in the sun the old male slept again.

Rooks were winnowing. Kia's daughter tripped warily, less neglectful of caution than One-Eye feared. Of human habitation she was not frightened, but the nightmare of the pond had left her sharply distrustful of other hunters, of the pool itself. Neither sunshine nor the homely clatter of rooks allayed suspicion. She found the stillness of the water as disquieting as the pitchy morning shadows where nettles rose. She distrusted tree stumps with hidden dens in them. She longed for company. Above all, she longed for Kine, the dimly recalled assurance of his presence, and she never stopped willing his safe return.

She looked back towards One-Eye. He was fond

of her. He let her show off, but he quickly grew tired and slept a lot. Wonder chuckled at his grumbles. She gave a skip, became festooned in leaves of ivy, halted suddenly. Her ears were cocked and her eyes, amid the growth, were suddenly flinty, devoid of mirth.

There was a small glade ahead, a place where rabbits had scraped and brashings had once been tossed, crushed by a fallen birch pole, still tenuously rooted, and partly leafed. Not quite on the ground, the slanting pole made a bridge beneath which, from lane to pond, and in direct line for Wonder, advanced Gru and her consort with shuffling gait. The little weasel watched stonily. Then, in a frenzy of haste, she was retracing her steps by the pool's edge.

She had to rouse the sleeping One-Eye. Beyond warning the veteran, her mind failed; it was a vacuum. But as she flew through the herbage, the first awakening of battle, of weasel defiance, bristled in Wonder: the urge to turn, spitting and clawing, in fighting trim. She could hear the monsters behind her, moving clumsily, her mother's slayers, and loathing mounted. Hatred churned in her. She reached the old weasel stiff with vehemence.

'Think coolly,' he calmed her. 'Did they follow you?'

'I outpaced them. They'll get the scent. A black fiend and a brown one – gigantic brutes.'

'Gru and Liverskin.'

'Let's hope I face them as bravely as my mother did.'

'Don't be foolish.' His eye scanned the bank. 'We're not facing two grown mink. They'll be heading for the marsh. The tribe will deal with them.'

'Shan't we defend the wood?'

'By self-sacrifice – a bit of a kitten and a creaking veteran?' He raised his neck, nostrils flaring. 'They're coming, Wonder. We'll slip them. Keep close to me.'

The mink paused by the Life Tree. Their heads cranked slowly, seeking the weasels with a deliberation verging almost on dispassion, then froze on their target. Wonder shuddered. The terror of their last call came back to her, a clammy fear she had to fight from the depths like a dreadful fascination, a macabre spell. They were motionless, impassive as the grey roots of willow, their eyes measuring the weasels with piercing scorn. It seemed to Wonder no evil on earth could be more terrible, yet to run would be wrong. 'Kia fought,' she exclaimed. 'I must live up to her.'

'You must *live*,' snarled One-Eye. 'Kia died to leave you the gift of life.'

'Come,' Gru interrupted coldly. 'She has her mother's weasel spirit. She craves to make the bold gesture. We bring that gift to her.'

'And I spit in their faces,' Wonder hissed, temper boiling. 'You've seen the way I dance, One-Eye – my agility. Let them see what I'm made of – that I'm the daughter of Kine, the mink fighter.'

'Of Kine,' rapped One-Eye, 'who'll never know you again if you're provoked to rashness by them. Come with me, Wonder. Fight another day.'

'Fight!' Gru laughed. It was a laugh like bones being crunched. 'When did the one-eyed ancient last do battle?' She waited for a flutter of leaves to subside. Rooks were silent in the oaktops, listening agog. A bough trembled. The trees settled and Gru said softly, 'Come, small daughter of the wood, your blood is younger; show your weasel paces to Gru and Liverskin.'

'Don't listen.' One-Eye moved to intercept, but Wonder jinked, bounding nearer the monsters, where she started to whirl with spitfire fury. 'Wonder!' He watched in horror. 'I beg of you . . .'

Gru said, 'Silence. Let the small one come closer. Let her dance for us.'

The old weasel sprang forward. There was despair in his action, but he could not turn away. He charged cursing, blocked by Liverskin, and in a flash Gru had struck, bowling Wonder on her back, towering over the she-weasel, poised to stab.

One-Eye's notion of what followed was imprecise. He was aware of the orange flame which seemed to belch from a thicket, the crashing explosion, the flight of rooks. For an instant, mink and weasels stiffened as pellets whistled. Then four creatures were bolting their own ways. One-Eye did not see Poacher. He watched the bush as he ran but no one rose from it. It seemed a miracle – miraculous the gunshot had missed, he thought.

CHAPTER NINETEEN

THE screen of reeds along the river had passed its glory. High waters had muddied and tossed the clusters. In the grey dawn they made tousled shadows where half-veiled banks flanked the smooth reach. A few tall tapers of rushes stood proud, or floated downstream, felled by water-voles. The gnawed stems formed dark rafts. One had lodged near the shrew, who kept closely to the cover at the water's edge.

The night had been long for Scrat. As the moon had illumined the gliding current, the dwarf had skulked by tarnished reeds, peering at the pump-house with deepening dread. Guards had moved in the fastness. Foul airs had wafted. Sounds had come from clay depths which made his skin crawl. Despite which – through mist, moongleam and bat's squeak – Scrat had stood firm. He ached with nervousness.

Morning did not reprieve the mini-spy. The first mink appeared with the eastern light. It drifted on the stream like a log, curled slowly beneath the surface, then slid ashore barely a hop from Scrat. He watched it through the stems of his reedy hide. The tasselled sedges grew thickly by the concrete embrasure of the outlet valve. Here, the monster shook before climbing the bank to the square fort where, pausing briefly, it slipped into the foundations through a crumbling niche.

Quietly, the river brimmed coastwards at Scrat's side. It seemed, through the shrew's pinhead eyes, an enormous width. It swirled out of focus, was lost to him. Fibrous reeds, nudged by eddies, mumbled restlessly. Their jumpy patter distracted him and he was glad when a woodpigeon came to drink. For a while its gaze swivelled, then, lowering white-ringed neck, it dipped thirstily. It drank not as other birds, who sipped, but with a steady inflow, like cow or horse. Sated, it rose heavily, and Scrat was alone again.

Within minutes the Watchman had touched down. Prepared for danger, he glanced round beadily. But if he spotted Scrat's hide, he did not draw attention to it. 'Stay under cover.' The rook pretended to drink. 'They've started down from the mound. If it's safe on this side, they'll cross immediately.'

'Safe?' Scrat dithered.

'Keep still.' The rook mimed the chore of bathing. 'Just keep calm and report. Are the mink inside? Is there a guard on? Don't get in a fluster, just answer me.'

'Exactly – a c-calm report . . .' Lumps of weed floated past, groups of pale opaque bubbles. Scrat's mind floundered. Bunda was dead, half his clan with him. The shrew had barely survived, his nerves in tatters. A calm report? Any minute the stream would ruffle with weasels, and slaughter and mayhem would strew the bank. It was all right for the rook. If shrews could fly, how boldly Scrat would soar the shore demanding calm reports! What vaunting song wings instilled in even small birds! But the shrew was wingless, a flightless midget, and stiff with fright. He gulped. 'Yes, they're inside. Woe betide intruders, Watchman. There's no escape from the monsters' lair.'

'That's not my business, Scrat, nor yours. If Kine's mad enough . . .'

'Kine's unharmed?'

'He's come this far.' The rook scanned Castle Mound with eyes incomparably keener than the grey dwarf's. There was no sign of movement and, admiring the fieldcraft of the raiders, the bird was gripped by suspense despite his dour nature. This phase was critical. Without achieving surprise the tribe would be doomed, its efforts squandered. But if surprise were attained, there was, in the rook's view, a thin chance. 'I never thought so,' he said, 'yet it's possible now. Kine's just mad enough, and the tribe's behind him. *If* they get in unseen. It's up to you, dwarf.'

'Yes . . .' The shrew clenched tiny cusps. Small rings dimpled the water; fry were feeding. He watched an empty can pass, burnished by the morning sun, like a silver ship. The light was brilliant; it swam in dazzling shoals on the tide, bringing tears to his eyes when they searched the current. 'I'll do my best.' He cursed the weakness of his sight. 'I can't do more.'

'Listen carefully.' The rook was brisk again. 'They'll steer for the reeds. Stay where you are until they land. Let them muster, then, if it's clear, lead them straight to the rear of the fastness, to the breach you've found. That's all you do, Scrat.'

'Except run.'

'It's their war.' The Watchman braced himself to take flight. 'We'll have done our bit for them. What will happen inside is best not thought about.'

The tribe came down the slope in jinking file. Each weasel kept low, darting snake-like through grass and scrub. You could have passed at a few paces and missed the raiders. They followed ruts, and held to folds in the ground where growth arched over them. They were invisible. Below, across the river, the roof of the pump-house was a grey slab, bleak as a tomb. The weasels could see the casing, the great screw. They glimpsed the iron-capped outlet at the river's lip.

They had climbed the mound wearily; they came down rested, charged with purpose and fighting zeal. They were as quiet as they were swift. Every small visage showed fierce purpose. Kine, scouting ahead, gave a churring 'All clear', and they raced on stealthily. A faint whiff of the bunker drifted over the river. Near the bank they formed line, inching forward towards the brink.

'With luck,' said Ford, 'the brutes are sleeping off a night's work.'

'A night's plundering,' Kine said.

'We'll soon find out.'

'Let's hope Scrat's in position.'

'We can do without him,' Ford grunted, 'the timid animal.'

'But brave.' Kine thought of Scrat's marsh inquiries. 'Without the shrew we'll have to search for the labyrinth. I believe in him.'

'He could be dead, Kine.'

It was possible. Kine turned to the sedge groves from which the tribe would breast the river. He did not like to think of the dwarf dead, but there had been many deaths – would be more as the sun rose. Revenge was close. He eyed the sedges. The morning of truth had dawned. 'If Scrat's dead,' he said, 'the rook will return. If not – if the rook flies away – the dwarf will be waiting. We go straight across.'

They scrambled to the groves, and the stripling from the heath slipped through the tough stems. He searched the stream impatiently. Kine, observing his tension, said, 'Easy, Young Heath, you'll get a swim in a moment.'

'This is it, Kine. My spine's tingling.'

'You're as good as a veteran.' Kine scanned the sky. 'Just keep behind me in the labyrinth, and stay cool. Remain close to Ford and me; we'll take care of you.'

'I can fight. I'm not worried.' His nose twitched back to the stream, towards the distant block which marked the fastness. 'We'll shock them, Kine. They won't know what's happening. There's just one thing . . .'

'Yes?'

'When it's over – will you visit the heath? I'd like to show you where I live. It's a fine land.'

Kine nodded. 'I'm sure it is.'

'The Watchman!' Ford was eager. 'There's the Watchman, he's climbing now.' Bright eyes followed the rook as he rose cumbrously from the far bank, wings labouring. He seemed to climb endlessly before making a circle above the stronghold. 'Come on,' Ford willed him, 'we can see you. Get on – what are you waiting for?' Slowly, the black shape wheeled, heaved north and flew off towards the ridge through the gathering light. 'Good for the midget!' Ford flashed his teeth. 'Let's get into them!'

Kine thrust his head from the sedges. Either side of him, pointed weasel noses, like the tips of levelled lances, stabbed from concealment. 'Go!' he rasped, launching forward. 'Keep down in the water, and make it fast!' He heard the soft swish of diving, was submerged for an instant, then surfaced, stroking powerfully. Around him, swimming weasels, living lance-tips, were surging for the distant shore.

The river was perfect for the assault: full, yet so smooth it seemed not to have awakened, but to glide in slumber through the silvery morning without a frown on it. Here and there a snag in the current, where plant or twig broke the gloss, was stroked away as if the day caressed it with tranquil hands. Kine swam thankfully. Drifting leaves crossed his bows with lazy carelessness. Shoals of muddy-hued fish ghosted under him. Abeam, the tribe cleaved the pale reach with rippling wakes.

At last, Kine believed, fortune had smiled on them. Storm and fire were behind. They had survived and, at the critical moment, their luck had changed. Scrat was waiting. Their final obstacle, the river, flowed favourably. As an omen of battle, it could only be good. He reviewed the course. They had been carried slightly downstream, and he swung against current to offset the drift.

The pump-house, high on the bank, was unmistakable. Lower, where weeds proliferated, the rendezvous agreed with the shrew was less evident. Each broad-bladed clump looked much alike, and Kine sought the valve emplacement to guide his eye. Even that, partly screened by sedges, was not easy to spot until the tribe reached midstream, when its shadowy gape became conspicuous. Water lapped the embrasure, half-concealing the throat and its hinged lid. Time had mellowed it. Incrusted with slime and rust, the four-foot cap merged darkly with the riverbank. Somewhere close to the outlet was the landing point.

'What's that?' Ford called quietly across the water. 'What was that, Kine?'

'Where?'

'From the bunker. A rumbling growl.'

Kine stopped paddling and listened.

Ford said, 'There! Hear the voice? They must have awakened. Swim faster, Kine.'

'Wait.' Kine heard the voice. It mocked his sense of changed fortunes and rising luck. It was the voice of disaster, and Kine, treading water, fought the sudden confusion which filled his mind. The engine whirred. Activated by the electrode in the dyke, the motor revved, engaged the screw with a jolt, rumbled steadily as the pump churned. Slowly, by the ton, liquid began to climb the great spinner from the marsh drains. Reaching the head, the flow would punch through the throat, force the valve, burst out across the stream with raging turbulence. Kine despaired. 'It's the voice of the machine. When the water hits the cap . . .'

The raiders had faltered.

'Can we make it?' hissed Ford.

'No time. We'd swim straight into it.'

'Then we can't get back, either.' Ford eyed the embrasure. 'I came for Gru and I'll get her. I'm going on.'

Kine was turning. Still the water was peaceful, gliding smoothly, but the throb of the pump beat with cataclysmic menace. Kine had watched the stream's fury when the dykes disgorged. Each throb brought it nearer. 'We can't get back but we must get as far from the force as possible. Go with the current, it's our only chance.' He saw weasels striking in all directions, swimming frantically. Ford alone maintained course. 'Don't be mad!' Kine's voice ripped over the surface. 'You'll meet it headlong!'

'I came to do battle.'

'You can't fight the outpour.'

Their exchange was lost in a rattle like death itself. As the force behind the valve began to challenge that outside, the hinged cap juddered violently, jets sizzling from the edges to form glittering fountains above the bank. They pattered down, like the first drops of a storm – and Kine saw Ford approaching the leaping jets.

Then, for a moment, the lid flipped, a gaping mouth belched and closed again. It was premature, but the discharge served warning on the calm stream. Shooting out from the embrasure, a rolling wave struck the current side-on, curled angrily and, boiling underwater, subsided only at the far bank. It threw the weasels aloft, dropping them so abruptly that Kine was seized and spun wildly in the undertow. He surfaced breathlessly. All around, the tribe floundered. Ford had disappeared. In the fleeting stillness which resumed, Kine heard a mounting roar and saw the iron cap first shudder then fly aside as a consolidated deluge from the screw arrived.

'Downstream,' he cried, 'with the current, and swim for life!'

The outpour burst on the river in a bellowing, boiling mass which seethed with explosive force. Tons of water, thousands of gallons, fought for freedom, punching beneath the surface in sludgy jets, leaping in foaming columns, churning in mammoth blisters and spitting bubbles. It was an evil brew, heaving and rolling with awesome vehemence, lashing reeds, raging out from the bank to consume the stream.

Behind its shock waves, a froth of scum marked the head of the outflow, thrust on turbulent ripples from bank to bank. Writhing and belching, the torrent swept the tide sideways, curled it back, sucked and dragged it relentlessly round again. Tongues of scum described at first sweeping circles, then tighter arcs. Knots of turmoil broke the surface. Still the throat raged, now creating a maelstrom which spanned the flow.

Scrat had run as spume enveloped him. Glancing back from the top of the bank, he glimpsed the cataclysm and ran again. In that fleeting glance he observed the tribe as helpless flotsam, specks on the deluge, and knew the raid was a lost cause. He saw one body, belly-uppermost, legs like masts in a hurricane. The pink gape of a lifeless mouth rose up. It drowned a second time. The specks were dwindling. Some writhed as the waters tossed them, their struggles oddly heavy.

The rook looked back as the pump spewed. Too far from the stream to see the animals, he watched the smooth ribbon torn by violence, and saw the boiling whirlpool which quickly formed. In its grey eye, the rook thought, was calamity, but the bird could do nothing. He hoped the weasels had crossed. They had more chance with the mink than in the maelstrom. Rooks flapped atop the oakwood. His job was done.

Kine was battling to stay afloat. Seething masses of water snatched him under, and he fought repeatedly to gain air. He could hear the pump throbbing, the grinding of the screw. Then his head was roaring and, swamped by the torrent, he sank again. He rose slowly to float semi-submerged and more than half drowned. He was drifting in a circle. The spinning current had gripped him. The vortex beckoned.

Ahead, a limp weasel body was revolving at greater speed. Nearing the guzzling hole, it spun wildly a moment and vanished suddenly. Kine coughed scum from his mouth. He had to break the whirling clutch, but his limbs were leaden and, paddling feebly, he continued to drift with coiling froth towards the cauldron's eye. Straining, he roused his sodden forelegs to stronger efforts. The stream of foam began to pass him. He was holding his own. But that was all – and, as his last despairing reserve of strength failed, the tow bore him on with increasing force.

There was no escape. It was, Kine thought, the end of all things in one spewing, tempestuous stroke of fate. He recalled that distant meeting at the gibbet in hay-scented gloom, the galaxies witness to the tribe's pledge: 'Death to weasel-killers!' He thought of One-Eye, rain dripping in puddles. 'You've a war to plan.'

Kine recalled them: the brave, trembling Scrat at the marsh gate when swifts were hawking and corn was golden. 'I understand . . . Kia was good to me, Kine . . . It's a spy's job.'

And the stripling: 'Please, Kine' – how young he had looked beside the Moon Pond – 'let me march with you. Let me be there – able, if I survive, to spread word of it. I don't mind danger. I don't think I mind death if it comes to that.'

They had planned the bold stroke, dared the consequences. Ford had been indomitable. Kine remembered the swamp trail as the flood rose. 'Wet!' Ford's phlegmatic comment had been typical: 'You're in a bog, not a garden of roses. Once you're wet, you're wet.'

And the dead were dead. They had been trampled, asphyxiated, burned alive; corpses left among sheep bones to trace the path. They had not complained. Their spirit had brought the tribe within a snap of its purpose. Fate had thwarted their mission. He drifted rapidly. It was all over, swept to nothing – the intention, the strategy, the sacrifice. The monsters lived, and the valley would quake to the rule of Gru.

He whirled faster, tumbling, gyrating closer to the hole in the spinning pool. It grew darker. The vortex of the maelstrom sucked greedily. The weasel's head drummed. The torrent whipped downwards, sucking him. Scum and twigs were being swallowed ahead of him. In the end, Kine supposed, the hole took everything.

CHAPTER TWENTY

TWO fluorescent strips gave the only light. In the centre of the cubicle, iron grey above a dustless floor, the electric motor was now inert. It was not the largest power unit on the marsh – some pump stations had twin screws and took more turning – but it shifted thirty thousand gallons a minute, a ton of water a second, when the spinner churned.

The engineer closed the door and stood eerily pallid in the robot light. Metal cases lined walls, some with dials in them. He admired the shipshape order, up-to-date as the gadgets in his own digs. He took a pride in the system, its efficiency. The spruce engine-room was immaculate. Only the speck of dirt his boots had dropped soiled this environment.

He worked unhurriedly. Reading the meters, he noted the figures on his report sheet, checked the fuses and tested driving belts. Then, replenishing the grease-pipe feeder, he swept the floor, turned the lights off, went outside again. It was like leaving a time machine. The valley hit him with untamed vistas and wild sounds. Locking the door, the young man surveyed the scene with ambivalence. It had a careless, diverse beauty whose logic defied him and which, unlike the motor, owed little to man's design. The engine was predictable. That had the power of seventy horses and was obedient. The vale was moody, as teasing as the girl herself.

Descending the bank, he checked the outlet valve. The pump had run that morning. Blobs of froth in still water at the edge of the stream told of the turbulence. Lighting a pipe, he watched the river as it flowed, ruminating on the spell she had cast on him. Or was it the place, with its brooding savagery? Why the cottage girl? The town was full of comely females with friendly eyes, yet he was haunted by old Poacher's scrubbing minx! Smoking thoughtfully, he returned to the pick-up and climbed into it.

As he did so, a scrap of velvet scuttled out of the reeds and crossed in front of him. Grinning, he let the gear in, swerved past the shrew and, shock-absorbers protesting, reached the marsh gate. A family of partridge rose ahead, young and adult birds. The young were well advanced. He watched their wings stab as far as the hedge then rest, to glide shallowly. Topping the rise, the driver accelerated, turned at the barn then braked suddenly. The girl had loomed without warning, and he wound down the window with feigned alarm.

Her own was real. 'The hens!' she wailed. 'I went to open the hut and the mink had been. It's a slaughter-house. Not a single bird living. It's horrible.'

'You've told the old fellow?'

'He's gone!' Her voice soared. 'I let the dog out, went in and – I've hollered till I'm hoarse. He isn't anywhere. Poacher's disappeared.'

'Is that possible?' He gave the cottage a glance and eyed her doubtfully. 'I thought he could barely move. Where've you looked for him?'

'All over.' Her anxiety was shrill. 'He's gone, I'm telling you!'

'I thought you said he was . . .'

'Never mind what I said,' she shrieked back through the window. 'We've got to look for him.'

The young man scowled. Reserving comment, he switched the engine off. Last time, he reflected, she had declared her independence by flouncing away from him. Now, as suddenly, it was 'we', and no sign of contrition, but her anguish was compelling, and he got out to join her with greater satisfaction than he showed. 'We'd better see, he said.

'He's not there.' She dogged his heels up the path. 'Oh, my God,' she muttered distraughtly, 'he's always been here, for as long as I remember, with his hens and his ferrets. Part of the valley. He can't play this trick. He belongs with us.'

'You've looked in every room?'

She said impatiently, 'Everywhere. Poacher's not there. I've got eyes, you know.'

'Yes.' They were wide and disturbed, the eyes of a sorceress. 'I know,' he told her, going inside all the same. 'You've looked, now I'll look. Then we'll be certain.'

He stood in the parlour. The low-beamed room was shadowy, heavy with old wood and dark cavities. He was not accustomed to the ghosts of ancient timbers, or mellow furniture. They smelled of age. Small pieces, steeped in private experience, glowered at him: a chipped jug, the burnished medals, a fading photograph in an ebony frame. He sensed the past, bygone hearth-beasts and peasants, and was hesitant. The girl fidgeted. Slowly, almost on tiptoe, the young man advanced.

The den enveloped him. It was as redolent of mystery as the marsh, thick with the spirit of Poacher. But unoccupied. The scullery was empty, and the back yard, too. The girl whined restlessly. 'Didn't I tell you? I told you, didn't I?'

'I'm going upstairs.'

'We're wasting time.' But she followed him cat-like up the steps and crouched in the attic as he looked round. He had to stoop. There was a chair, a rug on the boards, the dishevelled bed. 'Well?' the girl said.

'They could have taken him away,' he suggested. 'Maybe the doctor insisted.'

'There's been no ambulance.'

'You could have missed it.'

'He wouldn't have gone with them.'

'I don't know – if he felt bad enough.' Stubborn men, dying animals, ran out of fight at last. The young man's head brushed the roof. He could feel the ghosts there, hear their sighs and oaths in the cottage loft. Generations must have sheltered between those eaves, bred and perished there. He imagined cordy field women, woodmen, children like mice in thatch. For centuries such people had shared the vale with its wild creatures, surviving and dying on the same terms. He seemed almost to hear them, their moaning and squalling and guttural growls. Then, aware the girl was watching, he said, 'They may simply have grabbed him for his own good.'

'They'd have needed an army.' For a moment she pondered then stooped abruptly to the bed, hair thrown forward by the movement. 'The gun,' she breathed, 'it's not here. I hadn't noticed. He's got the gun with him.'

'Listen . . .'

'The dog – barking in the wood.'

'Come on, it may mean something!'

'Dear God, the fool,' the girl muttered, 'the rotten imbecile!'

The body lay on a pile of rubbish the river had washed up. For a while it looked as dead as the torn sedges and soggy twigs which formed its bier. Then a leg twitched, the mouth gasped faintly. Seconds later, the creature jerked, assumed a groggy but lifelike posture and shook a damp head.

Kine shuddered. Sight came dimly. He recognized the cove and the river's reach. Resting on the litter, he groped for memory. He remembered the maelstrom, spinning downwards in the hole, the black throat. Hope had died as the bowels of the cauldron sucked implacably. He had lost consciousness. His next recollection was indistinct. It was dark. He was still immersed but the drag had relented and, lungs bursting, he had started to fight again. He was rising, breaking surface. He remembered no more, except the quietness. The pump had stopped, and he must have been swept to the riverbank.

Feebly now, he crawled out of the reeds. The bank was slimy with scum, and leaves dripped on him. The sun had gone, the morning's promise blotted by dull clouds. Kine looked for other weasels. When none appeared, he started for the home wood, churring dismally. A thin mizzle blurred the marsh and his feet dragged.

A lapwing screamed. The cry spurred others to flight and, for some moments, the flock wheeled before settling, damp and unwelcoming, where the path rose. In the bramble hedge moist berries were overripe. The flies which sucked them had an alien glamour, with peacock abdomens. A scarlet leaf, like the cheek of a toper, blazed unhealthily. Kine shuffled. There was no threat in his step and the rabbits which watched him were contemptuous. The limp tail of the weasel signalled wretchedness. Their disesteem was conveyed in browsing lethargy.

Up the slope a tractor turned, charging misty rain. Kine scarcely noticed the derv fumes which fouled his tongue. Ahead, the plough drew glistening folds in the brown tilth. He plodded alongside, reminded of winter and the tyranny which would compound the frosts. Nothing more could challenge Gru. She was omnipotent. Gulls followed the tractor. A pair of crows, swarthy pirates, stalked the ridged soil. At last, by the stunted ash near the wood, One-Eye growled a greeting to the wanderer.

'You're safe.' The old animal sighed. 'It's been a long wait.'

Kine nodded. Safe and desolate. Beneath the ash tree of potent memory. He regarded it. It was hard to think of the spot as a bower of ecstasy, once resounding to the trumpeting of wild geese. Now the arbour was gloomy, bark weeping as rain seeped from branch to bough. A pool had collected on a shelf of fungus, overrunning in steady drips. The twisted grey trunk was doleful. He gulped back his emotion. 'It was a long trek.'

'An epic.' The single eye searched him gravely. 'You can rest at last.'

'Later.' Kine shook off the dampness. Later he

would sleep, for only sleep could bring forgetfulness, but the truth must be admitted, the news shared, before he dragged it ignominiously to some niche with him. He met the other's gaze. The sage seemed older, whiter than he recalled, and Kine doubted a winter was left in him. The old warrior was living his last campaign. The realization came with sudden and bitter clarity, and news of the disaster stuck in Kine's throat.

'You don't need to tell me,' he heard One-Eye growl quietly. 'I know what happened, and I'm proud. You would have vanquished them. All you needed was luck. It was a bold attempt.'

'A fiasco. I failed you, One-Eye – failed all of them.'

'On the contrary,' rasped One-Eye, 'you led them brilliantly.'

'I certainly led them.' He turned away, his ears flat. 'Oh yes, I led them. Led them over the river. Led them to Castle Mound. And then' – his voice was a hiss – 'led them back to the river and drowned them, One-Eye. I drowned the tribe. I led them back to the river and – that was my boldness, the guilt I bring you. That's my news of the raid and my damning guilt.' There was no reply. The tree dripped. The drip was steady, monotonous, insistent as the question which began to nag. He turned slowly to One-Eye. 'You *knew*?' he said.

'That none could have led with greater worthiness.'

'That the tribe perished?'

'Some perished,' growled One-Eye. 'Some returned before you did. Some may yet return.'

'Survivors?'

'They've straggled back.'

Kine felt the prick in his cheeks as relief stirred. Rising slowly on his haunches, he towered the long weasel neck and nosed the wet murk intensely, peering into it. There were shapes in the mizzle which might have been comrades or merely clumps of vegetation. 'Ford?' One was heaving towards him. He could barely pronounce it. 'That's not *you*, Ford?'

Ford laughed, thumping him. 'Who else? What were you saying on the river? I lost the gist of it.'

'That you were mad.' Bless the martyrs for Ford! 'That you were wholly and impossibly mad, Ford!'

'Then you were right, my friend, for I'd have taken them, fought them alone, if the tide hadn't swept me like a drowned bug.' Ford threw a paw, sparring clumsily. 'I was mad all right,' the bog-weasel granted, 'but unsinkable.'

'Indestructible,' said Kine, 'I might have known.' A breeze caught the mist, invading the ash tree with clammy breath. 'It's bad, Ford,' he said, perspective returning. 'The tribe's a remnant. Too many have died, too much sacrificed. As a fighting force we're spent. The vale's lost to us.'

'Not on your life.'

'Ask One-Eye.'

The old weasel shook his head. He was spared the need to reply by a commotion in the hedge and someone shrilled, 'It's Young Heath. The heath-weasel's safe. Let him through, he's exhausted.' Kine raced up to him. 'Lie still and recover. You're safe. Just rest for a moment. You're all right now.'

'The waves, Kine . . .'

'Don't worry.'

'I couldn't get to the stronghold. I tried, but I was carried away. Did we succeed, Kine?'

'Don't worry, you're safe. The pump defeated us all. You did well enough.' He watched the stripling revive. The rain had stopped. Far off, a great curtain of sunshine swept down, vanished, broke anew on the ploughland through scudding cloud. He heard the roar of the tractor as the shares bit the earth. The little group of survivors flinched. One-Eye looked towards the wood. He was hesitant, yet the old weasel had to speak, for at any time *she* might come, blunder into them, and Kine was unready for another shock. One-Eye glanced at him.

It should not have been difficult. And yet the veteran

223

had found words more readily in defeat than for the tidings still unrevealed. One-Eye braced himself.

Kine was saying, 'You did well, Young Heath. You should never have been with us; that was my fault. I take the blame for it. But you did well.' There was a catch in his voice. 'Praise the heroes, you're alive. And may others yet follow. It's not impossible.'

'It's possible,' One-Eye forced himself to utter. 'We must hope. Meanwhile, I have to speak of more than hope – of a miracle. I have to speak of a child of the tribe long thought lost, but returned like a star in the darkness to lift our hearts. A sign from the heavens, Kine. I have to warn you, for she comes at any moment. I'm expecting her.'

'She?' said Kine.

'Her?' The others were curious.

And Wonder stepped from the wood's edge.

Expecting only One-Eye, she came unselfconsciously, fey and dainty as a goblin, small snout high so her snowy bib dazzled, her arched back flashing, prancing skittishly. Here and gone in the herbage, she came unhurriedly, pausing to digress where some item took her interest. Once, she showed her dash in a bouncing sprint, crouched briefly in shadow, then danced again. Once, she climbed a stump, disappearing in the ivy which covered it. Popping out, she dropped lightly to earth, froze prettily, decided all was clear and made her neat way.

By the ash tree the weary remnant of the tribe watched her, mesmerized. She was, in the eyes of the stripling, a contemporary of dazzling charm. He chose the veteran's word for Wonder – 'A star,' he breathed.

Ford gawped at the vision. It was a long and testing time since the bog-weasel had seen her like, and he hung on each step, gazing slack-jawed at the spruce little female through glazed eyes. She came on through burdock and fox-tail grass. She was a wraith, a lump in Ford's heart, a haunting memory which rolled back the summer. She was the reincarnation of a heroine, he told himself.

Tired and battered, admiring survivors edged forward. Wonder halted. She had not seen them but sensed their surveillance and held herself in balance, poised and businesslike. Her eyes panned the grasses. Her alert head was high, forelegs straight, spine slanted to quarters prepared for quick flight. Every line proclaimed her hunting pedigree, her weasel trim. She was the spit of Kia, and Kine, faint with astonishment, gazed in awe. He had seen her double so often on that green slope: played and stalked with her, watched her ripen with his progeny. The likeness was uncanny. It was not possible.

Only one tiny soul had caught Kia's character. He still ached when he thought of the diminutive kitten, the imp of the litter, Kia's mischief in her. She would have grown to be – but that was impossible. None had lived.

He watched the female sniff warily. 'One-Eye?' Her call was apprehensive. 'Are you there, One-Eye? What's happening?'

'I'm here.' The veteran nudged Kine towards her. 'There's someone to meet you. He's coming out now.'

Kine went slowly, keeping low, as was the way between strangers, nose inquisitive. Pausing, he looked again at her. She had drawn back a shade and, suspicious of his manner, showed her teeth to him. She was not timid. He must, he thought, have presented a daunting front, haggard from the ordeals of the trail, begrimed by scum, yet she stood her ground so like Kia that his pulse jumped. She had Kia's snarl. It dared him to believe – to accept a miracle.

He took another step.

'Kine?' She was doubtful. Then, 'It is!' The snarl vanished and Wonder cried, 'It *is*! *It is!* You've come back, Kine – come back to me!'

He drank in her musky scent, the print of family. Next instant she had bounded forward and it was

Kine's turn to snarl, rebuff her lack of restraint, for it was not the style of the wild to accept familiarity before the proprieties of status had been observed. She would have none of it. 'Oh Kine,' she sang, 'I pulled your tail once, remember? I bit your ears! And you're back – I've found you again, Kine. Come, romp with me!' Kine dodged her, eyes misting. They skipped apart. For a moment the two animals seemed hypnotized. Then they fell on each other, tumbling, rolling, as the others inched nearer with twitching snouts.

CHAPTER TWENTY-ONE

WONDER told him, 'It's perfect here.'

She gave a skip, moving close to him. They were walking in the warmth, Kine's woes briefly forgotten in the joy of her. The grass was deep, lush with the last throw of summer, the path brilliant where sun glanced on shale and flint. Dragonflies basked on the stones, flitting up as the weasels approached and flying ahead to land again, shades of coral and lapis in their thin stems. The air was dense with that special pungency which daisies emit in certain atmospheres.

'Weasel country,' said Kine, 'since the birth of our kind. We've always hunted here.'

'You must teach me the secrets – the secrets of the mole and the rabbit's stop.'

'The secrets are endless and everywhere.' The valley was steeped in them. There were a hundred signs, a thousand mysteries. Kine could teach her the way of the badger and the yearning message of the vixen's howl. He could talk of mayflies swarming, partridge jugging, the adder's venom, the drumming which earned the snipe in summer the name of air-goat. He could tell of moonless nights when the owl stalked, and of strange banshee wailing in black bowers.

He could tell of the hedgehog's nocturnal prowl, of the jay planting acorns, of legless lizards which sloughed their tails if you grabbed them. Kine could tell of the tooth-clan and talon-clan. He knew the marches of furred midgets, the marsh haunts of feathered giants. Wonder might learn of the vale in its every mood from him. He thought of hot days, bright butterflies, steers with stockings of mud after wallowing; and of days when frost mantled hawthorn and the levels froze. He could have told all. Kine could have taught her the secrets of the territory, but to what end? 'You can't live here,' he told her. 'The war's lost.'

'If you can, I can.'

'I don't know about me.' He had thought only of Wonder since his return. 'But I know *you* can't. The line of Kia must survive. There's no place for my daughter under tyranny.' He did not look at her. It was too difficult. He looked at pastures, the noble canopies of great oaks. It was a cruel fate – to have found her and lost her birthright at a stroke, her valley heritage. The irony was bitter, but he would not have Kia's daughter bow to Gru's regime. He said as casually as possible, 'Young Heath will be going home. He's your age and he admires you. You could go with him.'

Wonder laughed. 'Now why should I want to do that? It's you I looked for. What would I want with a younger male?'

'You'd find out.' When the wild geese returned. 'Besides,' he told her, 'it's not far from here.'

'*Tchk*,' said Wonder. She took a step and said with petulance, 'I should think you'd be the last to suggest it. After the joy of our reunion! I should think you'd insist that I stayed with you.'

'I might come as well.' He hardly believed it, yet nothing could be dismissed. As things had turned out, emigration was an option. Kine had scorned it before, but the time for scorn had passed. The tribe was smashed. When its few survivors left, Gru would colonize the Moon Pond. There would be no safety in the valley, no place for scorn in his repertory. He had to find a home for Wonder. 'I *might* come,' he insisted. 'In any case, I'll be near. I've got to know you're secure. Your future's paramount.'

'Don't be stupid.' She eyed him with affection. 'You know you're not going to leave. As if you would! You were born here, so was I. I'll take my chances as Kia did.'

He knew better than to argue: she was too like her mother. 'We'll see,' he said.

228

Wonder purred smugly. 'Yes, we'll see. Now I'm going to Poacher. Will you come with me?'

He stopped in his tracks.

'I told you,' she added, 'he's been good to me.'

'I want nothing of Poacher.' He regarded her gravely. 'I know his craftiness. Poacher's kind built the gibbet, martyred the heroes with trap and gun. I've spent my life opposing Poacher. I'll not visit him.'

'One-Eye came with me.'

'Be wise.' His tone was reproachful. 'Forget the poaching man.'

She looked thoughtful. For a moment she hesitated then, shrugging, turned away from the cottage track and went into the wood instead. Kine caught up with her. 'You're wise, Wonder, weasel wise. Man's another animal.' They ducked through thickets towards the pool. The woodland light was a crystal green, like verdigris, where they cantered, and Wonder beamed. She showed no sign of vexation. 'Of course,' she murmured, stepping lightly, 'it's over now, but he did save my life. I don't think you understand. I can't leave him out here without a last call.'

'Poacher – here?'

The trace was faint but Kine smelled burnt cordite and, halting suddenly, found himself faced by the twin tubes. They gaped from the herbage with a grey metallic gleam of sullen ugliness. The only guns he had seen had been in the hands of men, not at close range, but he knew the smell of shooting and what confronted him. The muzzle was so close he could have pushed his nose into either of the barrels from where he stood. His hiss was furious.

'It's safe,' she calmed him. 'There's no danger now.'

Kine edged round the barrels, apprehensively skirting the wooden stock.

It lay where germander grew, snaked by brambles. He breached the tangle uneasily. His spine was bristling. Wonder was naive; her assurances glanced off him. His nostrils quivered. Something pale and forked, like the inverted foot of a vast bird, loomed stiffly in his path. There were five claws, bent up as if stilled in the act of clutching, each almost as thick as his own neck. It was a hand. He could have curled up in the palm. Hooked and withered, the fingers shimmered. He drew back. It was a cold and age-knotted human hand.

The great bough of the arm stretched away from the weasel to where a head, obscured partly by vegetation, lay on the mould. Poacher's twisted trunk sprawled like a fallen tree. 'He won't move,' Wonder whispered. 'The poaching man's dead. He won't move again.'

Kine inched closer to the bulk of his old foe. The scale and unfamiliar intimacy staggered him. He was overwhelmed. Kine had known the man as a dim shape in the dawn, a scarecrow figure with nets and ferrets; as a shadow in a window, or stooped across meadow, gun at readiness. He had known the smell of him, the outline of Poacher by bush or hedge. But those were abstracts. The concrete mass he confronted was another thing. Each line of feature, each knuckle and vein was a monument.

At that moment a rambler, lost in the wood, might quietly have paused and watched an odd scene. The body lay not far from the burrow so often plundered for rabbits, a bedraggled form around which, almost with reverence, the two small predators sniffed and scuffled like dwarfs at a giant's wake.

Respect mingled with distaste in Kine's sentiments. Poacher had been a rival of worthy cunning. In death the colossus unexpectedly affected him. It was as if size somehow amplified mortality. The weathered parchment on a cheek-bone, scratched by thorn, was stained with dark blood. Kine examined the sightless eyes. They were larger than a ewe's; the mouth, partly open, was a shadowed cave. He could have climbed into a pocket of the threadbare jacket and turned round comfortably. No carcase he had seen was so formidable. Its very lifelessness daunted him, it's massive impotence. It was as empty of soul as a snared rabbit.

The power had vanished, reclaimed by the valley, the living woods.

Wonder said, 'I owe my life to him. I couldn't pass by while he was here.'

'You knew?'

'He didn't move after the shot which drove off Gru and Liverskin.'

'Poacher dead!' It was said without elation, as if somehow the fact meant a loss to Kine. Like the barn-owl, Poacher had always existed, an adversary, yet so much part of life that it now seemed reduced. 'He belonged here, a valley animal. He had the venom of an adder . . .'

'He fed me, Kine.'

'Ah well – it's no place to linger.' He broke off, nose working. 'We're not alone,' he churred softly. 'Into the Life Tree! We've company.'

Wonder turned. 'It's the terrier.'

Peering from the hollow they watched the dog approach, sniff round the thicket and find the body. For a while the animal was nonplussed. Frustrated, he scratched up leaves, began to whine then, dismayed, set up a repeated bark.

The girl crouched by the body for a long time and, when she rose, one knee of her jeans was muddied by the moist ground. But she was calm – calmer, the young man thought, than she had been at the cottage – and her eyes were dry. She was resigned now, released from doubt. 'God in Heaven,' she sighed, 'the doctor warned the fool.'

'I'll call the doctor.'

'No.' She bent, fastening a button on Poacher's jacket. He supposed she was used to death's rawness – death in fur and feather, hedgerow and chicken coop. 'No hurry, let him rest,' she said from the germander. 'He always wanted to die here. Leave the gun by him.'

'He got a shot off.' Her companion had opened the breech and produced the cartridge. The gun was steadying. It felt true in his hands, light and balanced, as alive as the form on the ground was dead. 'He fired one. At the mink, perhaps.'

'And missed. There's nothing to show. Missed with his last shot.'

'No matter.'

'It would have mattered to Poacher.' She caught the dog and held it to her so the three of them – girl, terrier and corpse – seemed locked in privacy.

The young man felt no resentment. He could wait now. He eyed the trees, the thick columns and weathered bark. For the first time he noticed that vertical gardens grew on tree trunks: beds of spongy moss side-by-side with grey lichens in tiny round pads and crinkled beards. It had the quality of fantasy, all of it, yet he was there beneath the spell – as at school he had succumbed to the spell of verse.

Stones have been known to move and trees to speak;
Augurs and understood relations have
By maggot-pies and choughs and rooks brought forth
The secret'st man of blood.

'You didn't know him.' Her voice came from the brambles. She said, cheek to the dog's jowl, 'We were fond of him. We knew the beggar.' Her eyes were moist. 'Once,' she said, voice fading then starting again with greater steadiness, 'once, when I was small, I found a young bird. It had fallen from its nest in an apple tree. A missel-thrush. The nest was far out on a brittle bough. Poacher squirmed along the bough and replaced the bird. He risked his neck. And he saved the little weasel. I loved the idiot.'

She put the dog on the ground. 'He cussed,' she gulped, 'like a sore-nosed badger. He meant no harm by it. How he cussed that old willow! It had its way with him.'

'He had his own way.'

'I don't know – I've known rummer things.'

The man shrugged. Leaves were murmuring. '"*Trees*

to speak",' he reflected. It was rum, all right – the corpse, a patch-eyed terrier, a tree of life that brought death in a glade. A grieving girl-witch. He looked around, and a rook, with sidelong eye, returned his scrutiny. Something stirred in a recess by the pool. 'Shakespeare,' he explained. 'Read it at school. Came back to me.'

'Yes?' She looked up mistily.

'"*Stones have been known to move and trees to speak*".'

'He used to read. He was a rough old fool, but he'd got books. Grimed where his thumbs went. I seen them when I tidied. He was a dark horse.'

'A secret man.'

'Yes, that.' Her voice was husky. 'A secret man. Poacher could snare a pike with a copper noose. And snitcher eels. I've seen him lash an old sickle to a pole and go a-snitchering. Secretive as a fisher bird, but a conserving man. He took what he needed, no more – save sometimes a supper for dad and me. He wasted nothing, polluted nothing, despoiled no place meant for God's beasts. He left the valley as he found it, creatures flourishing.'

'As well he died before the mink got a grip on it.'

'He'd have stopped them. If he'd kept his strength, he'd have dealt with them.' She stepped to the pond's edge, fighting the emotion which welled suddenly. 'The bloody old fool! He didn't have to die yet. He could have lived to teach *my* children the secrets of marsh and woods.'

The man took her hand. 'There was no helping him.'

'Damn,' she sobbed, 'now what'll happen? It won't be the same, damn the idiot.'

'We must tell someone.' He pressed her warm, yielding fingers. 'That's our first step.'

'What'll happen to Poacher's den?'

'I don't know. I suppose some young couple could be cosy there.' He let her sniffing subside. 'A bit of paint, a new kitchen. Some couple who liked the valley and would take the dog. Weed the garden. Mend the chicken house . . .'

'And remember?'

'Look after the ghosts.'

There was a hush and Kine, peering from the willow, saw the couple reflected in the Moon Pond, the girl solaced in the arms of her companion, who said at last, 'Come on, I'm taking you home. We need a telephone. Then I'll come back and wait with him. Use my handkerchief – he wouldn't thank you for tears, by what I've heard of him.'

Kine watched them leave. For a moment the terrier lingered then, beckoned, disappeared and the wood was still. Only the scratch of blackbirds, seeking grubs in leaf-mould, disturbed the silence. Wonder had drowsed off. She was, thought Kine, too trusting of humankind, but her sleep suited him. Slipping quietly from the tree, the male weasel dropped into the plantains beside the pool, looked back briefly and crossed the glade.

He had no doubt what he must do. It had struck him forcibly while she curled, so like Kia, in the old nest. It had taken him back to a day, warm rain falling outside, when the brood was born. It had taken Wonder to rekindle the sadness and rage in him, his loathing of Gru in all its virulence.

He knew now what he must do.

And do alone, for it was his one chance of redemption, of repaying the fallen, his personal debt. He could ask no more of the survivors. It was his own task: to seek out the she-mink, and place his hold on her. He would perish, but he might just succeed in taking Gru with him. In which case, without their matriarch, the marauders would split up and leave for other camps. Some might tarry, but Gru was their spur, and the threat would wane.

He moved swiftly through the great trees. His head was cool. Wonder would inherit the wood, hunt his territory. Until One-Eye joined the heroes, he would counsel her. Then in spring she would mate, refurbish the line, maybe chatter a little of Kia and Kine. It was weasel country. He stopped at the track and viewed the rich tilth and pasture, the river winding where cattle grazed. It could happen. If he could penetrate the stronghold, then join his teeth until death in the black neck.

The tractor braked. It had crawled over the brow and turned near Kine for the reverse haul. For a minute, while the driver stretched and reset the plough, the radio in the cab blared the news of nations between jangling tunes. The ploughman stifled it. The news he enjoyed came with evening from the daughter he had not seen since he left at dawn. Mud vibrated on the rivets by his boots as the engine throbbed.

Selecting gear, he was preparing to move when he saw the weasel. It stood trance-like by the gibbet, still as a weasel will sometimes stand, as if dedicating some mischief to the bleak strips. It seemed frozen, white breast glimmering, a small knight at watch. Then, galvanized, it raced ahead of the tractor to the marsh gate.

CHAPTER TWENTY-TWO

KINE marched fixedly, unconscious of detail to left and right of him. He saw neither the grasses, grown high where sheep wire was rusted and punched by rabbit runs, nor the corrugated butt, green with age, of a felled oak. He was blind to sarsen and briar; deaf to the throb of the tractor. Purpose blinkered him. He knew what had to be done, and it transcended caution. Time was late for Kine.

Small birds, sensing his tension, chirped and fluttered in the hedge, their fear vicarious. They said, 'He's going for Gru,' and, tumbling ahead, 'He won't come back. No one visits the mink and comes back,' they said. Coiled where partridge had nested, the adder sneered. He was no friend of the weasel. 'Who cares?' he asked.

The way of the weasel was solitary. Once in many generations a tribe assembled, but the weasel's path was alone, and the hush of isolation enveloped Kine. He thought of Ford, of the survivors returning to their own realms. He thought of Ford's optimism, his rude belligerence. He thought of the stripling and his loyalty, and of One-Eye, unconquered in hoary age. Kine missed them, and was inspired by them.

He thought of Gru . . .

His pace quickened. The wood swept its hem behind him, and he passed the ash tree. Kine stepped doggedly. He thought of Liverskin, the she-devil's mate, and the saw-toothed bunker guards. He thought of their razor claws. In his mind he smelled the stench of the monsters, felt their breath on him. He went steadily. The chill of loneliness stabbed. His ears were closed to the birds. His eyes had flint in them.

A shadow slipped from the hedge and fell in with him. 'Keep going,' growled One-Eye, 'and save your tongue. I'm coming with you. The frosts of winter would get me in any case. Better die in the bunker than linger miserably.' His jaw was stubborn. 'You didn't think you could just sneak away from me?'

Kine's heart thumped. He made no answer. Side by side they went forward, masks inscrutable. Ancient briars, stems like birch poles with spikes, climbed beside them through blackthorn. A ditch was trickling. Kine knew each step. He knew each pothole. Fence palings were familiar friends, known by their knots, their diverse girths. He knew every tendril of every plant. It was Kine's trail. He could have plotted each nettle, each gangling burdock and tiny pimpernel. Every stone was a companion. He had no stomach for farewells and kept his gaze ahead.

Two weasels on a path. Then they were three. Young Heath, ghosting from the thicket, had joined step with the stalwarts. His manner, grimly determined, muzzled any argument. 'Three for Gru,' chirped the hedge-birds. 'Three for the citadel.'

The trio swung through the marsh gate, wheeling in silence for Mullen's dyke. There, by one post of the gate, was a small ravine where ditch flushed to culvert, and cress had rooted. A long-discarded 12-bore cartridge case had lodged there. The gully sighed and, as the three weasels passed, a dusty posse hauled over the lip, bounding after them. Ford led the rest of the survivors in ragged echelon. 'On, Kine!' It was imperious. 'You're not rid of us. On, or we'll head you to perdition and the devil's throat!'

They were advancing by spiky marsh grasses, where gicks and teazels flanked the path to the main cut. There were nine or ten in the troop, sore from trekking, disaster-haunted, the last of the tribe. Kine glanced over his shoulder. It was not as he planned, but they were fierce with resolution. There was no stopping them.

The wire braces of a pole which bore the power-line to the pump slanted upwards from the bank where the dyke began. A pile of hardcore had once been dumped there. Now gone, it left a scab without growth amid the vegetation. The weasels paused. They had a view from the clearing to the far pump. Great clouds knotted the sky. Kine scanned the dyke. Its banks ran true as the power-line to Gru's garrison.

It was a long charge. Kine stepped forward. He felt the others press behind him and quickened pace. Tall reeds bristled in clusters. He led the red troop at a jostling canter past the first pennoned clump, choosing ground between the bank and the path which bordered it. The dyke looked serene enough. Pink heads bloomed late on the umbels of flowering rush; midges danced. Nothing ruffled the water but Kine mistrusted it.

One-Eye bounded beside him. Ford was nearby. The rest followed, still bunched, but impatient to cut loose. 'Keep it steady.' One-Eye rumbled the warning. 'You'll be no good if you're blown. Don't make a race of it.'

He was right, but Kine's own blood was racing. The urge to sprint was overbearing. He restrained it with difficulty. The pump seemed to grow with painful tardiness. Momentarily he let his bounding stride lengthen, easing back with reluctance. The little troop had surged with him. 'Not yet.' Duck rose yelping from the water, whose sheen lay smooth and empty to the catch-grid, deceptively tranquil. 'Not yet,' he barked.

They were halfway there when Kine spotted the ripples and watched the creature break surface and reach the far bank. With a flick it shed water. It was a young mink, three-quarters grown, ahead of the weasels but aware of them. It was inquisitive. Sheep, browsing the escarpment, had trod shelving footholds and now the mink, ascending such a ledge, peered obliquely back across the water, curious.

Kine saw it rise on its haunches. Its nostrils worked as the weasels drew closer. Then it moved. It shifted suddenly. With a start, it had turned, scuffling quickly towards the stronghold, and Kine's command was simultaneous. 'Go *now*!' he screamed.

238

He was almost bowled over. Ford was surging ahead, and weasels, though drained by the swamp trek, lashed past with reserves of strength that surprised themselves. Neck stretched, Kine kicked down, accelerating to the front again. Sedges flashed by. He was flying, scudding along as sinews whipped, catapulting him. One-Eye dropped back. The survivors were stringing now, careering madly, streaming full-gallop towards the pump. Kine could see the screw looming, the concrete shoulders. He saw the warren nearby where the guards dossed. And as he charged they appeared, first eyes in the holes, then the shambling monsters, shaking sleep from them.

Ford was crooning as he raced, some bog-weasel war-song obscure to Kine. Others, battle in their faces, churred savagely. The Blood Fury was high and, ahead, the mink blinked disbelievingly. The weasels were crazy. That the puny band was bent on violence dawned late on the monsters, and stunningly.

Kine saw Ford peel off, loop towards the nearest of the brutes and tilt into it. Another weasel joined Ford with a flying leap. In a second, the survivors were everywhere, darting, stabbing, swarming the banks round the idle screw. Kine saw One-Eye plunge at a snarling mink. The monster reeled, backing into a tunnel, the veteran harrying. One giant spun like a dervish, two weasels clamped to it.

The sky loured. Sullen tongues of rain licked and the river tossed. The battle, raging by bury and water's edge, brought gulls baying from the floodlands. Crows slid overhead. There would be carrion, and the scuttling sallies, the glowering stalemates, excited them. They saw the sandy mink swivel, red eyes murderous. It had lost its twin in the weasel ambush. Rushing forward, it killed an attacker with a single stroke.

Then it was hurled on its back, weasels latched to it. Writhing – a twelve-legged fur-ball of fury – the struggling mass tumbled down the slope.

Ford was red at the lip, glazed with punishment.

Still he slurred out his war-hymn and charged again. Mink were mesmerized. The lurching bog-weasel was invulnerable. He had no nerve in him. Nothing stopped or dismayed him. He had one tactic: cut, crippled or concussed, he barged forward. A powerful scion of Gru's house confronted him. Ford went in swearing. Joined by One-Eye, now back from the tunnel, he routed the giant and looked for other mink.

Rain swept over them. One-Eye stomped in the moisture, dancing wickedly. The old warrior whooped. He was young again. Bygone battles stirred in him, distant victories. He had fought in woods, in meadows, on marsh and heath; fought against talon and poisoned tooth. But no memory matched this, the battle of battles, and One-Eye relished it. Mink were rallying. He saw their shapes in the downpour. 'Are you with me?' he asked Ford.

'To the death,' Ford responded. They charged again.

Elsewhere in the mêlée, the stripling paused. Mink heaved past, fangs threatening. Weasels chivvied. Someone was calling, 'Young Heath!' Looking back, he saw a late-comer sprinting from the marsh gate. The tumult eddied. 'Wait, Heath!' The cry was nearer, more compelling. 'Heath, wait for me!'

'You shouldn't be here.' His voice was a hiss. 'It's to the death,' he told Wonder. 'Stay out of it.'

'Don't be stupid. Why didn't Kine tell me?'

'He told nobody.'

'Where is he?'

'He wants Gru. I saw him enter the labyrinth.'

'Well, come on. He'll need us to help him. It's no good standing here.'

Kine thrust on, his objective the bunker and its occupant. There were several clefts between the bank and the base of the engine house, the largest opening the foundations to his swift probe. The black maze swallowed him. He was running on clay through a serpentine passage which muffled the sound of the clash outside. Walls of girded concrete entombed him, dank corridors. Charnel chambers were strewn with skins and picked bones. The labyrinth reeked of mink. He turned twice in quick succession. A steel-flanked aisle led him forward until the cramped space expanded. Kine stopped.

He could see nothing. The darkness was total. But this, he knew, was the bunker. He eased his rump to the wall. Every tooth was unsheathed. He said in almost a whisper, 'I've come at last.'

'How unwise of you.'

'Wisdom no longer matters.'

He thought of Kia, her last stand against that voice in the black void. That mattered – her weasel courage, her defiance to the bitter end. He thought of the heroes and the odds they fought.

'And what brings you here?'

'We must dance, Gru.' He heard her cackle of scorn. He was judging the distance. 'Dance the steps in the dark.'

'Steps?' the voice said.

'The steps of the death dance.'

There was a movement. Kine listened. 'Tell me more,' Gru invited, but the weasel was silent. The movement and Gru's voice did not accord. He ducked instinctively. Liverskin's jaws crackled over him. Kine felt the breath of the monster and, sliding into a corner, crouched motionless. 'Fool,' snarled Gru, 'you missed the ratling. Put an end to him.'

Liverskin cursed. He cast blindly in the gloom, hooked claws zipping. Kine heard them coming, slashing the wall, spraying concrete-dust. The mink was muttering. 'I can smell the weasel. I'm getting close to him.' Kine drew back. The boast was justified, each step more dangerous as the claws swept the darkness. The low grunting of the brute was foully intimate.

'The corner,' snapped Gru. 'He's in the corner.' Kine was flat to the ground. A hairy neck brushed his whiskers. With all the force he could find, he locked his teeth to it.

Liverskin lurched like a hooked pike. For a moment he shook violently, howling obscenely, then gave a long, deep shudder as the pain delved deeper.

'You've found him?' hissed Gru.

'He's taken hold . . .'

'Smash the weasel!'

'He's into me.' The mink jerked convulsively. Squealing, he threshed round the bunker dragging Kine with him. 'Get him off, he's in the nerve!' He barged wildly in the murk, slamming into the walls. Kine hung on. He was accustomed to the death ride. 'Get the weasel off!'

Gru laughed icily. 'Roll on the ratling. Smash the dandy hound.'

'Aaaeeh!' Her mate reared, shaking frenziedly then, plunging to the ground, tried to smother the creature which leeched to him. But nothing Liverskin knew could break the weasel hold. He crushed Kine, wrenched him, snatched him, hurled him down again. Dementedly, Liverskin bucked and flailed. A second time he coursed the bunker, scraping the leech against the rough walls. Kine clung on, scarcely knowing if he was still sensible. Stars were flashing, planets of the mind, and – far off, as it first seemed – weasel voices spoke.

'Kine, are you in there? What's happening?'

Wonder's voice.

Then Young Heath. 'I'll go first. It may be dangerous.'

Next thing, they were swirling to support him, tackling Liverskin. 'Hang on, Kine, we're with you. We'll stop the brute.' They danced like veterans. Wonder was a hornet, a spitting fury; the stripling pressed home with darting fearlessness. Kine felt their impact on the monster, his threshing violence. Fur was flying. Claws stabbed. Liverskin heaved massively. With savage force he started for the passage, dragging the three of them.

He never got there. Instead, the hulking body rose suddenly, swinging Kine against its belly, then slumped to the ground, the weasels locked to it. For several seconds the clawed feet kicked in spasm; at last they jerked and stiffened. The mink was motionless. Kine lay dazed against the neck. He heard the other two move, and Wonder shake herself. 'We've killed him.' The stripling's gasp was disbelieving. He echoed in the gloom, 'We've killed Liverskin.'

'For Kia.' Wonder stood breathless.

Kine collected his senses. 'And lost Gru,' he said, lurching round the bunker. 'The devil take her lieutenant, I want the she-mink. She can't have gone far. I'm going after her.'

He met the rain at a stumbling canter. It drifted in vaporous sheets which, after the bunker, were fiercely luminous. The light was steely. Through smoky clouds it touched reeds and rind of sallow with white streaks. It gleamed on skirmishers. Rain streamed on concrete, washing the bulwarks of the great screw. Pitched across them, a protective roof of mesh released a battery of droplets from metal links. They drubbed the flange of the propeller like drum-beats. Kine thrust forward, his eyes probing moisture, his nose alert.

The valley simmered. Vapour swirled, a vast curtain sweeping from the grey dome. Kine paused. The misty sheet obscured the dyke then, lifting suddenly, revealed the mink on the near bank. Gru glowered at him. Moist with rain, she gleamed dauntingly, bristling, feet wide-spaced, her claws splayed so the webbed interstices were evident. Her eyes were icy. They were compassionless, flintstones of menace. Her lip curled.

Kine found his voice. 'We've killed Liverskin.'

Gru cackled. 'His usefulness was done. You can have him. And this,' she said, tossing something forward, 'since we're speaking of the worthless. It belongs to you.'

'One-Eye!' Kine stared at the body with stinging eyes. His fury choked him.

'He thought he could stop me.'

'First Kia, now . . .'

Kine raged forward, was bowled backwards by the monster and, reckless with anger, attacked again. Gru ripped his cheek open. He lunged bitterly. The blow that hurled him away was aimed with the contempt of her superior power, and he sprawled on tilth, taking soil in his gasping mouth. The black mass loomed. Kine saw the gape of savage jaws. 'Move!' It was a weasel urging. 'Move, Kine!' He squirmed sideways, then was up, weaving groggily, Ford beside him. 'Keep moving,' Ford insisted. 'I'll cover you.'

His head cleared. Ford was screening him. The rain gusted, travelling along the dyke in trains of turbulence. He saw Gru foray in the squall, snatch the bogweasel and swing him bodily. Then, as suddenly, Young Heath was racing forward. Gru dropped her victim. She lashed out vengefully. Kine heard the heath-weasel squeal. A crimson line scored his flank. The monster followed him, but now another was charging, a spitting arrow, and as Wonder sallied, Kine supported her. Gru's back was to the water. Through bloody lips, Kine challenged the mink to stand and dance with them.

'With four weasels?' Her laugh was mocking. 'Come, Kine, I'll swim with you.'

She stood at the brink. Rain ruffled the surface, washed the catch-grid. If she dived, Kine reflected, she was lost to them. They could not match her – a tribe of weasels could not match her in the water. He remembered the torpedoes in the long reach. 'Shall we swim,' snarled the monster, 'and fight in the depths? Or shall it be later, when I return with a new consort and fresh followers? I'll be back, Kine. I've not finished with this valley.' Her gaze ranged the wet ridges. 'Or with you,' she rasped.

Kine was motionless. The hum of rain was in his ears – and another sound.

Vapour swirled. There was a click, the sharp whine

of a motor and, with a roar, the screw engaged, sucking water down the dyke in churning tons. Simultaneously the contents of adjoining dykes began to slide through culverts towards the main race. Floating plains of weed broke up and sedges threshed. Tunnels rumbled. With gathering momentum the complex streamed, became a torrent drawn seething to Mullen's dyke and the thunderous pump.

Kine caught his breath. The water mounted the spinner like a typhoon, tortured gushes leaping high through the roof of mesh. Waves boiled and spouted. Not even Gru could survive there. She had not moved. Spray was lashing her. For a second she hesitated then, scuffling awkwardly, fled the bank to the con-crete screw-housing and began to climb. Spume broke over her. The black monster climbed higher. At last she reached the mesh above the screw itself.

The weasels watched as she lurched on the trembling links. Foaming spouts rose like geysers. One slip and Gru would skid down the mesh, plummet into the cauldron, and feed the churning throat. On the other hand, if she traversed the mesh safely she would be free of them, her way clear to the calm stream above the pump. She had to be stopped. Water pounded as Kine sprang to the concrete, climbed the shoulder of the housing, and edged after her. Below, heaving and erupting, tens of thousands of gallons rode the great worm.

Claws groping, he stepped on to the wire. It was greasy, vibrating so the links jerked and pinched. Jets punched up at him. He was dwarfed by the turmoil – numbed by it. Ahead, his quarry moved grimly, inch by teetering inch. Kine fumbled. Heart in mouth, he missed his footing, thrust his legs between the links and, wire cutting his belly, hung on again. The churn-ing motion below was giddying. Gru was swaying. 'Keep back,' she hissed. 'If you grapple, we're done for. You'll fall with me.'

'Maybe,' breathed the weasel. He thought of One-

Eye. First Kia and now One-Eye. Next, Wonder? '*Maybe*,' he spat at her.

Ford flinched. From the ground, the bog-weasel and the others saw Kine leap and the two creatures tangle in swirling rain. Almost lazily, it seemed, they rolled down the shivering mesh, hovered at the edge, then were over it. Twice Gru twisted in the air before she was gone – and Wonder was screaming, 'Kine! He's still there! Hang on fast, Kine!' He was suspended by one foot from the fringe of the wire. Struggling upwards, the small creature regained the mesh and lay, sodden and dazed, above the thundering spinner. Wonder filled her lungs slowly. 'He's safe,' she said.

The grey clouds galloped. Pulsating thrusts drained the dyke to the river in a tortured flood. The outlet bellowed. From the reeds, the weasels watched macabre scum form writhing circles as the valve belched. Once, the raiders had floundered in that turbulence. Now all that floated was a shapeless black pelt, crushed and torn. It swirled soggily. Looping the maelstrom, it was caught by the current and borne limply down-river towards the estuary.

CHAPTER TWENTY-THREE

THE girl folded the open newspaper diagonally into a many-layered strip, bent it in the middle like a man's tie, and plaited the halves together. Kneeling at the hearth of Poacher's parlour she admired her work. In such a manner men had once balled the tails of plough-horses to keep the mud from them. Placing the chunky twist in the ashes, she piled it with kindling and put a match to it. The mornings were getting cold. While the cottage was empty, she looked after it.

Like a person, it needed warmth. She watched the wood burn. Her mother had taught her to twist paper fire-lighters; they were infallible. The ingle brightened with flame and she sat on the floor by the stone hearth. The room was quiet. She felt at peace, at home with the silence, the unseen. The flames murmured. She turned suddenly. There was a draught beneath the door and, intuitively, the girl knew she was no longer on her own.

'Poacher?' – It slipped out with habit. There was no sound, but like a cat she sensed a presence and her eyes gleamed.

At first she thought it was a spider, a blob by the skirting. It was too small for a mouse, little larger than a humble-bee, scuttling on tiny and frantic legs. Her eyes followed it, crinkling with amusement. Its tail was vertical. The legs raced like clockwork. A velvet goblin, the shrew paced the boarding with snuffling urgency, oblivious of the gaze of the crouching girl.

On all fours, she made a dart at it. Her clutching hands missed and, launching forward on her chest, she made another grab. Giggling, she let it slip through her fingers. It bumbled on again. Laughter hampered her. Slewing on her hips, the girl reached out and the shrew ran up her arm. She hooted helplessly. The dwarf dismounted at her elbow. Returning to the skirting, it resumed its march.

At last, palms cupped firmly round the midget, she rose gasping to her feet and went outside with it. Her eyes were watering. Her breath steamed in the sharp air. The ground was hard. For a moment she held the creature near her cheek, then, with a soft farewell, stooped and put it down. ''Tis spoken for, the cottage, my handsome. Try another place.'

Scrat's wail eluded her. 'Winter's coming! Time's running out! The days of doom are near!'

The badger ventured her nose outside, sniffed the leaves that had fallen and retired again. The set was scrupulously clean, devoid of ordure and refuse, the sow fastidious. More, it was snugly warm. The leaves, by contrast, were cold and crisp with the first frost of autumn; the wood draughty where its skirts frayed. The pond in the glade was chill. Sunrise had yet to touch it, and the weasel, slipping from the plantains, sipped sparingly. Reflected in the water, the sharp head twisted; it was joined by another and the two drank together.

At length Wonder said, 'I've never seen such a morning, so bright and frosty. I wish One-Eye was here to enjoy it.'

'You haven't lived through a winter.' Kine climbed the bluff. 'There's no pleasure in frost when you're old. It saps the strength from you.'

'All the same . . .'

'One-Eye knew about winter. He made his choice.'

They rambled to the lea. It was silver-grey – the dark mole hills in sharp relief. Wonder goggled. Each sliver of grass was a crystal blade. As the sun rose, the owl winged to roost. They watched the great pale bird dissolve in white haze. 'He chose battle,' Kine reflected of One-Eye. 'He was a warrior.'

'He was a hero,' breathed Wonder. 'I miss his old face.'

Squirrels stirred among acorns, brisk and stiff-tailed. The air was pleasantly fresh, moving gently as it warmed, extending the glide-paths of falling leaves. The marsh shimmered. Life was vigorous. Mallard, in fast-rising formations, welcomed the sun with sweeping circuits of the valley; swans preened in meadows. Far above them, a heron barked. The weasels went down the slope. 'And Ford and Heath,' added Wonder, 'I miss all of them.'

'They'll be back. You'll see that pair next spring.'

'I don't know.' She danced prettily.

Kine knew. 'You'll see,' he said.

The female shrugged and they passed harrowed tilth where lapwings waited to breakfast when the surface thawed. Graceful birds, they stood in dozens, crests tilted, patient while the sun unlocked the soil for them. Nearby, a young hare, animated by the frost, capered boastfully. Bounding forward, he leaped high, intoxicated by his prowess, then raced again. Enraptured by his own speed, he chased from sight.

'You'll see,' Kine reiterated. 'They'll remember you.' They would not forget Kia's daughter. He shook his head. Fur would fly over Wonder, he told himself.

'If I'm here. I might be anywhere.'

He looked askance at her. Thickets rustled and ditches shrilled. You could not have gone far that morning without hearing the squeaking of voles and shrews. Wonder beamed at him. An iced puddle intrigued her and she slid on it. 'They say Kia was a rover,' she cried, whirling blithely, 'I want to travel. I want to see places, visit other lands. I'll come back, of course.'

'Travel in winter?'

'I've proved myself.'

'In strange terrain?'

'Stop worrying!' She whisked over the rink, churring merrily. There was a crackling snap and she bounced from the ice with feigned terror. Wonder laughed. 'It can't be so bad, if this is winter . . .'

'It isn't, Wonder. An early frost isn't winter.' He frowned at her. 'I've seen the winter. Sap freezes, the cold is vicious, the land a wilderness. The belly aches. You walk in a naked world.'

Kine knew the winter. His frown deepened. He knew the dark season, days which died without a struggle, dawns and sunsets alike starved and fugitive. Then the gloom drooped from snow-clouds and life decayed. He knew the winter, the mystery and agony of the long nights. Kine recalled the bitter solstice, as Wonder frolicked: the hoot of brown owls across stiff plough-land, the barked alarm of a distant dog, the thin notes of a robin in grey emptiness. In winter, stone crumbled. In winter, earth and blood froze. The thrust perished. Rooks sought middens, the muddy vapours where steers wallowed, while woodmice, stores expended, gnawed elder rind. Wild life hungered. Like fought like in the winter and the weak died.

'When ice clings to your coat,' he said, 'and paws burn with cold – when hunger grips like a talon – *that's* winter, Wonder. Be prepared for it.'

'Don't worry. Come on,' she protested, 'the sun's shining, the mink have gone! The country is Kine's again.'

He marched broodingly. They reached the river and stood where the frogs had croaked. Snipe corkscrewed from the sedges; a moorhen dabbled. The stream was clear, minnows glinting in shallows, and a pike prowled. A far ripple marked the plunge of an otter in search of food. Wonder's eyes were understanding. 'It's in the past, Kine; it's time to forget, to start afresh. The weasel hunts alone. This is your kingdom. I must leave, but I'll not be gone forever. I'll drop by,' she purred, 'if you'll have me.' She regarded him fondly. 'If you'll put up with my chatter,' she said at last.

'Yes.' He smiled at her.

She was right. He faced the wood and the ridge. She spoke with Kia's voice, and he knew before his gaze reached the slopes that the frost had cleared from them.

Kine returned to the crest with weasel energy. Autumn blazed in his land, crowned his inheritance. Through history his family had hunted there. He knew the deep places, the fortress of the mole and the rabbit's stop. He could interpret the signs and the valley sounds. '*Tchk*,' he sang. He was free and alone. He churred as he forayed. '*Tchk-kkkk*.' He was unbowed. He heard the yaffle of the rainbird, the vixen's holla. None moved with such lightness, such dexterity. Kine moved hungrily. '*Tchk-kkkk-chk*.' He was small, his song proclaimed, but formidable.

Author's note

Kine's country exists. From the windows as I write I can see the owl barn, the wood and rookery, a hare on the slopes, the marsh and pump-house, and the sweep of the vale towards the coastal flats where Kent and Sussex meet. The story is imagined; the dykes and thickets are real, as are their denizens. I share their land.

The weasel has many names. Shakespeare called him a mousehunt; gipsies called him a dandy hound. When I was a boy the weasel, male or female, was a kine in our neighbourhood. Gamekeepers were his foes but farmers welcomed him. For the maligned weasel is not only attractive and full of character but our natural ally against rat, mouse and rabbit – three great plagues of agriculture where they proliferate.

Smallest of his species, the weasel is bolder than the stoat, his larger cousin, and often lives near human dwellings. Many times I have watched him work my garden, or hunt the farmyard and nearby wood. I have heard the female swear at my dogs and scold her own young. The weasel does not always please – I object when he climbs after bird nests in my thorn hedge – but he fascinates and I make him my hero without apologies.

Stories need villains and, I fear, in this neck of the country the mink is so cast. That is not the fault of the mink, who did not ask to be brought to our island, but of those who imported him. The first imports to fur 'farms' in Britain occurred in the late 1920s. Escapes were soon reported and, though wild mink do not reach the six or seven pounds of ranch mink, they are too voracious to suit nature's balance here. The mink is also courageous and intelligent. Indeed, he could be the hero of a different tale, and it behoves us to control him by humane means.

While I have seen stranger battles in the countryside,

the mink-versus-weasel war is a fantasy. Weasel packs, however, are not imaginary. Mention of them can be found in various memoirs and country books. And mink certainly frequent the pump-houses here. Similarly, the struggle with the barn-owl is based on fact. The naturalist Arthur Thomson recorded the taking of a weasel by a barn-owl which lived to rue its temerity. That splendid bird is my nearest neighbour. I should not care to confront him were I weasel-sized.

It is a long time since I was taught to make and set the rat snare Poacher uses. In those days rats infested farms and scarcely a sack of corn or meal was spared by them. Before threshing, farmers would run wire-netting round the base of their ricks to contain the rats which harboured there. When the last sheaves were dislodged there might be more than two dozen rats in the enclosure. The slaughter was formidable. As a lad I was paid twopence a rat's tail and did well from it, mostly using gin-traps (now rightly outlawed) and the improvised hang-snare.

The Founding Twelve marsh frogs in the story are historic fact. In the winter of 1934–35 a dozen specimens from Europe were released into a stream near here, on the borders of Romney Marsh. By 1975 their progeny were widely distributed over more than a hundred square miles of the marsh and adjacent levels. On a warm night their voices fill the valley, and they are often vociferous on sunny days. The ventriloquial effect is remarkable. Frequently I have failed to spot marsh frogs though their croaking has seemed at my very feet.

One more animal, perhaps, deserves a personal note: the scuttling shrew, possessed, whenever I have found him, by Scrat's urgency. Sometimes he comes indoors. Not long ago I put one determined intruder out of the house several times, each time to find him back almost instantly. At length I released the shrew in the lane beyond the gate – a route-march from the farmhouse for the mini-tramp. Within minutes he (or was it she?) was back in the living room. Shrews have short lives, and dead specimens are often found lying untouched, perhaps because they are unpalatable to scavengers.

Hares, rabbits and rooks have been the subjects of various instructive books. There are many hares here, and my observations have been helpfully informed by Henry Tegner's interesting *Wild Hares* (John Baker, 1969), while, for those not all too familiar with rabbits, a good introduction is *Rabbits and Their History* by John Sheail (David and Charles, 1971). Rooks and other members of the crow family make fascinating reading in *Crows: A Study of the Corvids of Europe* by C. J. F. Coombs (Batsford, 1978). Unfortunately I have yet to find a book on weasels, but for informative sections on other interesting creatures, including mink and marsh frogs, I recommend Christopher Lever's excellent *The Naturalized Animals of the British Isles* (Hutchinson, 1977; Paladin paperback, 1979).

Finally, a tame weasel is an extremely rare phenomenon. Last year a tiny male, a week or two old, was rescued from a cat and hand-reared by Steve Scott of Leeds. The now mature weasel is at home with people and I am indebted to Mr Scott for allowing me to study his fine specimen.

A. R. Lloyd
Kent, 1982

FICTION

GENERAL

☐ Chains	Justin Adams	£1.25
☐ Secrets	F. Lee Bailey	£1.25
☐ Skyship	John Brosnan	£1.65
☐ The Free Fishers	John Buchan	£1.50
☐ Huntingtower	John Buchan	£1.50
☐ Midwinter	John Buchan	£1.25
☐ A Prince of the Captivity	John Buchan	£1.25
☐ The Eve of St Venus	Anthony Burgess	£1.10
☐ Nothing Like the Sun	Anthony Burgess	£1.50
☐ The Memoirs of Maria Brown	John Cleland	£1.25
☐ The Last Liberator	John Clive	£1.25
☐ Wyndward Fury	Norman Daniels	£1.50
☐ Ladies in Waiting	Gwen Davis	£1.50
☐ The Money Wolves	Paul Erikson	£1.50
☐ Rich Little Poor Girl	Terence Feely	£1.50
☐ Fever Pitch	Betty Ferm	£1.50
☐ The Bride of Lowther Fell	Margaret Forster	£1.75
☐ Forced Feedings	Maxine Herman	£1.50
☐ Savannah Blue	William Harrison	£1.50
☐ Duncton Wood	William Horwood	£1.95
☐ Dingley Falls	Michael Malone	£1.95
☐ Gossip	Marc Olden	£1.25
☐ Buccaneer	Dudley Pope	£1.50
☐ An Inch of Fortune	Simon Raven	£1.25
☐ The Dream Makers	John Sherlock	£1.50
☐ The Reichling Affair	Jack Stoneley	£1.75
☐ Eclipse	Margaret Tabor	£1.35
☐ Pillars of the Establishment	Alexander Thynn	£1.50
☐ Cat Stories	Stella Whitelaw	£1.10

WESTERN — BLADE SERIES by Matt Chisholm

☐ No. 5 The Colorado Virgins	85p
☐ No. 6 The Mexican Proposition	85p
☐ No. 7 The Arizona Climax	85p
☐ No. 8 The Nevada Mustang	85p
☐ No. 9 The Montana Deadlock	95p
☐ No. 10 The Cheyenne Trap	95p
☐ No. 11 The Navaho Trail	95p
☐ No. 12 The Last Act	95p

NAME ....

ADDRESS ....

....

Write to Hamlyn Paperbacks Cash Sales, PO Box 11, Falmouth, Cornwall TR10 9EN.

Please indicate order and enclose remittance to the value of the cover price plus:

U.K.: Please allow 45p for the first book plus 20p for the second book and 14p for each additional book ordered, to a maximum charge of £1.63.

B.F.P.O. & EIRE: Please allow 45p for the first book plus 20p for the second book and 14p per copy for the next 7 books, thereafter 8p per book.

OVERSEAS: Please allow 75p for the first book and 21p per copy for each additional book.

Whilst every effort is made to keep prices low it is sometimes necessary to increase cover prices and also postage and packing rates at short notice. Hamlyn Paperbacks ....rve the right to show new retail prices on covers which may differ from those ....ly advertised in the text or elsewhere.